BUFFALO JUSTICE

ALSO BY W. MICHAEL GEAR AND KATHLEEN O'NEAL GEAR

BUFFALO JUSTICE

W. MICHAEL GEAR
KATHLEEN O'NEAL GEAR

WOLFPACK
PUBLISHING
— EST 2013 —

Buffalo Justice
Paperback Edition
Copyright © 2025 by W. Michael Gear and Kathleen O'Neal Gear

Wolfpack Publishing
1707 E. Diana Street
Tampa, FL 33610

www.wolfpackpublishing.com

Paperback ISBN 979-8-89567-078-1
Ebook ISBN 979-8-89567-077-4
LCCN 2025934823

To
The Historic UXU Ranch.
A special place for us to relax and enjoy a
Moment's Peace.
And
To
John Hoskins for making it so.

BUFFALO JUSTICE

CHAPTER ONE

Black ice triggered the Maserati's all-wheel drive when Ryman Banks the Third took the turn from Wilson Creek Road onto his private lane. January in Montana was like that, and with the coming of nightfall, the roads turned slick south of Bozeman. Encountering dry blacktop, Ryman punched the accelerator, loving the sound as the Ghibli Q4's twin-turboed V6 charged forward. Nothing sounded like a Maserati. And, by damn, tonight he needed to hear that harmony exhaust.

He wound through the winter-bare cottonwoods and headed up the lane toward his home. The house was an architectural masterpiece—thrusting prow roof, windows with log accents, majestic custom stonework, all framed by some of the best landscaping in Montana. Set against the high snow-capped Gallatin Range that rose from the southern horizon, the property, valued at two-point-eight-million dollars, was the symbol of his success.

Right.

Because the rest of his life was sure as hell shit.

————

The day had started miserably. After spending the last three nights romping with Charlotte Zypanski, Ryman had stepped out of Charlotte's shower to the ringing of his cell phone. Picking it up with wet fingers, caller ID tagged it as being from Jennifer, his soon-to-be ex-wife.

"Sorry to pull you out of your skank girlfriend's arms so early in the morning," Jennifer's voice had been like ice. *"Got your latest legal broadside, you son of a bitch. You weren't there for your son back before I filed for divorce. Why do you want to go to war over spending time with Bailey now? Just 'cause I'm moving? Or is it spite because I'm marrying a real man, for once?"*

Yeah, he'd admit it. It was payback for dumping him. He left women. They didn't leave him. The divorce would be final in the coming week, and she'd already planned a May wedding to Ryman's one-time friend, Tormey Tanner. It was like a thorn driven deep under Ryman's thumbnail. Of course she'd move up to the head-quarters for the Plains Wilderness Project. And little Bailey would be starting preschool next year.

"I want to see you in person. I don't care if it is Sunday morning. Meet me at the bakery in an hour."

Ryman hoped she was about to give in on visitation. Damn it, he needed a win. Some consolation he could point to. To get it, he'd threatened her with one hell of a lawsuit, a filing to delay the divorce proceedings. Figured she'd meet him half way rather than suffer through the litigation.

When he'd arrived a little before eight, he was

surprised to find her accompanied by a new attorney, William C. "Billy" Blood. While Jennifer gave Ryman loathing and hateful ice-blue looks over a cup of coffee, Blood informed him that not only was Jennifer moving to the project, but if Ryman wanted to see their three-year-old son ever again, he'd have to travel to northern Montana to do so. The boy would be homeschooled, and if Ryman wanted a lawsuit: bring it on.

On his way out the door, Ryman heard her tell Blood, "Wish someone would put a bullet in his brain. Save us all a lot of misery."

Jennifer had called his bluff. Bitter she-bitch that she was. Worse, she'd totally turned the tables on him. Her new husband-to-be was probably going to give her all the money she'd need to afford the best—like Blood—and drag it out in court.

In a foul mood, Ryman checked his expensive watch and headed for ICoHR's Main Street offices. Ten till nine.

His phone was ringing when he walked through the door. Turned out to be the icing on the cake for a real shitty morning. Timothy Little, PhD, was the geneticist that ICoHR had worked with and depended on for years. Little had patented a Third Generation DNA Sequencing technology to identify cattle genes in bison; it proved what geneticists called "introgression." Or non-purity of the genome. Hybridization, of course, had been going on for millennia, and really took off in the 1500s when Spanish cattle started mixing with wild bison herds. To make matters worse, ranchers—going all the way to Charlie Goodnight in the 1880s—tried to breed buffalo and beef cows into something called a "beefalo" or some-times "cattelo." The idea had been to capitalize on a beef

cow's placid disposition and gain a bison's tough surviv-
ability in a harsh western Plains environment.

Unfortunately, there were fertility problems between
the species, which made it useless to ranchers. For the
conservation movement, however, those residual cattle
genes were pure gold. It gave them a weapon and a cause
in their battle to get rid of commercial beef and bison
ranchers and turn the West into a vast unsullied American Serengeti. Finding cattle genes in bison allowed
conservationists to claim that it was evil ranchers who
were tainting "pure" bison genetics, and gave the movement a reason to bilk millions out of outraged animal
lovers. For decades they'd been flooding ICoHR with
money to protect the last wild herds of pure bison in
federal parks.

Tim Little's voice sounded uncommonly humble. "*Uh,
Ryman? The Third Generation Sequencing tech I developed is
the backbone of our case against the government, right? You
know, proof that Yellowstone bison are the most genetically pure,
wild bison, in the world? Well, you're not going to want to hear
this, but a new study by Oxford University...*"

By the end, Dr. Little's scratchy high-pitched voice
had taken on a wheedling screech. The kind that made
Ryman wince.

In a wooden voice, he'd asked, "But the study hasn't
undergone peer review yet, right?"

"*No. But it will,*" Little said. "*Six months? Maybe a year.
Then it will be published.*"

Ryman killed the call and fixed on the implications of
Tim Little's mealy-mouthed explanation of the science.
His recent suit filed on behalf of International Coalition
on Habitat Rescue—or ICoHR—against the National
Park Service and the US Fish and Wildlife Service—had
been processed by the United States Court of Appeals

for the District of Columbia. A new court date had been set. The suit was a legal petition to have Yellowstone bison listed as a distinct population segment, or DPS, under the Endangered Species Act.

Without purity, that suit was dead meat. There were close to five hundred thousand buffalo, or bison if you wanted to use the scientific name, in North America. Why would anyone believe they were endangered? Purity was everything.

Steps pounded down the hallway outside his office. He looked up to see his partner and chair of the ICoHR board, Carly Joyner, burst through the door.

She stopped short just inside, eyes going wide in surprise. Her jaw dropped. "My God. What are you doing here?" She placed a hand to her heart. Squeaked, "You should be... I mean..."

"Yes, Carly?"

"On a *Sunday*?"

"So what if it's Sunday? It's a fucked-up morning."

She swallowed hard. Then, recovering, her expression hardened, and she pointed an accusatory finger. "Have you seen the accounts? The bottom line? I just came in here to pull all your files. The accountant sent the year-end report. Spent all night going over the figures. My, God, Ryman! That's close to a quarter million in the fourth quarter alone. Gone. Like...where is it?"

"Relax," he told her in a calming voice. "You know the game. We filed suit in September. We're on the docket. You know the rules under 34 CFR § 21.1. Under the Equal Access to Justice Act, the government reimburses us at the rate of seven hundred and fifty bucks an hour. And we've got a lot of hours into this. Should net us a little over a million."

"Yeah, when we can prove the government's position

is not justified. First, we have to win, Ryman." She'd stomped across his expensive carpet, braced her arms, palms down, on his polished mahogany desk. Propped herself there like a blonde harpy, her six-foot-tall beanpole body tense and vibrating. "Meanwhile, we're broke! Get it? We can't even pay the light bill. What the hell were you thinking?"

"Justifying our fee reimbursement. DC is an expensive place. We had to have the team there for close to a month." Ryman waved his hands in a shooing manner that told her to back off. But a cold shiver had traced down his back. It all hinged on Tim Little's fancy Third Generation Sequencing study of Yellowstone bison. On his DNA test...which was now apparently junk.

Christ! This case has to make it to court before that study is peer-reviewed and published, or we're dog shit.

To mollify Carly he adopted a soothing voice, adding, "Public donations will carry us through in the meantime. Especially if it looks like we're on the ropes. I've got the folks at Montana Ads producing a nice video of newborn bison calves. Footage of their little orange bodies frolicking in the wildflowers. You know, that video we—"

"That was shot on a buffalo ranch in Colorado. It wasn't even Yellowstone."

"So? Who's gonna know?"

"Maybe someone will geolocate the mountains in the background? Identify the Gore Range? Call us out for frauds? We're perched on the edge here, Ryman. The economy's in the toilet. Given a choice between paying the rent, putting food on the table, or sending fifty bucks to save one of the last pure bison, what do you think John Q. Public is going to pick?"

"Then we'll run the video segment with the hunters field-gutting that bison cow. With the telephoto, we got some great close ups of the guy in the NRA hat pulling out the guts. Lots of blood. Focus on the sightless eyes and the cow's tongue lolling out. I was waiting to release that later this spring for tourist season."

When she said nothing, he considered telling her Tim Little's latest news, but decided against it. Science would just complicate the discussion, so he said, "How many times do I have to tell you? Publicity, publicity, publicity. It's all about generating sympathy. Making people feel sorry for the animals. We're the underdogs fighting to save an American icon against ignorant, make-a-buck, gun-toting ranchers. We stand up for helpless endangered bison, for wilderness, and the future of planet earth." He chuckled. "We want to make them feel good about giving us money. Like they're making a difference, you know?"

Carly's lips, thin and pinched, quivered. Her icy blue glare ate into his resolve. He saw the moment it happened, as if something inside her snapped. She'd always been the glazed-eyed idealist, but in the last year she'd become obsessed. A martyr dedicated to the cause. But what could she do? Like it or not, she couldn't fire him. Without him and the income his lawsuits brought, ICoRH would wither, shrivel, and blow away like dust in the Montana wind.

Hard to believe that once upon a time they couldn't keep their hands off each other. But that had been in the beginning, before Jenn. Before all the others.

Her voice went oddly soft: "You know what this movement means to me. I'll do anything I must to save ICoHR. Unlike you, I believe in our mission." Then her eyes took on that wet glitter, as if she was seeing something sad in her mind. She jerked a short nod, spun on her heel, and strode for the door with grim purpose.

That put Ryman off his feed.

It wasn't even nine thirty when he locked the office and headed back to Charlotte's. He found her lounging in a fluffy white bathrobe at her breakfast table, the low morning light streaming in through her townhouse window. He poured a cup of coffee and joined her. It was nice to spend the day reveling in the company of an attractive and provocative woman who didn't hate him. Or at least tolerated him. But Charlotte was always about what was best for Charlotte. Maybe that's what made them click. They understood each other.

———

Ryman's mind was on their last frantic coupling as he pulled the Maserati under the imposing port cochere that protected his front entrance. He revved the engine one last time to savor the throaty rapping exhaust. Killing the ignition, he sat in silence, hands gripping the steering wheel, and stared off to the southwest where the sun was vanishing in a dying orange haze behind the cloud-obscured mountains. Looked like it was snowing up there.

Problem was, Charlotte wasn't a long-term prospect. She was tiring of the relationship. Soon someone newer, wealthier, and more athletic would be spending time at her Bozeman townhouse or her condo in Big Sky. But then, he had been plowing other fields, too.

He stepped out into the cold, his sheepskin coat open, and walked slowly up to the ornately decorated teakwood door. The thing was a masterpiece: A mighty bull bison stood in carved relief, it's head high, right hoof raised in a three-quarter pose. It had taken a year from the time Ryman commissioned it to delivery and cost him close to thirty thousand.

He tapped in his code, surprised when he didn't hear the lock click. He'd left it open all this time? What the hell had he been thinking? Grasping the cast bronze handle, Ryman swung the big door wide...

The blast caught him squarely in the chest.

CHAPTER TWO

Carly Joyner checked the Subaru's dash clock as she followed the blacktop out of town in the morning half-light. The rising sun still lingered behind the highest peaks, the winter horizon glowing in shades ranging from pale gray to pink. Traffic on Wilson Creek Road this time of morning was still light with only occasional commuters heading into Bozeman. She had to wait while the school bus with its flashing red lights picked up a batch of kids. When the lights went dark and the foldout stop sign swung in, Carly accelerated, headed south.

Her phone buzzed, the disposable red one from Walmart, and she glanced down. Saw the text alert for *The Buffalo Warrior.* Stressed as she was, the last thing Carly needed was another inflammatory inquiry asking for an elaboration of things she couldn't explain.

Why was it that all the men in her life were either scumbags or half crazy?

But then, glassy-eyed fanatics had their uses. Even if they didn't come cheap.

She turned her attention back to the road. *Focus. Don't lose your nerve.*

Time.

The clock read 7:35.

Time was critical. Carly dug in her purse for her iPhone, instructing it, "Call Beth."

She listened to the ring tone, once, twice, three times. "Come on, Beth. You gotta be there."

"*Hello?*"

"Hey, sister. What's up?"

"*Carly? Why are you calling this early? It's...uh...*"

"Yeah. Sorry. It's six thirty where you're at out on the coast. Listen, I wasn't thinking. But I've got a busy day coming up. Lots of meetings. And I wanted to talk to you about Dad. He kind of worried me the other night. I don't know what's going on in Pennsylvania, but I wondered if you'd talked to him lately."

"*Yeah, about a month ago. Why?*"

"Do you think he sounded okay? I mean, last time I called he kept losing his thoughts. Confused. Like, you don't think it could be Alzheimer's do you?"

The expected silence on the other end lasted maybe ten seconds. Long enough that Beth was really thinking it through.

"*I know he's been having a rough time with retirement, but he sounded really good to me. What did he say that worried you?*"

Carly flipped on her blinker, slowed, felt the Subaru slip a little on the patch of ice before the traction control kicked in. She passed the two high brick pillars on either side of the gate. Shook her head in disgust. Brick pillars? Like it was an Old World European estate? Ryman had always pissed her off with his ostentation. Thinking back, she'd have been rid of the son of a bitch years ago if he hadn't been such a freakin' fine lawyer. He'd *made* the International Coalition on Habitat Rescue through legal reimbursements ensured by the Equal Access to Justice Act and his acumen when it came to publicity. Sure, they'd lost some, but losing brought international awareness. Awareness brought donations. They couldn't have paid for better publicity.

Publicity, publicity! The world ran on it.

She chuckled dryly. Ryman had been right. It all came down to publicity.

"Carly? You still there?"

"Beth? I'm just driving up to Ryman's. Got an unpleasant meeting with him before we talk to the accountant about our taxes. Gotta go."

"You serious about Dad?"

"Gotta go, baby sister." She ended the call. Checked the time.

Seven forty-three.

She pulled up behind Ryman's Maserati, noticed the great wooden front door was open. Felt a tingle of anticipation as she shifted the Subaru into park and killed the ignition. Taking a deep breath, she fought the fluttery feeling around her heart. Seemed like she couldn't make her hand reach for the door handle.

"Gotta do this," she whispered to herself, fighting the urge to slip the car in reverse and back away. Jaw clenched, she opened the door, grabbed up the folder full of financial statements, and stepped out. Yes, she had all the paperwork the accountant had sent. Right down to the penny.

She made three steps around the rear of the Maserati.

Stopped short.

The blood! There was so much of it. Pooled and frozen around Ryman's sprawled body. But it was his open mouth and staring wide eyes that really freaked her out. The pupils were ice-gray. Inhuman. She wasn't prepared for this.

Carly staggered back, placed a hand on the Maserati's fender to brace herself, and bent double before she threw up.

...

CHAPTER THREE

T he late January sun hung low in the sky as Jillian
St. Clair Masterson found the address off
Wilson Creek Road.

"This is definitely the place."

The roadsides were lined with media vehicles
sporting radio call signs and a local KBZK TV van with
its dish. The reporters stood in a knot by the high brick
pillars that marked the entrance to the lane, held at bay
by a miserable-looking deputy standing by his cruiser.
She could see the interest, some of the reporters
recording her Department Durango with its official state
plates.

Jillian slowed, lowered her window, and flashed her
credentials at the deputy who secured the drive. He
barely looked at the Montana Department of Justice
badge as he waved her past.

She'd figured from the two elaborate brick pillars that
it would be a high-dollar property. But dang, when the
main house came into view it was stunning. Jillian wasn't
sure what the style was called, but the construction was

all custom logs sealed in honey tones. The foundations and lower walls were clad in gray and white river stone, as was the imposing chimney. Not to mention lots of glass. The roof looked like it was sheathed in copper. From the curve in the drive she could just see the high windows fronting the soaring great room with its magnificent Gallatin Range views.

The lane, however, was a tangled mess of sheriff's office cruisers and pickups, a couple of police vans for the evidence collection team and an ambulance. The sea of flashing red-and blue lights reflected from the snow and windows. Two deputies, breath fogging in the cold air, stepped out of the closest vehicle and walked down to meet her.

Jillian offered her credentials. "Agent Jillian Masterson, Montana DCI, Major Case Section. I need to speak to whomever is in charge."

The first deputy—a guy in his fifties with way too much gut hanging over his duty belt—glanced at her credentials and shot her a measuring look. His name tag read Clark.

Yeah, yeah, she knew what he was seeing, knew that skeptical look. What was an attractive woman in her late twenties, dressed in slim brown slacks with a fitted wool blazer, doing working for the Investigations Bureau? And, more to the point, why was she here?

"You drive all the way from Billings?" The deputy handed her badge folder back before shifting his hat higher on his head. His younger sidekick, Jones according to his tag, was giving her the eye, too. What they called "Male Gaze." It pissed her off.

"Just tell me who's in charge. Sheriff Wain on scene?"

Clark turned and pointed. "Sheriff's up at the house.

You can pull off here. We're trying to keep the road open."

And doing such a great job. Jillian barely bit off the retort as she eyed the jam ahead. She replaced the badge folder in her jacket and shifted the Durango into four-wheel drive, easing off just far enough onto the crusted snow to keep from getting stuck.

She stepped out and pulled on her coat before nodding stiffly at the deputies, Then she walked the gauntlet of vehicles to the house. As she passed the ambulance, they were just loading a bagged body into the back. Dr. A.C. France, "Doc AC" as the coroner was known, was standing to one side, reviewing a list of notes as he listened to his ear buds. Probably ensuring that he'd recorded everything from the scene.

Stepping around the last of the vehicles, she encountered a late-model green Subaru with Gallatin County plates parked behind a maroon Maserati. The port cochere rose high above and jutted toward the northern sky. Several officers were bunched on the stamped-and-dyed concrete, standing wide of a large bloodstain before the door. Plastic evidence markers had been placed on the concrete and the outline of a man's torso could be seen in the clotted blood. Looked like he'd been on his back, left arm extended.

Damn.

Jillian stepped wide, ignored the stares, and entered the foyer past the ornately carved door with its artisti-cally rendered buffalo bull. Another evidence marker stood by a loose string that ran from the inside door handle to a Molesworth-style chair no more than ten feet back on the polished Italian-tile floor.

Jillian veered wide around the string. One of the crime scene techs was staring through his goggles as he used a hand-held laser to inspect the double-barrel shotgun duct-taped to the chair. The laser was a common tool used to document fingerprints. The guy rocked back on his heels, shifted the goggles up on his forehead, and shook his head in frustration.

Jillian could see that the string ended in a loop tied around both triggers with a slipknot. Fingerprint powder dusted the gun, chair, and tape. Looking back, she could see the double barrels aimed chest-high at the door.

"Son of a bitch," she whispered to herself.

Vague images stirred in her memory.

Something dissociated.

Unreal.

It's as if she's standing there, the foyer oddly silvered and watery. Time seems to slow, distant voices, half remembered, are too indistinct to understand. Something important hovers just beyond her comprehension.

Jillian tries to fix on it. Yes. Important. Something she should know...

"Ma'am?" The voice makes her jump.

And she was back in the foyer, heart beating wildly in her chest. She blinked, fully aware of the fancy wainscoting, the great door, the string and shotgun. And there's the crime scene tech, crouched over the shotgun, his soft brown eyes fixed curiously on her.

"Sorry," she said, and forced herself back to the room, to the scene. "Happens sometimes. I was just..." She gestured her embarrassment.

"Looked like you'd just checked out. Like you weren't here, I mean. You okay?"

"Yeah. Just tired," she lied.

"Good thing they took the body away. It even weirded me out. Really made a mess." The tech went back to studying the shotgun. "I mean...that's cold. Two barrels, right to the chest."

She tried to shake off the trancelike feel.

Come on, Jillian, get your mind in the game.

"Yeah," the tech continued. "The guy that rigged this knew what he was doing."

"Any clues?"

"Nada."

She made herself concentrate on the wooden-walled foyer with its sconce lighting. Curiously, an evidence marker had been placed behind the door. Number 22, it rested on

the ornate tile beneath the coat rack.

Hearing voices, Jillian proceeded through the arched entry into the great room. Spacious, with a soaring ceiling, it what might have been a centerpiece for a *Cowboys & Indians* architectural spread. Custom tooled-leather furniture that hinted of Molesworth influence rested on intricate Navajo rugs, and a huge buffalo hide covered the floor before the giant river-stone fireplace. Decorated with antler art, a Cody High Style wet bar dominated one corner of the room. Expensive-looking bottles gleamed on the mirrored backbar. Across from it, floor-to-ceiling windows offered spectacular views of the Gallatins. An incredible elk-antler chandelier hung from the high log center pole, the ceiling all finished in knotty pine.

Two officers were seated across from the giant sofa with its rich Cordovan leather. She recognized Sheriff Bert Wain, his florid face looking even redder under the creamy white Stetson he'd pushed back from his forehead. He had unzipped his nylon uniform coat with its badge and patches; the elastic band was tucked tight at his duty belt. A curled cord ran from the mic at his shoulder to the com box on his belt.

The female deputy—Sampson according to her nametag—was a heavyset blonde woman in her mid-forties who leaned forward in the chair beside him, concentrating on the woman who huddled on the couch.

The fortyish woman curled on the cushions reminded Jillian of a terrified mouse. Suspect? Witness? Dressed in a stylish leather coat with tan slacks, the woman was tall and thin. Her face, while not unattractive, had a severe expression. Her blonde hair was cut short with bangs and fashionable curls around her ears. Tension tightened the lines around her fatigued eyes. The thin woman's knees were pulled up, and she kept rubbing her hands up and down the backs of her arms while looking drained, empty, and distraught.

A folder of paperwork was spread over the stone slab top of the coffee table. Looked like accounting.

Come on, think, Jillian. Get a grip and remember why you're here.

Wain looked up, and Jillian could see the hesitation in his eyes, as if annoyed at her arrival. She fished out her credentials as the sheriff stood and walked over. Jillian figured him at about five-foot-seven without the additional two inches lent by the dogger heels on his polished black western boots. Without a word, he glanced at the familiar Montana DOJ badge, then gave her a wary appraisal before asking, "Why are you here, Agent Masterson? Why is the Investigations Bureau interested?"

With a tilt of her head, Jillian indicated the corner of the room next to the wet bar. Sheriff Wain followed her over, the question growing behind his brown eyes.

Turning, Jillian told him, "I was headed home to Billings on I-90 when I got the call. My boss, Supervisor Meyer, had just gotten off the phone with the governor.

Meyer wanted me to ensure that the victim was really Ryman Banks the Third. If it is, I'm to act as liaison between the Gallatin County Sheriff's Office and the Major Case Section. I'm to offer you every assistance."

"Shit." Wain exhaled, glanced around the room with weary eyes. "Okay, so it's Banks, all right. No doubt. That's Carly Joyner on the couch. She's Banks' business associate and the CEO at the International Coalition on Habitat Rescue. It's a nonprofit environmental organization. You know. The one that's in the news all the time. She found the body this morning."

"What was she doing out here?"

"Says she wanted to go over the books. That's what those papers on the coffee table are all about. Says the accountant has issues about how much the organization spent during a legal campaign in DC last year. Says that Banks didn't answer her phone calls last night, so she thought he was brushing her off. Figured to catch him at home first thing this morning."

Jillian looked around at the house. "Looks pretty plush for a nonprofit, don't you think? Ryman Banks have another source of income?"

"Don't know," Wain admitted, sticking fingers in the back of his duty belt and rocking onto his toes. "Joyner says Banks gets reimbursed by the hour like any other attorney. But we'll run that down."

"Time of death?"

"Doc France estimates it was last night based on body temp, but he'll refine that back at the lab. Says that figuring it precisely might be complicated by the front door being open all night. Didn't matter that we had a low of five degrees. Hot air would have been blowing out through the open door. Ambient temperature wouldn't be constant."

Wain paused. "You saw the shotgun? It's an old trick. Probably been in use for as long as there have been firearms. My evidence guys have been going over the room with a fine toothed comb. Everything's wiped as clean as an operating room floor. We're having trouble finding so much as fibers, let alone anything as blatant as fingerprints. Might get lucky back at the lab. Might be a partial on the shells or maybe on the shotgun's standing breech."

"And no one heard the shots?"

Wain waved out through the windows. "Out here? Closest neighbor is a mile away. But we're checking."

Jillian chewed her lips. "Whose shotgun?"

"We think it belongs to Ryman Banks. I mean, did you get a close look at it?"

"Side-by-side, looked to me like a 12 gauge." She shrugged.

"It's a Merkel. German. Expensive. Engraved. All the slots in the screws are what's called 'regulated.' Means they all align in the same direction when they're torqued to spec. The wood's top-grade walnut. Really fine. Think big dollar signs. On rare occasion maybe you'd find something like it in the Gun Library at Cabela's, but you're not going to buy a Merkle in the sporting goods department at Wal-Mart."

"So..." she mused, "whoever set the booby trap knew where Ryman Banks kept his guns."

"Yep. Safe door was open in the gunroom when we got here. Got prints from the electric combination lock. We'll run them and see what turns up." Wain's lips curled into a humorless grin. "So, if we assume the safe was locked, that means our perp knew the combination. That narrows the suspects down to a handful. We get a print, we got the shooter."

Jillian nodded, shifting her gaze to Carly Joyner. "Did you ask her if she knew the combination?"

Wain followed Jillian's gaze to wilted-looking bean-pole woman on the couch. "Says she has no clue when it comes to the safe. Says she and Banks didn't agree about guns. Claims she donates regularly to the gun control lobby and votes for anti-gun Democrats. We'll check it out, but given her other political stances, I suspect she's telling the truth."

Wain's eyebrow lifted. "The code to the front door? That's a different thing. According to Ms. Joyner, the keypad code was 111222. We checked after we dusted for prints. That's it, all right. Joyner says it wasn't any secret in Mr. Banks' circle of close associates and lady friends."

"Was Joyner one of those lady friends?"

"Don't know."

"What about other enemies? A guy like Banks? Given what he does? With their lawsuits ICoHR has made a ton of trouble for ranchers, developers, politicians, Yellowstone, the Park Service, the Forest Service, you name it."

Sheriff Wain took another deep breath. "Yeah. Banks was kind of like a lit stick of dynamite bouncing around southern Montana. You never knew whose porch he'd land on or where he was going to go off next. I've got a whole file full of threats, restraining orders, and the stuff posted on social media would make your hair stand up. A lot of people wanted Banks dead."

"Anyone outstanding on that list?" Jillian asked.

Sheriff Wain shrugged. "Got one piece of the puzzle that doesn't fit. A hat."

"A hat?" Jillian glanced again at the view of the Gallatin Range, fading now in sunset.

"Yep. Evidence marker twenty-two just inside the

front door. A custom black beaver cowboy hat made by Kevin O'Farrell out of Santa Fe. Custom hatters, you see, they put the name of who they made if for in the sweat-band. In this case, the hat was made for a John B. Cody. One of my guys called O'Farrell's. Seems they've got really good records. John B. Cody is John Bernard Cody from down in Sunlight Basin, just across the line in Wyoming. I thought the name rang a bell, and sure enough. Cody has been a thorn in Ryman Banks' side for years. Testified against the ICoHR in a number of their lawsuits. Cody and Banks despise each other."

"So, how did Cody's hat end up here at the murder scene?" Jillian noticed that on the couch, Carly Joyner had turned her attention from the female deputy to her. Even across the room, the woman's gaze had the intensity of lasers. Something about it was downright haunting.

A shiver ran down Jillian's back as the woman's weird pale green eyes seemed to burn right through her.

She barely heard Sheriff Wain say, "Yeah, that's the question, isn't it?"

CHAPTER FOUR

An impenetrable haze of blowing snow obscured the highway to a depth of about five feet. In the Ram 3500's headlights, it was an opaque wall of rushing white that blew in waves across what was now invisible blacktop. Beyond the headlights' feeble reach, the night pressed down so inky black a person might have rolled down the window, reached out, and touched it.

In the driver's seat, John Bernard Cody blinked, squinted, and checked his speed. The big dually pickup with its heavy gooseneck stock trailer in tow was barely doing thirty, and that, he figured, was too damn fast. Especially since he was pretty much navigating by the occasionally visible reflector post and the rumble strips that marked the centerline and road edges.

Not for the first time, Cody wondered if he was an idiotic fool for being out on the road on a night like this. Maybe he was. The only other traffic was the occasional semi-truck and trailer. The over-the-road guys had elevation going for them, sitting high enough to see over the wind-blown snow. And they had weight. Weight meant traction.

Cody glanced into his driver's side mirror. The clearance lights burned a gleaming amber on his twenty-eight foot stock trailer. The all-steel Titan was the "Bull-rated" heavy-duty model. The one with three full-width compartments. Just the sight of those lights in the middle of the darkness and storm reassured him. Along with the cab and fender clearance lights, they kept other drivers from running into him. As long as he, in turn, didn't crash into some stalled or stopped auto in the middle of the lane, he'd be all right.

And so would his. They now rode back in the trailer, uneasy, stressed out, and headed for a new home. They'd have been more stressed out if bison only understood what black ice and ground blizzard really meant. Since they were riding back there in blissful ignorance, John got to do the worrying for all of them.

There were various qualities of soul among the people who raised bison.

Some, mostly the super-rich and the occasional make-a-quick-buck entrepreneur, looked at the bison as curiosities, economic units, or a tradable commodity. Just potential dollar bills wandering around on four feet. The wealthy bought the animals because they looked exotic and epic while grazing on their multimillion-dollar Western ranches. Call them appropriated cultural icons used to ensure that the agricultural tax exemptions saved the owners tens of thousands a year over what they'd pay for "recreational" property. After all, these were ranches they visited for a week or two, or wrote off as a corporate retreat, before climbing onto their private jets to fly back to their mansions in the New Jersey horse country, the Hamptons, Marin County, or outside of Austin.

On the other hand, the get-rich-quick folks only cared about the money. Bison usually sold anywhere from two to three times what beef brought on the open market. To the entrepreneurs, a buffalo was a walking short-term investment. Raise them to slaughter-weight on as little feed as could be grown or scrounged, load them into a truck, and send them off to the plant. Then cash the check.

Those were the soulless ones, devoid of empathy, who traded buffalo with no more emotional investment than they felt when buying and selling stocks, bonds, toasters, or washing machines.

For most ranchers—or producers, as they were called in the business—bison were precious. For some, they were a tie with America's ancient past. After all, buffalo had been here for around two hundred thousand years, compared to beef cattle that'd been in America for only a few hundred years. For others, bison were fascinating creatures imbued with a haunting spiritual presence. And then there were the producers who just plain thrived on the animals and the unique challenges they presented. Like the fact that if you were going to ranch bison, you'd damn well better have a well-developed sense of humor. Because with buffalo, you were going to need it. They were, simply put, smarter than humans.

To John Cody, bison remained a wonder, living beings for whom he was responsible. Maybe that quality made him and those like him such good stewards. And there were four of the shaggy critters riding back in that Titan trailer: a Canadian grand champion two-year-old bull; a gold-trophy-winning bred two-year-old heifer; and two yearling heifers. Of the later, one was the Grand Champion female from a ranch in southern Colorado, the other a hard luck case who had just caught Cody's eye.

Didn't matter that her pale coffee-and-cream brown coat was lusterless, or that she'd been nutritionally deprived, she had the structure and potential. Sometimes, with bison as with people, all an individual needed was a chance.

Cody had been high bidder on all four at the National Western Stock Show sale ring. Each would be an addition, bringing traits he admired to his ranch herd. Now his responsibility was to get them home to Pilot Creek Ranch in safety.

He just hadn't figured on roads like this. Frickin' black ice so slick a serpent couldn't slither across it.

"Hell, I never was much good at metaphors," he muttered. Yawned. Blinked his eyes.

Ground blizzard. Endless waves of white. Undulating and hypnotizing. Look at it long enough and you'd start to see things: Shapes. Faces. Ghosts. Especially when a feller was on the end of a long week. And, damn, given his "extra-curricular" activities, this year's stock show had been longer and harder, with less sleep than normal.

He was trying not to think about sleep. How good it would be as the blowing white rippled and wavered in the headlight's glow. What started as shapes and lines misted together into eyes, nose, could see her mouth. Speaking. The words lost in the low moan of wind and engine.

"Mom?" he whispered, and looked into his mother's desperate eyes.

She was trying to tell him something, the words muffled by the windshield and roar.

"What?" he demanded, grip tightening on the wheel.

And as quickly, a gutter of wind whipped her away into the billowing streamers of endless white.

Cody took a deep breath. His heart hammered

against his sternum. A shiver played down his back despite the truck's heater.

"Damn it, Mom," he told the vanished apparition. "I'm getting close. Not sure you'd like how I did it, but I got a name."

He blinked, fought a yawn as his fear subsided. The quick trip had taken two days. Right in the middle of the conference, he'd slipped out. Made that mad all-night drive up I-25 clear up to Montana. Arrived in Hardin at the cheap motel just at daybreak. Dewey Tarbeau had still been in bed. Cody had pounded on the door of room 27. The miracle was that he hadn't awakened the entire motel.

Tarbeau had opened the door, his glittery light blue eyes red-rimmed and puffy.

"Got my money?"

Cody had handed him an envelope.

"Come on in," Tarbeau had told him, stepping to the side and, after scanning the dawn-grayed parking lot, had closed the door.

Cody would remember that room. The musty smell of old tobacco, mold, and unwashed human. The one lamp on the nightstand. The wadded bedding.

And Dewey Tarbeau. Greasy black hair hung in strands over the man's collar, his faded blue denim shirt wrinkled and unwashed, stained here and there with old food, the cuffs frayed and dirt-rimmed. The blue jeans hanging on the man's bony hips had been grease-shiny, worn, with the knees out.

Cody thought the guy looked like a rat with his thin narrow face, broken nose, and missing teeth.

"Have you got what I need?" Cody had asked as Tarbeau's dirty fingers counted the bills in the envelope.

The man sniffed, wiped a sleeve under his nose, then fixed Cody with those glittery blue eyes.

"I gotta have more money. This ain't enough. Not when what I know could git me kilt."

Dewey Tarbeau's head almost popped off his neck when Cody hit him. The skinny man had never seen the blow coming. He may or may not have seen the ones that followed.

But John Cody left that dingy stinky old motel with a name: Jerry "Crank" Laumer.

"So, Mom, I haven't forgotten."

No. Anything but.

Debts had to be paid. It all went back to that responsibility thing. Stuff John Cody really hadn't wanted to do. Not that week. Not ever. But there hadn't been a choice.

Back at the conference hotel in Denver, Gus Cooney had said, "Missed you." That had been Thursday night just before the fun auction banquet. "Where you been the last couple of days?"

"Around," John had told the grizzled old rancher. It hadn't been a lie. As a term, "around" covered a lot of ground. Then he'd added, "You know how stock show is. Walked the Coliseum. Caught the rodeo last night. Been looking at the livestock in the Pavilion and checking out the exhibits. Never knew there were that many breeds of chickens."

Cooney had nodded. "Wanted to talk to you about that bull you brought this year. He's outta your Red Canyon Silvertip line, isn't he? Got that long woodsy look about him."

"Yeah. I call him Sun Dancer, out of that old Moss cow and Fire Dancer," he'd said easily and started into the bull's weight, gain, and structural assets.

Funny how a person in the midst of people could just

disappear and reappear. It had been as easy as that. John had fallen into the conversation about bloodlines, sires and dams, and old Gus had never batted an eye.

For a second Cody thought he saw Gus's face form in the blanket of flickering white haze.

John shook his head. Damn. By now Gus was enjoying two fingers of bourbon at his ranch in Belle Fourche, South Dakota. Sun Dancer would have been unloaded in a new corral, happy to be out of the trailer, smelling other buffalo, sniffing a different wind filled with new scents.

At least, that was the hope. Gus had pulled out early, should have been ahead of this weather.

Cody jerked, half startled by the buzzing of the cell phone in his breast pocket.

Damn. Should have turned it off back at the Ghost Town truck stop when he fueled up before leaving Casper. He eased the wheel, steering right as the driver's side tires rumbled on the hidden centerline. Caught the barest glimmer of light from one of the reflector posts off to the side. Then a big blast of wind hit him from the right, pushing hard on the big stock trailer.

Adrenaline charged him like a live wire as the outfit slipped sideways.

Carefully, he feathered the throttle to keep the diesel off compression, let the truck and trailer coast, steering with the skid, bringing the Ram dually back into line, and catching the edge of the rumble strip as he did. Damn, that had been close.

Exhaling, he eased the throttle, accelerating from the fifteen miles per hour he'd slowed to. Another reflector post gave him his bearings.

Only then did he remember the phone call. Taking a chance, he reached into his pocket and retrieved the phone. Tapping the screen, it brought up a 406 area code. Montana. Funny, he'd just been thinking about Montana. The number didn't trip any memories. He checked the "recent" phone log. What the hell? In the last hour, while he'd been out of cell service, there'd been a whole string of calls from Montana. Same number. Someone he'd met at the show and sale? Somebody wanting meat or hides? They could wait.

Without a thought, John slipped his phone back in his pocket. On road like this he needed two hands on the wheel. Couldn't chance a distraction.

Checked the time. A little after ten thirty. At this rate, he was still four to five hours from home. He wondered. When he got there, would anything be the same? Or, like with the death of his parents, had his activities this last week marked another change of direction? And had he been good enough, smart enough, to make it work?

Jerry "Crank" Laumer.

Now, all he had to do was find him.

CHAPTER FIVE

I n her room in Bozeman's Hilton Garden Inn, Jillian Masterson sat perched at the desk. On the laptop, Montana Governor Nick Brewster's face filled the left half of the screen while her boss, Gaylen Meyer's, filled the right. The pizza she'd just eaten across the street at Old Chicago should have smothered the butterflies in her stomach.

They weren't.

It was unsettling to be looking into the Governor's eyes, a man who could break her career with a single word.

For his part, Gaylen Meyer had an uncharacteristic ruffled look behind his normally placid gray gaze. He kept reaching up, smoothing back the silvered hair at his temples and shifting as though uncomfortable.

"*A shotgun, huh?*" Governor Brewster said incredulously.

"Taped to a chair, sir. It's an old-style booby trap. The problem with such a set up is that it kills whomever opens the door. Indiscriminate. That's really got Sheriff Wain concerned. Turns out that lots of Banks' friends knew the door security code. Could have been anybody who walked through that door."

"I just talked to the sheriff," Brewster told her. "He's taking this for the full-court press. So far he's got a short list of suspects. You were there, Agent Masterson, what do you think?"

"I think the sheriff's a good man. He's covering all the bases, sir."

"That's not what I asked." On the screen, Brewster's eyes narrowed, his trademark twitching of the lip when he was annoyed very apparent. "What do *you* think, Agent Masterson?" He looked down at something out of sight on his desk. "Says here that you're a recent graduate of the criminal justice program at the University of Montana in Missoula. Is that why Gaylen hired you?"

Director Meyer broke in, speaking carefully. "Jillian has my complete confidence, Governor."

"Why'd you pick a rookie for this, Gaylen? Some special reason? You know what this case means to me. Ryman Banks was more than just a donor. He was a close friend."

Gaylen nodded. "I know, sir. Jillian was headed back to Billings after a meeting here in Helena. Our Bozeman Section was already committed to a fentanyl ring working the university. I took a chance that Jillian could swing by." He cleared his throat. "If you will recall, you only asked for a report, sir. We only knew that the Gallatin County SO was investigating Ryman Banks' death. Not that it was a homicide, let alone one as sensational as this."

Brewster sucked at his lips, brow furrowed. "It does look like someone wanted to make a point, doesn't it?

One of these right-wing hillbilly God and guns groups? You know, Ryman's ICoHR just sued the US Fish and Wildlife Service, the Park Service, and Forest Service over the Yellowstone bison. Or could this be something from one of the landowners? Maybe that Dan Butler fellow just this side of Gardner?"

Gaylen checked something out of sight. "ICoHR put the guy out of business. Ruined the value of Butler's ranch by having it declared critical habitat for several species of endangered wildlife migrating down from the park. Butler is currently under a court restraining order to stay away from Banks and anyone from ICoHR."

Jillian surreptitiously made notes. Dan Butler. The image stuck in her mind: a tall lanky old rancher wearing a cowboy hat being hauled off by Bozeman police. They'd been tipped off. Arrested outside the ICoHR offices before Butler could enter with a semiautomatic shotgun and some pistols. Said he'd lost everything, so why not his life?

"I want every lead run down." Brewster shook his head, a sad look in his dark eyes. "I want the son of a bitch who did this caught, Gaylen. Put your best on it."

Later, Jillian would ask herself what could have possibly goaded her to say it, but she did.

"I'm already on it, sir."

Brewster had straightened, a roiling behind his eyes. "I guess that remains to be seen, doesn't it, Agent Masterson?"

The image flicked off, Gaylen's face now dominating the screen. His bushy right eyebrow raised, a deadly hint of humor in the lift of his lip. "Jillian? If I would have known this was going to be such a hot potato..."

She took a deep breath. "I've got it, sir. Whatever it

takes. Consider me the governor's eyes and ears on this case. I can do this."

"Yeah, well you and Sheriff Wain better wrap this up quick. I know Nick Brewster. You screw this up? In the whole state of Montana you'll be lucky to so much as find a job washing dishes in a truck stop."

CHAPTER SIX

It worked! The story was all over the evening news out of Billings. Seated at the table in his house outside Clark, Wyoming, three and a half hours from Bozeman, Seeley Atherton stared at the image on his computer screen. The place wasn't much, an old frame ranch house, white-sided, with three rooms and a worn green asphalt-shingle roof. But it was at the end of the road miles from the nearest neighbor, with a splendid view of the majestic Beartooth Mountain Range rising just to the west.

He'd killed Ryman. Odd to think that he'd known the man, talked to him, been to his house on social occasions in support of ICoHR. Shared his victim's food and drink. He should have felt something. It should have filled him with a sense of sadness or loss.

Instead, the only thought in his head was, what the hell had taken so long?

He considered that as he checked the sizzling medallions of backstrap cooking in the skillet. Seeley preferred to eat wild meat for health reasons. This was freshly cut from a dead bighorn ewe lamb's carcass that he'd poached a couple of days before. Killed the lamb with a single long shot across a high meadow. She'd never known what hit her. The tender meat smelled heavenly. It mixed perfectly with the feeling of relief that ran through him. What if the wrong person had opened that door?

What if he had left a clue?

But the information he'd been given had been perfect. The code to the front door—God bless electronic locks. The combination to the big gun safe. Everything just like the instructions had lain out.

Seeley had taken no chances with the job. He had worn a bouffant surgical bonnet lest he shed so much as a single hair, and plastic HAZMAT suit with booties to contain pollen, fibers, or other contamination. Had pulled cotton gloves from their plastic packaging and worn them over nitrile gloves to avoid any chance of leaving a fingerprint. Even then, he'd wiped everything down and even vacuumed the foyer.

The suit, hat, booties and gloves had gone into the burn barrel the moment he'd come home.

Satisfied with the searing on the tender meat, he turned off the burner and used a spatula to pile the sizzling steaks on his plate. Pouring a cup of coffee, Seeley was just about to seat himself at the table when his phone buzzed to announce a text message.

Payment made in full.

Pick up at the usual place.

One more thing to cross off his list of worries. Payment had always been made through a dead drop. In this case, a package left in a partially silted-in culvert on Forest Service land just outside of Bozeman.

On the TV, the reporter was standing at the entrance to Ryman's property, talking in that serious way reporters did. The lined brow, the serious nods of the head, the expressive brooding and pursed lips.

Seeley reminisced, thinking back to better times he had had on the property. Those had been days of celebration that had followed various victories in the endless battle to save the land, its animals, and water. Ryman Banks had been a leader in the fight. A true warrior.

Sometimes it became a warrior's duty to die for the cause.

Seeley would have. In a heartbeat. So he couldn't feel particularly sorry for Ryman.

And this was war.

He rubbed his eyes, aware of the scars where his thick black eyebrows pinched under his frown. Maybe it was reminiscing about Ryman, but he hardly tasted his breakfast. He pushed back the dining room chair and picked up his morning coffee. The house was redolent with the smell of frying meat as he placed his plate in the sink.

Walking over to the dining room window, he stared out at the jutting slopes of the Beartooth Mountains just to the west of his small house. A thousand feet up, clouds obscured the peaks, and feathery tendrils of snow blew down across the slabs of uplifted Permian limestone. That view had always impressed him. The incredible amount of force it took to shove that much rock upright for a couple of thousand near-vertical feet. Not to mention that the core of the uplift was solid 2.7 billion-year-old granite and gneiss. Like looking out at the very bones of the Earth.

A gust of wind made the window shudder, and a few flakes of snow blew across his yard. He could see more clouds flowing from the mouth of the Clark's Fork

Canyon, fluffy and roiling as they spilled out through the great V of stone that marked the river's emergence from the mountains.

He stared sightlessly at the vista. Banks was dead. It would change the entire dynamic, provide a martyr for the struggle.

"No man is irreplaceable," he told himself. "Someone's gotta carry the fight to the enemy."

Banks had done that.

So had Seeley. First as a kid when his father walked out and left Seeley and his mother to fend for themselves. Then with Charley Mace when the man had taken them in and started abusing Seeley's mom. When young Seeley tried to do something about it, old Charley had beaten him half to death. Lotta hard lessons learned there. But Seeley had gotten Charley in the end. Filmed him smacking Mom around and ripping her clothes off. Then Seeley had taken a twenty-four-inch pipe wrench to Charley, all the while screaming, "Leave her alone! That's rape, you son of a bitch!"

The beating had put Charley in the hospital; the cell phone video had given the DA enough to file charges of battery and sexual assault that got Charley put away for two years. Seeley, of course, walked free as a hero. He'd been a celebrity in high school because of it.

Funny thing about Mom, though. She'd never really forgiven him. Or trusted him, either.

In the Army he'd taken every challenge. Earned his Ranger Patch and been assigned to some pretty hairy shit when they sent him downrange. Then, in Afghanistan, somehow the rules had changed. He wasn't sure when that had happened. Couldn't pick out the moment when good and bad had gone fuzzy.] When does white turn gray, and when does gray become black? How do you know where that fine line is?

He thinks back to the moment he knew he'd crossed the line. Remembers. He hears the thunder of the M4 as he bursts into the squalid, flat-roofed stone house. Sees the movement, barely hears the screams over the banging muzzle blast. Just bodies dressed in stained off-white and tan robes. Smudged images. Moving, screaming. And then they are dead. Shot down as his thirty-round mag runs dry and the bolt locks open.

He drops the mag and inserts a second out of instinct. The bolt snaps closed. The acrid smell of burned powder is cloying, thick in the room.

The silence is deafening. Ears ringing, he can't hear the faintest rustle of cloth on the sleeping pallets, or the soft exhalation from blood-frothed lips.

He can only see the twitching and quivering of legs and arms, the weak grasping of the fingers as they tremble and go still. Blood, ghostlike in silence, begins to spread on their clothing.

Seeley squints in the half-light. Cranes his head as his heart rate slows, and hears the first plaintive cry from the baby. Locates the infant back in the corner of the room where it kicks and waves tiny fists.

Then he looks again at the five bodies sprawled in a tangle before him...and realizes they are all young women and teenage girls.

A search of the room turns up no weapon. Nothing more lethal than a rusty bread knife.

Gray is such a perplexing color.

Seeley comes back to the present, to Wyoming, eyes once again seeing the patterns of snow blowing down from the Beartooths.

Fighting for the right side. That's what mattered. Somehow he'd lost that in Afghanistan. Found it again when he moved here. To the West. To a place where all that was good and clean and wild and free lay defenseless before the rapacious greed of the ranchers who shot the coyotes and denied wildlife the graze they needed to survive. Defenseless against the miners, the developers, and the multitudes who would pollute the last free place. A land that needed warriors and sacrifice. A land that needed someone like him.

And now Ryman Banks' death signaled to the world that what once had been an abstract environmental movement, was now a life-or-death struggle for the future.

The only thing that would make sense to them was that Banks had been too much of a threat to the ranchers and developers. To the old guard and exploiters. If you couldn't win a fight straight up, you took out the enemy's advantage. Like with Charley so long ago. With Banks dead, people would think ICoHR had lost its most powerful asset.

"But you haven't won," Seeley promised as he sipped his coffee. "We've just raised the stakes."

As if the universe were listening, his computer dinged.

Seeley walked back to the table, bent down, and opened his messenger. Saw the text.

Possible complications.

If needed can you assist?

Usual rate applies.

Setting his coffee down, he typed:

Whatever you need. I'm your warrior.

Then the reply.

A few loose ends need to be dealt with.

Seeley grunted to himself and deleted the exchange. It wasn't as if he hadn't expected this.

He washed his coffee cup and did the dishes before entering his bedroom. He'd made the twin bed that morning after rising, of course. A narrow aisle separated the small bed from a reloading bench with its press, dies, powders, and components. A large gun safe stood in one corner. Seeley pressed in the security code on the safe, opened the heavy door, and selected a scoped Ruger American bolt action in 6.5 Creedmoor that was still wrapped in the manufacturer's plastic, a handgun case, and equipment bag.

His bug-out bag was already packed.

Fifteen minutes later, his house locked up behind him, the metal gate chained closed, Seeley was on his way to Montana.

And the next stage of the fight.

CHAPTER SEVEN

*S*he is staring wide-eyed at the darkness. Her heart beats
frantically.

   ThumpityThumpityThumpity!

It's dark. Black.

She strains but only hears the sounds of the house.

Pull the blanket up. Crawl under it. Hide!

Blankets are safe. Magical.

Please, God. Make it safe.

*Her heart beats even faster, and the shiver makes her whole
body shake.*

She freezes at the noise. Hears the bedroom door open.

She doesn't breathe.

Doesn't think.

Hears the heavy exhale of his breath.

Please, God. Please...

And the blanket is ripped away.

Magic is a lie...

Jillian jerked awake, stifled a cry. She sat bolt upright,
staring around the room. On the ceiling the smoke
detector blinked its pale green light. The microwave

clock flashed 2:37. She could see the light from the parking lot outside seeping in around the drawn curtain.

Breathe!

Jillian sucked a deep breath into her half-suffocated lungs, and she panted for air. Damn, how long had she been holding her breath? With a trembling hand, she pulled her hair back, realized it was wet, and she was sweating. Hot. The room heater kicked on, the sound of the fan reassuring.

In her mind, images froze, the dream slowly faded against the reality that she was in the Hilton Garden Inn. In Bozeman. That she's all right. That she wasn't a little six-year-old girl. Not in that bedroom. There is no man, no blanket.

Not now.

Not here.

"Get it together, Jillian," she told herself.

At least she wasn't on the floor. That happened sometimes. Or she'd find herself under the bed, having no idea how she'd gotten there.

Pushing the covers back, Jillian swung her legs out and climbed to her feet. She plodded barefoot into the bathroom, emptied her bladder, braced elbows on knees and propped her head on her hands. For what seemed an eternity, she sat there. Fought the shivers as fragmented images played ghostly games in her head.

"Why do I dream that?"

But she did. Over and over. And there were other recurring dreams, some just as unsettling. It had been worse when she was taking classes that focused on crimes against children. She'd barely slept that entire semester. Thought maybe she'd been going crazy. Drank too much. Gotten the worst grades of her entire college career.

God, yes. A drink. What she wouldn't give.

And right downstairs in the lounge, there were all those bottles locked up behind the cabinet.

Maybe she could talk the night manager into just one...

"Stop it! God, Jillian! It was just a fucking dream. Your subconscious playing games with your head."

Finally, she flushed, got up, and sucked down a glass of water. Then she walked back out into the room. She found her shoulder holster hanging from the chair back and shucked her service pistol. A forty caliber Glock 23.

The cool weight in her hand felt reassuring, solid.

She had a love-hate relationship with that Glock. Cradling the compact pistol to her chest diluted any sense of helplessness. She was no longer a potential victim, but capable of protecting herself. And the forty-caliber bullet was a proven man-stopper. But, damn! She hated the almost painful snapping recoil when she shot the thing. It had taken her three tries to qualify at the range, not to mention that it was cumbersome to pack. Even wearing jackets, the shoulder holster rig was uncomfortable and awkward.

Ripping the cover off the bed, Jillian retreated to the chair in the corner, wrapped the coverlet around her, and tucked her legs under her. She blinked at the night, blanking her brain. Clutching the Glock close to her chest, she stared vacantly at the room clock. Watched the numbers flip from 3:05 to 3:06.

Don't sleep.

If you do, he might come back.

And the blanket won't protect you.

Fortunately, there are a lot of numbers on the room clock, and they change to a new one every minute.

CHAPTER EIGHT

John Cody cranked an eye open, seeing faint light through the curtains. From out in the yard, he could hear the sound of a diesel. Had to be old Danielle Redweed out on the tractor attending to her morning chores. Cody grunted to himself. Images of dreams that should have only been dreams, but were not, whirled away into wakefulness.

He scratched his stomach as he wandered into the bathroom and stood at the toilet. Through the little window he could see snowflakes drifting down between the house and the thicket of fir trees out beyond the yard fence.

Across the yard, he could see the John Deere 540, the chained tires clinking musically as Danny made the journey from the stack yard to the east pasture gate. A big round bale of grass hay bobbed on the spike as the tractor passed.

Dressing, Cody ambled into the kitchen. Large for a ranch kitchen, it reflected the fact that Pilot Creek Ranch had once catered to dudes and hunters, so the old white-painted wooden cabinets were large. The vintage Wolf stove on the back wall had six burners and an oversized Sub-Zero fridge stood across from the sink. The oddity was the big mirror in the corner behind the small table where he and Danny usually ate breakfast. Set at an angle, he supposed his mother had mounted it there so she could look out one of the windows and see the reflected mountains while she cooked.

Cody made coffee in the Capresso machine, listening to it grind, steam, and infuse the beans. Then he scarfed down a burrito filled with canned refritos, Ortega diced chilis, and a slab of cheddar. Fit for the day, he paused, seeing the number of messages on the answering machine. That same damn 406 number. Screw it. They'd wait.

At the front door, he checked the thermometer: twelve degrees.

From the crowded coat rack, he pulled down his heavy buffalo coat, one Merlin's Hide Out had built from old Leo's winter hide. Leo had been a particularly dark bull, having a little Orcheski blood in his lineage. Buttoning the coat, John clamped his hat down tight. The feel of it brought a growl to his lips. Didn't matter that it was labeled 100% beaver, it didn't feel like it. And brand-new off-the-rack hats never fit quite right and were always too damn stiff.

Slipping into his packs, he opened the door and headed out through the pristine snow across the yard to the corrals. His truck and trailer, mantled in white, stood where he'd left them. It had been close to three am when he'd unloaded the last compartment and locked the two-year-old bred heifer in her pen. The Titan was still backed up to the corral load-out gate.

Cody paused long enough to knock the snow off and

climb into the Ram. He waited for the pre-heat before starting the diesel. Cody let it idle while he clambered over the corral. He could see Danny Redweed's tracks in the newly fallen snow. The old Shoshoni woman had already made the rounds and checked out the new arrivals. Cody followed the tracks down the alley to the first pen. The two yearling heifers stood in the back, side-by-side, watching him with a wary stare. Each had a dusting of snow on her back; their eyes gleamed as breath fogged from each one's nostrils.

"Morning, girls," Cody greeted. "Good to see you're up and at 'em this morning."

The heifers shifted, unsure if they should bolt.

Cody could see that they'd been into the hay, and the water was open where the tank heater kept it from freezing.

Then he crossed to the opposite side. The bred two-year-old, tag 208, stood alone and panicky. She immediately tried to flee, trotting from one side of the pen to the other. Cody paused only long enough to ensure her water was open and that she'd been in the hay. Bred heifers were always ringy—and as good as her confirmation and breeding might be, the ranch she came from was run by a bunch of wild-West cowboy types who shouldn't have been in the bison business. Best thing for her was to leave her alone. Let her figure out that she was safe.

The next pen down, the 214 tagged bull, the one Cody figured he'd call "Rumbler", was standing in the back corner, head up. He watched Cody approach, his nostrils blowing fog as he scented the air. Damn, he looked magnificent and full of himself. At the show, the bull had crossed the scales at nineteen hundred pounds, and that was after a two-day haul from Saskatchewan. Rumbler came from one of the best ranches in Canada.

What they called a "woods cross" because of the fiction the Canadian government maintained that "Woods" bison were different from "Plains" bison, even though no one had found any significant genetic divergence.

"How are you doing today, big guy?" Cody called. "You happy to be out of that trailer?"

Rumbler exhaled twin gusts of fog, but his head dropped to a more relaxed pose; he shifted, snow groaning under his weight.

Again, the bull had been at the hay, and the water was open.

"Always want to check, big fella. Make sure you new folks are eating and drinking. And don't you worry. You've got a couple of weeks to ease into the place. Figure out that no one's going to hurt you. Then we'll start to work getting you acquainted with the rest of the herd a little at a time."

Past the bull's pen, Cody walked to the end of the alley and stared out across the pasture. At first glance, everything looked good, and the sight never ceased to amaze him. Out in the snowy landscape he could see the herd. Not that he could get an accurate count from this far, but there should have been close to a hundred bison in the twenty-acre pasture. This was winter graze where he left the third cutting of meadow grass standing.

For the moment, they were milling around, following the tractor as Danny drove the hay bale over to one of the big round metal feeders. After a week of Cody being gone, the other feeders were partially full, indicating that Danny had been on the job.

Following the tractor, the bison crowded around in a free-for-all, butting each other, trying to get at the fresh bale. The dominant animals chased the subordinates away, charging, shaking their heads. It was pandemonium as individual bison leaped this way and that. Cody heard the metallic thump, watched as one of the cows leaped through the round steel feeder.

Then Danny raised the implement and artfully tilted the bale spike so the big round bale slid off to thump into the feeder.

"Looks like you all made it," Cody told the animals.

From the tracks, he could see that the entire herd had been packed around the corral during the night so they could smell and talk to the newcomers. Bison, dogs, wolves, and people. They had to be the most social animals on the planet.

His cell phone buzzed where it rested in his pocket.

Cody reached inside, pulling it out. Reception this far up in Sunlight Basin was hit or miss. For whatever reason, this morning the phone had a full bar of signal.

"Hello?"

The sound was scratchy and he could only catch bits of it. "...*Cody, this is the...sheriff's office...*" then it went away completely until, "...*talk to you...*"

"You're breaking up. How about you call me on my landline in ten minutes? I've got to move my truck and unhook the trailer. Like I said, you're breaking up. Call. My. Landline." And he gave them the number.

Putting his phone back, Cody sighed and propped his boot on the lowest railing. "Sheriff's office?"

He rocked his jaw, wishing he could have heard exactly *which* sheriff's office was trying to get hold of him. Images of Tarbeau's bloody and bruised face swam up from his memory. Damn, the bastard hadn't ratted, had he?

Grinding his teeth, the first tendrils of worry ticking his gut, he sighed and headed back up the alley to move his outfit, park his trailer, and unhook the pickup.

CHAPTER NINE

Checking the mirrors one last time, Seeley ensured the Forest Service access road south of Bozeman was empty. Just a snow-packed crowned-and-ditched gravel road that snaked its way between stands of fir, narrow-leafed cottonwood, and sage-covered slopes. Enough traffic had passed that last-night's dusting of white had been packed into a smooth sheen.

Seeley let his truck roll to a stop where the culvert ran under the road. Took one last look up and down the road to confirm he was alone and shifted into Park. He left the engine running, opened the door, and stepped out into the cold morning. He could see where someone had climbed up over the windrowed snow piled by the plow. The tracks had been curiously stomped in a manner that left them irregular and unidentifiable.

Taking care, he stepped into the same tracks, climbed over the crusted snow, and followed in his predecessor's footsteps down to the culvert.

Again, he glanced around.

Across the creek, the snow was unbroken around a grove of willows and narrow-leaf cottonwoods. He could see no tracks on the far slope where sage and rabbitbrush poked through the snowfield. To either side, the willows screened any view of the culvert.

Bending down, he found the package right where it was supposed to be. A large manila envelope, the flap sealed, was encased in a clear plastic wrapper to protect it from moisture. Thick, it felt right.

With care, he retraced his path, ensuring he didn't leave anything like an identifiable footprint. Climbing over the windrow, he slid into the driver's seat and slammed the door. Shifting to Drive, he motored off. For good measure, he followed the road up toward the next campground, carefully looked for tire tracks or any place someone might have turned off, left the road, and perhaps been waiting to catch sight of whomsoever might have collected the package.

He found nothing. At the campground—closed for the season with a chain across the gate—he pulled in as others had, shifted to reverse, and backed out to head back to Bozeman.

He waited until he was in town, pulled into the parking lot at a Maverick convenience store, and opened the package. The money was there, correct to the dollar. And so was a Post-it note on which were scribbled two names in pencil. The block-print letters were thick, looked forced, and obviously meant to disguise the writer's penmanship from any kind of analysis.

Seeley studied the names and instructions, frowned. They didn't make sense. Not to mention the increased risk. Doing what the client asked was playing with fire.

Then he looked at the stack of bills. Well, what the hell?

He was the warrior.

Glancing at the brand-new Ruger rifle, still encased in plastic, he figured it wasn't his job to judge.

CHAPTER TEN

J illian Masterson watched Sheriff Wain replace the handset of his office phone in the receiver. Muted gray morning light shone in through the window. Outside, a light snow was falling.

The sheriff's office might have been right out of a movie set. The desk was cluttered with papers, a Rotary Club cup served as a pen and pencil holder. A slightly dated Dell unit with Post-it notes on the monitor margins was centered across from his chair. An irregular stack of file folders, some brimming with paper and plastic marker tabs, extended dangerously over the edge, as if just waiting to be knocked onto the floor. A pile of opened envelopes, some with the letters sticking out, rose to Wain's left. An acrylic display held photos of Wain and two girls dressed in white cotton blouses and jeans that Jillian took to be his daughters. Others of the family included a portly gray-haired woman who leaned close and clutched Wain's arm. In the background, a life preserver ring with "Welcome to Curacao" painted around its circumference and a beach could be seen.

On the wall to Jillian's right a series of diplomas, certificates, awards, and photos had been framed and hung. Among them, photos of Sheriff Wain with all three of the previous governors before Brewster. Next to a photo of Wain—wearing orange, kneeling behind a massive dead elk—was a shot of him shaking Ted Turner's hand. And there were other celebrities. Various movie stars who made the area home, as well as some big name politicians.

After setting the handset back in its cradle, Wain stared thoughtfully at it. "That was Doc A.C.. Says he's narrowed the time of death down to between five thirty and seven last night based on core temperature, rigor, and lividity. Cause of death? Massive trauma to the chest, heart, and lungs from two shotgun blasts. Terminal ballistics and wound pattern are consistent with what you'd expect from both barrels of the shotgun we recovered. The double-aught buck pellets are tungsten-nickel consistent with the Heavy Shot hulls we recovered from the murder weapon."

"Did you find a box of that in his gun room?"

"Yep. Open and sitting on his reloading bench." Wain glanced at her. Reached for his cup of coffee. "And, before you ask, we got zip from either the box, shells, or fired hulls. Whoever did this was meticulous. Lab was on it all night. You know those fingerprints on the lock plate of the gun safe? The ones we were so anxious to match? They were identifiable as Ryman Banks'. Smudged, so the best guess is that our perp wore gloves. Probably cotton."

Jillian gave him a knowing look. "Let me guess. You didn't stumble across a pair of cotton gloves during the search yesterday, did you? Maybe isolate some fibers?"

"Nope. But I've got a deputy out there this morning

looking. Just in case they're there and no one made the connection."

She took a deep breath. "Don't worry, something will give us a break. Crime scenes are never perfect. The victim, the perpetrator, they all carry part of the puzzle on their clothing, in their cars, or leave it behind. It's just a matter of finding—"

"Yeah. Recent graduate from Montana U. Isn't that what I heard?" Wain was giving her a slight grin.

Jillian tensed. "Yes, as a matter of fact. I was—"

"Summa Cum Laude. I know." Wain leaned forward. "Now, don't let me rain on your parade, but out here in the real world things don't always work out like the text-book examples would lead you to think. Here we've got defense attorneys, bored crime scene techs, deputies who are preoccupied because their spouse just filed for divorce or their kid's marrying a low-life. Tags fall off bagged evidence while they're being shipped to the lab. Hell, we've even had a family dog contaminate a crime scene."

She met his gaze. "Yes, yes. And it all boils down to the DA's judgment as to whether you've got enough to prosecute, let alone convict. I know these things. But Sheriff, this time, we've *got* to catch the bad guy." She ended passionately, then forced herself to relax and sink back into the chair.

His sliver of smile weakened. "Yeah. Your supervisor gave me a call. Told me that you'd managed to hang your ass on the line with the governor. Gaylen said that he'd expedite anything we need through the DCI. We'll nail whoever did this."

"I don't get it." Jillian raised helpless hands. "Okay, so the guy was one of the governor's friends. Everything I've read about Ryman Banks paints him as a kind of greasy wheel."

Wain's chair squeaked as he shifted. "I'm not implying anything about Nick Brewster, but sometimes the difference between winning and losing elections comes down to endorsements. Sure, good old Ryman Banks the Third contributed generously to Brewster's campaign. Call him a major donor. But it was the endorsement that really put Brewster over the top. The fact that Ryman and ICoHR backed his campaign brought in a substantial part of the liberal environmental vote. Gave him the margin he needed."

Wain's expression turned quizzical in reflection. "And from everything I saw, they genuinely liked each other. Peas out of the same pod. They enjoyed basking in the limelight. Being seen with beautiful women and celebrities. I remember when Brewster was campaigning here and Banks held a fundraiser for the movers and shakers to come meet the candidate. Those guys got along, both cracking jokes, hamming it up like two freshman frat boys. Instant best buds, and you could tell they had the same egos."

Wain reached for the phone when it buzzed, answering, "Yeah?"

A pause.

"Put him on." To Jillian, he said, "Seems we've finally got ahold of the mysterious John Cody."

Wain hit the speaker button. *"Hello?"*

"This is John Bernard Cody?" Wain asked as he pulled his notepad front and center and started jotting notes.

"It is. What's this about?"

"I'm Bert Wain, Gallatin County Sheriff's Office. With me is Agent Jillian Masterson with the Investigations Bureau of the Montana Department of Justice. I need to inform you that this call will be recorded. We'd like to ask you some questions about Ryman Banks. Could you tell me your whereabouts over the last forty-eight to seventy-two hours?"

A five second silence was followed by, *"Banks, huh? What's the son of a bitch into now? And what does it have to do with me?"*

Jillian shared a look with Sheriff Wain at the hostile tone in Cody's voice.

Wain said, "Ryman Banks was murdered the night before last. Someone used a booby-trapped shotgun tied to his front door. We know that you and Mr. Banks had an antagonistic relationship."

Again, silence.

"Cool character." Jillian mouthed the words.

"Antagonistic? Yeah, you could say that. He and Tim Little did more damage to the buffalo industry and the animals than anyone since the hide hunters back in the 1880s. But why would you think I had anything to do with it?"

"Among the evidence we collected was your hat. It was found in proximity to the shotgun, not five feet from Mr. Banks' body."

The silence stretched even longer before Cody asked, *"Black O'Farrell hat? One hundred percent beaver, with a five inch brim, northern Plains crease? It's got a blotchy kind of stain on the front of the crown that looks like a buffalo blew bloody snot all over it?"*

"That's it. It even has your name on the hat band."

"Son of a bitch!" The tone almost had an amused quality. Jillian's mind raced, trying to imagine a face to match with the voice.

"Would you like to explain how your hat ended up at the murder scene?" Wain asked.

"Yes, Sheriff, I most definitely would. And I'd bet we'd both

find that explanation really interesting, 'cause that hat disappeared from the Doubletree Hotel in Billings almost a month ago. I was at the Montana Bison Association banquet. I'd placed it under my chair."

"Why would you do that?" Jillian ventured to ask.

"It's called etiquette. Some of us were taught that it's rude to wear a hat while seated at the dinner table. I'm traditional. When I got up to leave, the hat was gone. As to who, or how it got took? Nobody saw anything. It was just gone. Had to buy me a new hat off the shelf at the feed store. I'm sure the lady clerk there remembers, given the way I was cussing."

Wain rolled his eyes, then noted. "You still haven't told us your whereabouts for this past week."

"I was in Colorado. National Bison Association meetings in conjunction with the National Western Stock Show down in Denver. I got back to the ranch a little after two this morning with a load of buffalo that I bought at the auction on Saturday. I've got the receipts to prove it. You can check if you like."

"Oh, yes, Mr. Cody, we will indeed." Wain's voice changed. "Mr. Cody, can you think of anyone who might want to cause Ryman Banks harm?"

Jillian was taken aback by the laughter. *"Sure, Sheriff. Half of Montana. The landowners north of the Park boundary that he's trying to destroy. The beef producers whose land Banks and the conservationists are trying to turn into critical habitat for bison. Or maybe the hundreds of thousands of people he's bilked into donating millions. All these years, he's told them that the last of the pure bison are on the verge of extinction when it was all a bald-faced lie. Wouldn't you be pissed if you discovered you'd been duped?"*

Wain had been writing furiously. "That's quite a list, Mr. Cody."

"Good old Ryman Banks was quite a guy. Takes a real piece of work to make a list of enemies like he had." A pause. *"Oh,*

and then there's the wreckage of his personal life. I don't envy you for what you're going to find when you start looking under the rocks he left on his back trail."

"Anything you know of in particular that would motivate someone to kill him?"

"Sheriff, that would be malicious gossip if I did." Another pause. *"We done here?"*

"For now. Thank you for your cooperation. If you think of anything that might be of interest or contribute to the case, please give me a call."

"Will do."

Wain hung up, shot Jillian a wary look. "Somehow, that was just too pat."

"How?"

Wain shook his head. "I'm not sure."

"The news that Ryman was murdered didn't surprise him at all."

"Yeah. That's what bothers me."

CHAPTER ELEVEN

Cody hung up his old landline wall-mount phone and stared out the kitchen window at the falling snow. So, it wasn't Tarbeau. Different sheriff. Desultory flakes drifted lazily down, the surrounding mountains obscured by low gray clouds.

Walking to the door, he shrugged on his buffalo coat and clamped the irritating store-bought hat with its too-stiff mass-produced felt onto his head.

Stepping out on the porch, he was halfway across the yard when the green John Deere rolled in from the winter pasture. Cody waited while Danny climbed lightly down from the cab and closed the gate. Then she waved, walking his way as she called, "See you made it back."

"Yep."

Danielle Redweed's real shape couldn't be seen through the layers of insulated Carhartts, thick buffalo vest and clunky snowpacks. Under all that was a whip-thin and muscular body that belied the woman's sixty-five years of hard living. Beneath the bison-fur hat, Danny kept her long hair in braids, though the once-midnight black was now streaked with white. Tough as old leather and railroad spikes and uncommonly strong she might be, but close to fifty years of ranch life had taken a toll on bones, joints, and organs. She squinted up at him, a gleam in her hard black eyes.

"So, couldn't keep your hand down at the auction, huh?" She gestured toward the corral. "The bull's nice, and so's that one yearling heifer. That bred two looks about as stable as crystalized dynamite. But that last yearling heifer? The scrawny half-starved one? Did someone pay you to take her, or did you buy her for meat? You seen the color of that ratty hide? Somebody was pretty stupid. Bad feed program. She was probably getting straight alfalfa. Too much protein. Her gut must hurt like crazy. Poor girl. And I swear, her hooves have grown out so long they look like skis. Six'll get you a half dozen she's been foundered."

"Nope. I just think she's a better animal than she shows."

"There goes that eye of yours again, huh? Sometimes I think you can see right through the hide and meat to the genetics. Got a feel for an animal, you do." Danny gave him a slight nod, reached in her pocket for her can of Copenhagen, and put a pinch behind her lip. She spit the excess to one side. He'd never been able to talk her out of chewing tobacco. Or the hard liquor. And what she lacked in social decorum was made up for with brutal honesty.

Cody had inherited her with the ranch. His parents had originally hired her to look after the few bison and keep an eye on the property when they were away. Since he'd taken over, he'd never found reason to replace her. Didn't matter that Danny was in her sixties, she could still buck bales with the best of them, knew her way around a tractor, and was a real buffalero when it came time to work the animals through the chute for vaccinations, doctoring, or testing. That latter was a special skill. Bison weren't beef, but wild animals that panicked if spooked. Working them in the pens and alleys took patience, a calm demeanor, and that special sense for what a buffalo was thinking and feeling. Try and "cowboy" them with whistles, yells, and waving arms and the result was a hell of a wreck with broken, bleeding, and dying bison.

The old woman shot him a sidelong glance. "What about that other thing? You find out anything?"

"Yeah. Did an overnight fast trip to Hardin. Got a name. Crank Laumer. You ever heard that before?"

Danny's glance went to the tree-covered slopes that rose toward Jim Smith Peak, tracing the contours of the mountain's flank, the snow-packed and rugged heights hidden by gray cloud. "Can't say as I have. But you listen to me, *taipo*. You go messing around with this thing, it's like reaching under rocks in summer. Do it enough, you're gonna grab onto a rattlesnake and wish you hadn't."

"I'll be careful."

"Uh-huh. Your father told me that." She fixed her obsidian-black eyes on his. "And look where that got 'em." Then she turned, feet crunching the powdery snow as she headed back for the tractor.

Cody squinted up at where the clouds twisted and roiled. Over the years he'd had enough of being cautious, of waiting for something to break in the case. He crossed to the corrals and went through the small side gate that gave access to the main alleyway between the pens. 208, the new bred heifer, immediately started to dart back and forth within the limits of her pen. That was expected, she wouldn't start to settle down until she had some company. Bison, with the exception of old bachelor bulls, hated being alone. They developed friendships just like people did. He'd discovered early on that if he separated two heifers that were best friends during breeding season, neither would get pregnant. They were just plain lonely.

"You're all right, girl." He spoke softly, stepping wide and moving slowly to keep from adding to her anxiety. That left him standing in front of the Canadian two-year-old bull's pen.

To John's delight, the bull he called Rumbler watched him from the far corner, his head up, but not showing any alarm. Damn, but he had good lines. Thick in the shoulders, long in the body through the primals, with a good length of hip and a well-boned frame.

"You seem to be a pretty good-natured guy. Did I mention I'm thinking about calling you Rumbler?"

The bull shifted, grinding his teeth just loudly enough for Cody to hear. Buffalo did that when they were nervous or stressed, and sometimes if they were bored.

"So, Rumbler. I just had a call from the Sheriff up at Bozeman. Seems someone used a shotgun to blow old Ryman Banks away. You wouldn't have liked him. He'd have taken one look at you, labeled you an impure buffalo, and sent you off to the kill pen. Something wrong with those people. If you're not in a conservation herd somewhere, they think you're not worth shit as a bison. Damn fools."

Rumbler shifted again, the snow starting to build up on the thick black hair atop his massive skull.

Cody braced himself on the gate's top rail, listening to the silence. Somewhere in the snowy distance, a raven gave that chattery clicking call.

"Now, here's the twist that no one anticipated. Somehow my hat ended up in the same place where piece-of-shit Ryman got himself blown away." He shook his head. "Funny, isn't it? You can plan things down to the last detail, and then something like that comes blowing in from who in the hell knows where to really screw things up."

Rumbler snuffled out a fog of breath and carefully licked his nose, a gleam that might have been interpreted as understanding behind his dark eyes.

"Now, what do you suppose is going to go wrong next?"

But for that, Rumbler had no answer.

CHAPTER TWELVE

Jillian closed the door on her Durango and locked it with the fob. She'd parked just off Main Street in downtown Bozeman and walked to the corner. She had to admit, the downtown business district in Bozeman still had character. Something Billings had lost sometime in the last century.

Something caused her to glance up as the older red-and-white Ford pickup seemed to slow. She couldn't make out the driver through the tinted side window, but thought she saw the shape of a cowboy hat. Could feel his eyes on her. As she squinted, the truck growled forward, stopped for the red light, and turned west on Main.

God, it was Bozeman. A college town filled with attractive young women. Couldn't the guy get his fill without ogling every female who walked the streets? But then, what woman would waste her time on that kind of man in the first place?

Among the offices, quaint eateries, outdoor equipment

shops, and shoe stores, she found the redbrick building where the International Coalition on Habitat Rescue maintained their headquarters. Not that it would be hard to miss. A collection of flowers, notes, cards, and candles had been laid against the wall, partially blocking the sidewalk on either side of the door. Posters with Ryman Banks' photo and block lettering declaring "Enough is Enough!" and "Heinous Murder!" along with calls for swift and terrible justice had been taped to the brick.

Two young women wearing North Face parkas, tattered jeans, and sneakers were staring wide-eyed at the makeshift shrine as Jillian ignored the hastily scribed "Closed" sign and let herself in. She was surprised that the door hadn't been locked. She crossed the small foyer and stepped into the office.

The first impression was of organization: the file cabinets, desks, and chairs all perfectly placed. In the window, potted plants looked healthy, and the walls were decorated with wildlife photography. Most of it featured bison, but some showed grizzlies, moose, and a magnificent bull elk caught in the act of bugling.

The now-familiar woman behind the closest desk stood as Jillian entered and pulled her gloves off.

"Agent Masterson," Carly Joyner said wearily. "You are prompt. Won't you have a seat?"

"Thank you for seeing me. I can't imagine what it must be like..."

The phone rang.

Joyner stabbed the mute button as she re-seated herself. "It's constant. The voicemail is already full. I've got calls coming in from all over the country." She laughed. "Hell, all over the world. ABC and CBS are sending crews and asking for interviews." A pause.

"You've seen the news? Yahoo. Google. We're all over social media. Not to mention the local press."

Joyner tapped her computer screen in emphasis. "Since the news broke, we've received close to a million dollars in donations. All in Ryman's name to carry on his work. It's brought me to tears several times already. People really loved him. If only he could have seen this."

Jillian shrugged out of her coat and removed her notepad. "Yeah, well, booby trap shotgun murders of high-profile lawyers aren't everyday fodder. And, you'll admit, what happened to Ryman Banks wasn't just gruesome, it's pretty sensational."

Jillian thought she saw a flicker behind Joyner's lips, a sharpening of her eyes. But then, she was the one who'd found the body. While Jillian hadn't seen it first hand, she'd reviewed the photos. Carly Joyner had a right to be shaken.

The woman's voice almost cracked. "Funny how you can see things in retrospect. Ryman had his faults. You can honestly call him a flawed human being. But look around, Agent Masterson. Without him, none of this would exist. Tens of thousands of acres of critical habitat for endangered species would still be locked away and denied to the wildlife that depend on it in an ever-hotter and hostile environment."

"Flawed how?"

Joyner ran a hand through her short blonde hair, a distance in her pale green eyes. "Yeah, I know I just sang Ryman's praises. But, honestly, he was a self-serving egotistical son of a bitch. A pain in the ass to work with. In spite of all that he made the world a better place, and I'm sure that's why John Cody killed him."

"Cody?" Jillian leaned forward.

"I overheard the deputies talking out at Ryman's.

When they called that hat maker. The son of a bitch left his hat right there by the shotgun, didn't he? On any given day you can read about criminals losing their wallets, or leaving their cell phones, bragging to Facebook, or some other dumb thing at a crime scene."

"Who else might have had enough motive to kill him?"

Joyner half nodded to herself. "Outside of Cody? First person to come to mind is Dan Butler down outside of Gardiner. He tried before. Next in line, would be Ryman's soon-to-be-ex-wife Jennifer. Um, she'll be Jennifer Tanner now. Once the divorce is final, she'll marry Tormey Tanner. You know who he is?"

"Sure. He's the guy who owned half of Silicone Valley before he sold out his tech companies and real estate. Then he started buying up cattle ranches up on the High Line in Northern Montana. He's trying to make some sort of free-ranging Northern Plains zoological preserve. He's locked in a tooth-and-nail fight with some of the remaining ranchers up there." She glanced at Tormey Tanner's poster promoting The Plains Wilderness Project where it hung on the opposite wall. "Thought you people worked hand-in-hand with the PWP."

"We do." Joyner's smile looked forced. "Or we did until Jennifer divorced Ryman and took up with Tormey. Now, I'm not going to tell you what I think of dear Jenn, but let's just say that she never turned down an opportunity to better her station in life."

"So...bad blood between Tormey and Ryman?"

"It's no secret that it was a nasty divorce. Ryman walked away with everything but the boy, Bailey. That's the thing about Ryman. I don't know how he did it, but he had compromising video of Jenn and Tormey Tanner. Stuff they didn't want admitted in court. So Jenn folded.

She just packed up her apartment here in town to move up to the project. Ryman slapped her with a custody suit over Bailey. Sometimes Ryman never knew when to quit." Joyner's eyebrow lifted. "I'll bet Jenn never shed a tear when she heard he was dead."

Throughout the interview, the incoming call light on the phone hadn't stopped blinking. Joyner kept glancing at it, as if fascinated.

"What about this geneticist? Tim Little? According to Ryman's phone log, he received a call from Tim the morning before he was killed."

Joyner exhaled, rubbing the back of her neck as if to ease a headache. "That's complicated. Without Dr. Little's groundbreaking genetics tests we wouldn't know the first thing about the threat that beef genes pose for bison. That test is our bedrock, Agent Masterson. But something happened. I know that whatever they said in that conversation, Ryman was disturbed. Wasn't long after that, and I showed him the accountant's report, that he checked out and left for Charlotte's."

"I read your testimony from yesterday. That would be Charlotte Zypanski. Ryman's girlfriend."

Joyner arched a questioning eyebrow. "Girlfriend? I guess that term can cover a lot of ground. If you ask me, they feed of each other like vampires. Or I should say, fed. She'll have to find someone new to screw and milk for a good time."

"I have an appointment to see her tomorrow."

"Don't waste your time. It was Cody. Has to be." Joyner fixed Jillian with that piercing pale stare, as if to make the point. "The bastard's hat was lying there on the floor, wasn't it? I think he left it on purpose. Whatever psychologist was it who said that the criminals couldn't help it? That it was an almost subconscious desire to be caught."

"We've talked to Cody. He has a pretty airtight alibi for last week. Says he was in Denver at the National Western Stock Show. Seems the bison association has their yearly conference and buffalo show there."

"Stock show? That was...last week?" Joyner asked incredulously, looking off to the right where a wall calendar hung. "But..." She drew a half breath. Then closed her eyes, leaning back in the chair.

Jillian watched the woman struggle. "But?"

Joyner chuckled, forced herself to relax. "Damn them. Damn them all. The producers. The bison ranchers. The meat packers. Everybody in the business of buying and selling bison. All of them wanting to make a buck off of America's iconic national mammal. Just the sight of anyone in a cowboy hat makes me want to puke."

Joyner leaned forward, pointing a hard finger. "These commercial herds, they're the greatest threat to the bison since General Phil Sheridan pleaded for the extinction of the entire species back in the 1870s. His words to the hide hunters were 'Let them kill, skin, and sell until the buffalo are destroyed.' Bison barely made it. Now these ranchers are in the process of taking an iconic species and ruining them."

"How's that?"

"They're turning bison into another kind of domesticated beef cow, Agent Masterson. They're breeding them for docility. Crossing those remarkable bison with beef cattle. Diluting the wild gene pool with Jersey, Holstein, Hereford, and most of all Charolaise cow genes. Why Charolaise? Because they're white. White! So they can breed these mutant hybrids and call them 'Sacred White Buffalo.' Sacred? Bullshit! They're an abomination!"

Joyner had half risen from the desk, her face reddening. "And that bastard, John Cody, he's fought us tooth and nail. He's at every public hearing. So, hell yes! Now, seeing he was about to lose on the ESA listing of the Yellowstone herd given our latest lawsuit in DC, he's taken the last desperate step."

"You think he killed Ryman to stop the lawsuit?" Jillian watched Joyner reseat herself.

"Give me one good reason why he wouldn't? He's got the most to lose."

"How?"

"His ranch down in Wyoming lies just outside of the Park boundaries on the head of the Clark's Fork. That's up above Sunlight Basin almost to Cooke City. Yellowstone bison drift out of the Lamar Valley in the park and utilize habitat in the upper Clark's Fork all the time. Cody is constantly fencing to keep his genetically tainted domestic bison from mingling with the wild ones. You ought to see his fences. But once the Yellowstone bison are listed, John Cody's ranch becomes critical habitat. It'll be ours!"

Joyner snapped her fingers. "Just like that, Cody and his cattalo are out of business. He'll be forced to slaughter or move his genetically polluted hybrid herd and tear down his fences. If that's not a reason to rig a shotgun to kill Ryman, you tell me what is?"

CHAPTER THIRTEEN

L ow overcast skies smothered dawn's arrival in a somber gray. Occasional flakes of snow drifted down, and the drive past the fancy brick columns up to Ryman Banks' sprawling house was covered by an inch of new-fallen snow.

Jillian had spent the previous afternoon reviewing the evidence, thinking about what Carly Joyner had told her. After making her report to Supervisor Meyer, she'd turned in early. In the middle of the night, something from one of her lectures in class had come to her.

Put yourself in the perpetrator's position. Walk in his shoes. See the crime scene from his perspective.

So, here she was. Jillian stepped out into the cold, her breath fogging, and unhooked the yellow crime scene tape, setting it aside. Glancing around, the road, the winter-bare trees, and morning-gray snow-covered fields looked somber and depressed.

No tracks marred the pristine snow as she hooked in the four-wheel drive and drove up the winding lane to the house. Ryman's Maserati remained under the shelter of the jutting port cochere. Jillian stopped behind it, shut off the Durango, and studied the entry where crime scene tape had been strung from the wall to the Maserati and back to the far wall, boxing off the front door where Banks had been killed.

"Okay, so how did the killer see this?" She got out of the Durango, stepped over the tape, and walked up to the massive front door with its defiant buffalo bull carved into the wood. The bloodstain had darkened until it looked black on the cold concrete. The silhouette of Banks' body sent a shiver down her back. Banks' ghost? Watching, filled with anger over his untimely death?

Anxiously, she glanced around at the still morning, the skeletal trees, the frozen snow and landscaping. Nothing moved. The only sound was the distant passing of a vehicle out on the road.

Did Banks, alone like she was, pause like this? Hesitate?

With a quivering finger, she tapped 111222 on the electronic lock pad set into the stonework beside the door. It clicked. Reaching, Jillian grabbed the sculpted bronze door handle and pressed the thumb tab that worked the latch. The door opened. She couldn't help herself, stepping to the side, as it swung wide on silent hinges.

Nothing. The foyer was black, empty, and ominous.

Jillian took a deep breath. "It was that easy. What were you thinking, Ryman?"

Just like the felon had, she stepped inside, flipped on the light switch and closed the door. The string, chair, and shotgun were missing, having been hauled off as evidence. So, too, where the evidence markers. The room was pristine, just as the killer would have found it.

Jillian took her time, really got a look at the house without the bustle of the techs. She'd never been in a millionaire's mansion before. It wasn't just the house itself that was impressive, but its furnishings. As she wandered from room to room, each filled with custom Western furniture, she stopped to stare at the artwork. Some of the paintings and artists she recognized. Kevin Red Star, Howard Terpning, Mark Kelso, Harry Jackson, Nicholas Coleman, and even a pedestaled bronze with a brass plaque claiming to be a Charlie Russell original.

The kitchen was a revelation in itself. Not only were the appliances top-of-the-line, including Wolf, Sub Zero, and Cove, but also the central island was sheathed in beaten copper, as were the hood, sinks, and cabinet knobs. The floor gleamed, tiled as it was in an exotic highly patterned marble that had a lucent quality. The faucets might have been solid silver for all she knew, and the espresso coffee machine on the back counter gleamed of chrome and polished brass. What appeared to be handcrafted cutlery clung to a slabbed piece of what looked like petrified wood inserted with magnets and hung on the wall.

The office was down a short hall off the kitchen: a well-lit room worthy of a Wall Street tycoon, the walls and floor-to-ceiling bookshelves of some exotic tropical hardwood with strikingly patterned grain. The legal volumes, books on conservation law, and associated tomes looked impressive. Turning to the desk, she found it to be a cherry-wood monstrous thing with sides and legs carved in an intricate floral design. The chair behind, of course, looked marvelously plush, expensive, and upholstered of soft leather. On the wall opposite, a collection of Native American busts by Dave McGary filled an entire shelf. Antique oak file cabinets lined the fourth wall, each drawer labeled by an alphabetical topic.

Not surprising, the master bedroom was almost

mind-blowing with its giant four-poster bed, thick carpeting, and mirrored walls. Expensive Tom Ford, Armani, and Zegna suits hung in the closet. The attached bath she called sybaritic. The guest bedrooms, though not as stunning, were each done in a different shade of opulent.

As was the theater room. Like, a real theater, complete with rising rows of chairs, giant wall screen, and wet bar to the side with popcorn maker.

And then she found the gunroom downstairs. The walls were decorated with wildlife paintings by Shawn Gould and Sally Maxwell. Shooting jackets hung from hooks along one wall, as did historical cartridge-board collections from Winchester and Remington. In a glass case she found mounted cap-and-ball revolvers that looked old and authentic. Boxes of ammunition were shelved by caliber across from the big Browning gun safe.

Just like the killer was supposed to have done, Jillian stopped before the gun safe and, with her index finger, tapped in 111222#. The light flashed as the lock clicked. Turning the handle, Jillian swung the heavy steel door open. In the illuminated interior, she could see several shotguns, some side-by-side, some over-under all with well-figured wood, each looking expensive. Across from them were fancy rifles. She looked closely at the makers: Weatherby, Blazer, Rigby, and Krieghoff. An engraved and gold-plated Colt 1911 sat in a special display box on the top shelf.

Oddly, the second shelf down was empty.

As was a single slot in the rack of shotguns. Where the killer had removed the Merkel?

Jillian turned, looking at the shelves of stacked ammunition boxes.

"Just like that." Standing there, she could imagine the

killer, lifting out the shotgun, reaching for the box of 12-gauge double-aught buck.

Again, she asked, "Banks? What were you thinking?"

It mystified her that anyone—especially an attorney with known enemies—wouldn't have been more circumspect with passcodes, let alone have the same code for the front door and safe.

Jillian locked the safe, crossed the room, and flipped the light switch. As she closed the door, she heard the voices. Faint. Two people talking.

Instinctively she patted her jacket where it covered her duty pistol in its holster by her left breast. Then, feeling that uncomfortable acceleration of her heartbeat, she started up the stairs. At the top, she caught the last of the sentence.

"...Will all be yours, little man."

A woman's voice.

Then a giggle, sounded like a child.

Jillian found them in Ryman's office. The woman was bent over one of the antique oak file cabinet drawers, thumbing through the folders. Maybe thirty, she was dressed in a tailored fawn-colored wool jacket and wore chic slacks that fit her long legs and accented the dress boots on her feet. Long red hair was confined at the nape of the neck by a golden clip. Even from the rear, she looked like a knockout.

The kid was maybe five, towheaded, wearing an insulated nylon coat, oversized blue jeans, and rubber boots. Just then, he was sucking on his knuckles, watching studiously as the woman searched the drawer. She stopped, squinted at a tab, and started to pull a file from the drawer.

"You had better have a very good reason for being here." Jillian crossed her arms, blocking the door.

At the words, the woman jumped, yipped. The little boy screamed, not even bothering to look as he leaped to cling to the woman's leg. The redhead whirled, eyes wide, expression startled. The little boy began to cry.

"Jesus! What the fuck?" the redhead cried. "Who the hell are you?"

Jillian tilted her head, meeting the woman's panicked blue gaze. "Agent Jillian Masterson, Montana Department of Justice. And you are?"

"Jennifer Banks. I live here. This is my house." She bent down, prying the kid loose from her leg. "Shh. It's okay, sweetie. You're all right. Everything's fine."

The kid went from squalling to muffled sobs.

"This is a crime scene, Mrs. Banks. And I was under the impression that you and Ryman Banks were separated. That you were just days from finalizing a divorce."

"We were," Jennifer straightened, glaring at Jillian. "Key word: Were. Apparently, given the turn of events, I am now Ryman's widow." She smiled, gesturing wide. "And, apparently, with his death, this is now my property. Can I help you with something, Agent Masterson?"

The kid was now staring at her with big blue eyes, back to sucking his knuckles again.

"How did you get in here?" Jillian asked.

"Ryman wasn't one to change the code on his locks." Jennifer pointed at the computer on the desk. "One, one, one, two, two, two. Or when the passwords have to be more than six characters it's Capital R, small case y, capital M, small case a, capital N, small case b, and so forth before he added one, one, one, two, two, two. For as smart as he was, Ryman had some absolutely simple solutions to aspects of his life." The woman laughed bitterly. "You should have heard him scream and curse when one of his passwords was rejected. I mean the man went ballistic."

"So that would be the same for the gun safe downstairs?"

"Sure. Everything. Even that lock box. Like if someone opened the safe, they could have opened his precious little box, too. I mean, what kind of crazy is that?"

"Lock box?" Jillian asked.

"The one he keeps on the second shelf of the gun safe. Which reminds me. I never had the courage to see what was in the ledger he kept locked in that box. Some kind of accounts." She gestured at the file cabinets. "I thought it was odd he never kept them here."

Jillian frowned. The empty shelf in the safe? She'd seen no lock box.

"Can you account for your whereabouts during the week before he was killed?"

Jennifer gave her a bewitching smile, eyes twinkling. "Sure can. But you'll have to ask any questions regarding my relationship with my late husband in the presence of my lawyer."

Jennifer reached across to the desk to retrieve her purse. Jillian figured the woman had to be close to five foot ten, and that was without the heels.

From inside, Jennifer produced a card and handed it over. "That's the number and address for William C. Blood's office here in Bozeman. I will be happy to cooperate with the authorities in any way possible, but only in the presence of my attorney."

"You don't seem terribly upset about what happened to your husband."

Jennifer studied her for a moment with a squinted eye. "You know, with the right makeup, a bit of eyeliner, something to bring out the glow in that perfect skin of yours, you'd be his type. Of course, the bulky jacket and those absolutely ordinary Wal-Mart slacks have to go. And I understand that for professional reasons, you're trying to de-emphasize the girls, but give them the support they deserve, and it would do wonders for your figure."

Jennifer forced a plastic smile. "Not that Ryman would have cared. He'd fuck any cute bit of tail for the hell of it."

Jillian said, "Mrs. Banks, this is a crime scene. What folder did you just locate, and what do you intend to do with it?"

Jennifer turned, pulling the file free. "This is the title to the house and property. *My* house and property. I'm sure they have it on file at the courthouse, but I thought I'd pick it up just to be sure."

"Put it back," Jillian told her. "And you will immediately leave the premises."

"Hey! I told you, I'm Ryman's widow. This is all mine."

"That's not my problem, Mrs. Banks. Evidence is. And yes, this might be yours, and I'm sure you can have access to any documents you need. But you can touch nothing until the scene is cleared by the Gallatin County Sheriff's Office." Jillian lifted the card. "If you need something from the house, I suggest you call your attorney, Mr. Blood, and have him make arrangements with the SO to have a deputy accompany you. Do you understand?"

Jennifer's cold glare would have frozen molten lava.

In a clipped voice, the woman said, "Come on, Bailey. You and Mommy have to go."

Jillian stepped aside to let them pass.

As she followed them to the door, the little boy said, "Mommy, why was that lady mean to you?"

Jennifer shot a glance over her shoulder, expression promising revenge. "Oh, honey, just like Daddy, she'll get hers."

It was the tone of voice. Like Jennifer Banks wasn't the kind to forget a grudge.

After seeing them out, Jillian ran it all through her head again. Then she made her way back downstairs. In the gunroom, she flipped on the lights and crossed to the safe. Pressing in the combination, she opened the steel door. The second shelf down was still empty, but looking closely at the felt padding that cushioned any contents Jillian could see the impression where a square box had once set. She had seen no such box listed in the catalog of property removed for evidence.

"Now, what do you suppose that means?" she wondered.

CHAPTER FOURTEEN

Jillian braced her elbows on the table and cradled her cup of coffee. The restaurant called Jam! was filled with the lunch crowd. Across from her Sheriff Wain was making a valiant effort at demolishing the four-egg pulled-pork omelet. She had barely managed to finish off the biscuit sandwich. There was something bulldoggish in the way Bret Wain ate that reflected on how the man approached life, his job, and maybe his leisure hours as well.

"Must make you a very good sheriff," Jillian mused before sipping the dark roast-with-a-shot that she'd ordered.

"What's that?" Wain asked between mouthfuls.

"I was thinking about tenacity. Seeing the job through. You learn that from your father?"

Wain chewed, studied her thoughtfully. "Nope. My father was a no-account failure at everything he ever did. Except maybe when it came to cadging drinks. Couldn't keep a job. Spent every last dime in the roadside casinos in Billings, gambling and drinking. And don't ask about my mother. When it came to life she didn't have the sense God gave a rock."

He wiped his lips with a napkin, brown eyes going soft. "No, I got the break of a lifetime when I was five. Mom had moved us in with a guy called Fred Paint, another of her boyfriends. That was in a trailer house set on blocks in South Billings, and that guy wanted me gone. Told Mom that a rancher friend of his would take me for two weeks. A sort of summer camp, he called it."

"You've got to be kidding?"

Wain gave her a steely-eyed look. "Not hardly. The rancher's name was Tyler Tippetts. I'm not making that up. Had a fifteen-hundred-acre cattle ranch in the Bull Hills. Said he'd take me for the two weeks in lieu of the two hundred dollars he owned Fred for a saddle."

"And?"

"And Mom and good old Fred never came back."

"Jesus! They just abandoned you? What about social services?"

Wain shrugged. "It was just Tyler and his dogs up there on that little fifty-cow outfit. His wife had died the year before. He kind of took to me. Maybe I was just another stray. But he put me to work that summer and got me started in school that fall up in Roundup. Musselshell County's kind of strange. Tyler finagled the paperwork somehow, maybe in collusion with the County Clerk. However he did it, he ended up as my legal guardian."

"With the hope that no one ever gave the paperwork a proper scrutiny?"

Wain's eyes twinkled. "Yep. That's a really good call. Maybe you should think of a job in law enforcement? Anything I ever became was because of Tyler and the lessons he taught me on that ranch." He paused. "How about you?"

Jillian pushed her empty plate to the side. "My story is nowhere near as exciting. Dad was from Minneapolis. He'd just finished his BA in anthropology from Colorado State and was traveling through Wyoming when he saw a sign for the Powwow at Fort Washakie. Mom was a grass dancer. Just turned twenty and freshly divorced from an abusive husband. Dad said he'd never seen anything as enchanting as the way Mom was dancing. How her eyes sparkled, her feet flew, and her hair shone."

Jillian reached up, fingering her straight black hair. "This came from her."

And to hell with what Jennifer Banks said. She liked her hair as it was.

"I guess what followed was just like a fairy tale. White guy and Shoshoni girl, star-crossed lovers who fell for each other at first glance. Ran off, head-over-heels in love. Married. And then had to figure out what to do with each other. They tried living on the rez. Dad never fit in. They tried Minneapolis. Then Denver. Then Dallas. Mom couldn't take it. She left in the middle of the night." An icy tingle, like cold fingers ran down her back. No need to tell him the rest. She never told anyone the rest.

"So, what happened?"

Tensing muscles to forestall the incipient shiver, she tried to adopt an offhanded tone. "Dad filed for divorce, moved us back to Minneapolis, got a job selling insurance, and married his high school sweetheart. Mom went back to the rez, and I never saw her much."

Jillian changed the subject to forestall the images that flashed in her memory like video clips from a horror movie. "So, what's the story on Jennifer Banks? She really inherits?"

"Apparently so." He gave her an unhappy look. "After your run-in this morning, her lawyer has been making himself a pain in my ass. Deputy Sampson is meeting them at the scene this afternoon to go over the house. What a lucky lady. Not that she wasn't already in the process of trading up. Leaving millionaire Banks for billionaire Tanner is like ditching a Jaguar F-Type for a Bugatti Chiron. Picking up the house and property is just a bonus."

"That house and property—not to mention the furnishings and artwork—has be worth close to three million." Jennifer lifted an inquisitive brow. "In my book, that's motive."

"Yeah." Wain pinched his nose as if to stifle a sneeze. "Jennifer's attorney, good old Billy Blood, already explained to me this morning that his client, who is planning a May wedding with Tormey Tanner, by the way, is hardly in need of such a paltry sum. In short, she's about to be worth hundreds of millions. What's a measly seven-thousand-square-foot log-and-stone designer house on an acreage outside Bozeman?" He sighed. "We should all have such problems."

"Something else," Jillian noted. "Jenn said something about a missing lock box from the safe. It's not on the evidence sheets, and it wasn't in the safe. You know anything about that?"

"Nope. But Jenn and Banks were estranged. If it wasn't there, and it's not linked to the crime, why would it be important? She tell you?"

"No." Jillian gestured with her fork. "Motive is more than money. You didn't see the look in her eyes when she was talking about her husband. Think of how many cases you see where all that mattered was the payback. People don't always act rationally or in their own interests. Sometimes, getting back at someone is all that counts."

"I'm with you, but before we can bring her in and tear her apart in the interrogation room, we've got to get past her lawyer. And Billy Blood's one of the toughest and brightest west of the Mississippi."

Wain's phone buzzed. He checked it, using a thumb to scroll through a lot of text. Looked up. "They finished the lab work. They've got nothing. The prints? All of them are Ryman's. Every other surface has been wiped clean. We did get some hairs. Long. Blonde. And some traces of prints in the bedroom and master bath that had been overlaid with Banks'. We're thinking maybe Charlotte Zypanski. Carly Joyner said Charlotte and Banks were hot."

"Last person to see Ryman Banks alive? Zypanski agreed to see me this afternoon."

Wain shook his head. "I don't get it. Somebody always leaves something at the crime scene. That's basic transfer-of-evidence theory. We had a clean start on the preliminary investigation. Documented the hell out of the crime scene and came up with no associative evidence. Nada."

"What about the hat? Isn't that like a big shining beacon?"

Wain shoveled in the last of his omelet. Swallowed. "Is it? Come on, freshly graduated Investigator Masterson. Answer your own question."

Jillian scowled. "All right. Cody says the hat disappeared almost a month ago. Anyone could have taken it. Maybe even Ryman Banks himself. What's the lab say? Any trace evidence on it that points us in a direction?"

Wain lifted his own hat to run fingers through his

hair. "They're still looking at sticky tape through the scope, but the last I heard was that they had brown hair, pollen consistent with montane environment, dust, an old blood stain that tests negative for human, but they're waiting for a bison reagent to test it further. Sweat and body oils. DNA is pending, even with the Governor's help to expedite running the samples. We expect it all to match Cody's when we finally get a sample from him. It's his hat after all." He paused. "Oh, and microscopic particles of fecal material."

"Microscopic what?" Jillian squinted.

"Most likely buffalo shit, given Cody's ranch life." His grin turned wry. "What? You had a more romantic notion about what would really be on a working ranchman's hat? You'll never look at Clint Eastwood with the same romance. Ever."

"All that, but it's still a dead end?"

"So far."

CHAPTER FIFTEEN

S eeley Atherton stood three doors down from the entrance to the restaurant. He'd watched the tall woman with raven-black hair park, don a down coat against the cold, and enter the establishment. That was all Seeley had needed. From where he stood on West Main, his cellphone to his ear, he could see her black Durango with its state plates. That was the thing about cell phones. A man could stand for as much as an hour, phone to his head, and people never looked twice. To the Bozeman lunch crowd, he might have been invisible as they hurried past.

And now, here she came, wearing a camel-colored parka. And, to Seeley's surprise, she was accompanied by a man in a sheriff's office uniform.

When they turned his direction, Seeley ignored them, focusing on the second story office building across the street. His heart never so much as skipped a beat as they approached.

"Oh, sure, Bill," he said as they came within hearing. "Right now we're just dickering price. I think they'll take the deal given what I'm getting for the trade-in on the Toyota."

He never so much as made eye contact as they passed. Heard the woman say, "After this interview I'll write up the notes, make sure you have a copy."

Seeley got a look at the name on the officer's nylon coat: Wain. The Gallatin County Sheriff himself. A competent-looking man given his age, brown eyes, and florid strong-jawed features.

Seeley kept the phone to his ear, never letting his gaze wander from the second story windows lest the woman or sheriff look back. He found great satisfaction in that. The two of them had passed within an arm's length of Ryman Banks' killer and never known. Now, that was real power.

Sent a tremble of delight down his backbone that tingled clear through his pelvis.

From the corner of his eye, he saw the woman walk out, open the door of the Durango, and slide behind the wheel. He didn't need to watch. Instead, he tapped the screen on his phone. Accessed the app that let him follow the air tracker he'd placed on the inside of her front fender.

An older model Ford F250 parked next to the curb rumbled to life, signaled, and pulled out into traffic. Seeley couldn't see who might have been driving, given the tinted windows, but it had the used look of a ranch truck, right down to the missing tailgate.

The phone chimed. Tapping in the password, he watched as text appeared in a little box at the top of the screen.

Change of plans.

A wrinkle needs ironed out.

Name one: Action upgrade to full retirement.

Pay scale to be commensurate.

Seeley stared at the name and photo that accompanied the text. Who would have thought?

The tingle started down under his belly, ran electric through his muscles and bones.

"Oh, God, thank you," he whispered. "Now, let the fun begin."

He pocketed the phone and headed for where he'd parked his pickup. Reacquiring the woman would be easy. With the airtracker, he could pick her up anytime, anyplace.

CHAPTER SIXTEEN

J illian checked the address as she locked the Durango and crossed the parking lot. On the street, a white-and-red older model Ford pickup slowed, the cloud-filtered sunlight reflecting from tinted glass. Then the throaty exhaust rumbled as it accelerated away. Given the missing tailgate she could see bits of hay and a rusty ball hitch for a gooseneck trailer.

Jillian climbed the steps and was reaching for the bell when the oak door swung open to reveal a tall Nordic-looking blonde with remarkable blue eyes. The woman wore a blue-and-white designer sweater that conformed to every curve. Fine wool slacks hugged her hips, flat belly, and muscular thighs as though sprayed on. Not that she needed it, but high-heeled black leather boots rose to just below her knees.

Jillian fixed on the woman's perfect features: straight nose, high cheekbones and forehead, full lips and firm chin. But it was those eyes, penetrating, somehow dismissive and formidable beneath the glossy mane of dark-blonde hair.

"Agent Masterson, I presume?"

"Yes, ma'am." Jillian offered her badge folder. "I take it that you are Charlotte Zypanski?"

The woman barely glanced at Jillian's credentials before turning and calling, "Come on in. I already told the deputy who was here this morning everything I know."

Jillian closed the door behind her, following the woman into the plush living room. It might have been furnished by a designer obsessed with the latest edition of *Contemporary Living*. The wild angles of the couch and chairs looked anything but comfortable. A snow-white carpet contrasted with the angular black, yellow, red, and green stripes painted on the back wall. The lamps came off as shining chrome monstrosities and cast cones onto the almost reflective floor.

All in all, Jillian would have called it hideous.

"Have a seat," Charlotte indicated a chair that looked something like an elongated and angular S. "Drink?"

"No, thank you." Jillian settled herself on the creamy fabric. It felt somewhat rubbery and bent her legs at an uncomfortable angle.

"Suit yourself, but it's well past noon." Charlotte crossed to a small wet bar, pulled down a bottle of Stolichnaya Elit, removed the stopper, and poured two fingers over ice in a tumbler.

"Sanctions be damned when you can drink the best, don't you think?" Charlotte rattled the drink as she settled onto the chartreuse-toned couch. "Now, what can I do for the governor?"

"The governor?" Jillian asked, pulling her notebook from her jacket pocket.

"It's all over the news that he sent you to find

Ryman's killer." Charlotte's lips quivered in amusement. "Have you met him?"

"The governor? No. I was just—"

"Fun guy." Charlotte pulled her long legs up and tucked them, despite the boots, to one side. She reclined against the curved back of the couch. "Good old Nick, he and one of his ladies came down and spent a weekend with Ryman and me at the condo in Big Sky. Turned into quite the wild fling. Polyamory can be really liberating." She paused, studying Jillian with that intense gaze. "And, oh, he'd like you. You're his type, you know?"

What was it about the women who had been in Banks' life?

Jillian took a deep breath. "I could care less about the governor's type."

"Really?" Charlotte ran full lips over the rim of the glass as she sipped. "That would make you different from most young upwardly mobile women. And, I have to tell you, there's worse guy's when it comes to—"

"Cut the horseshit. You were the last person to see Ryman Banks alive. What time did he leave here?"

"A little before five that night." Charlotte gave her a challenging smile. "But, let's cut the horseshit, as you said in such a cavalier manner. What you want to know is if I could have killed Ryman." She cocked her head in an offhanded manner. "I'm not sure. No one has ever pushed me that far, and Ryman certainly didn't. We were still having fun. And the sex was great. He didn't mind experimenting, if you know what I mean."

"That doesn't sound like much of a relationship."

"Experimenting? Oh, you'd be surprised. Doesn't matter what most men fantasize, when it actually comes to performing? They really can't keep it up. Not even with pills."

Jillian struggled to keep her expression blank. "Were you in love with him?"

"Heavens, no. But that isn't to say that his death isn't disturbing. I mean I was in bed with the guy mere hours before he was shot to death. It's a most peculiar sensation when you realize that a dead man's sperm are still swimming around in your uterus."

"I'll take your word for it. Did Ryman ever tell you that he'd been threatened?"

Charlotte laughed in response. "Oh, Agent Masterson. Or can I call you Jillian? Death threats? He got them constantly. This is Ryman we're talking about. Remember that rancher? Dan Butler from down by Gardiner? The police caught him outside the ICoHR offices with a shotgun and two handguns just moments before he was about to break the door down. And he was swearing to shoot both Ryman and that frigid bitch he works with on the spot." She shrugged. "Ruining a fifth generation rancher's land and income? Prohibiting grazing, leasing, subdividing or development? Essentially turning a fifteen-to-twenty-million-dollar property worthless by having a court declare it critical habitat? That's grounds for murder."

"Yes, I suppose it is."

"And you've got to consider his ex, good old Jennifer." Charlotte rattled the ice to settle her drink. "You met her yet?"

"Briefly."

"She's a jewel." Charlotte's lips twisted wryly. "They coined the definition of gold digger with her in mind. Jenn's got the body, the looks, and the game. She latched onto Ryman that first summer when he and Carly started ICoHR. Grabbed him by the cock and led him straight to the altar so that their child 'would have a father.'

Then she took over the finances. Got to admit, she was smart with the money. Built that house, ensured they had the best of everything. Pissed her off royally when Ryman got the goods on her and Tanner. Ryman ended up with everything she'd built." Charlotte shifted her drink to point with a slim index finger. "Now, there's a lady with motive, even if she did end up with a billionaire."

"We have a lot of persons of interest."

"I'll bet you do." Charlotte cocked her head. "They have any clues? According to the news, it was a shotgun wired to the door."

"Who could have had access to the house? There are no signs of forced entry."

"Could have been anybody." Charlotte swirled her vodka. "Ryman gave the door code to anyone and everyone. He'd say, 'Let's have drinks at my place. The key code is 111222. Make yourself at home until I get there.'"

"How long since he last updated the code?"

Charlotte gave another shrug. "I'm not sure he ever did. He always said, 'It's easy. Tap the first two numbers three times.'"

"What about the gun safe? Same security code?"

"It wouldn't surprise me. Ryman wasn't a complicated kind of guy. It drove him nuts when he had to change a password on any of his online accounts. Swore it would be the end of world civilization when somebody accidently launched a nuclear warhead and no one could find the password for the self-destruct."

"Ms. Zypanski, can you tell me where you were that day?"

"Never left the house. Jenn woke us up when she called at six that morning. Wanted to meet Ryman for breakfast. He left an hour later. Then he was back a little before ten, pissed as hell." She smiled in satisfaction. "God, he was a great fuck when he was mad."

"So, he spent the whole night here with you before he was murdered?"

"Night?" Charlotte arched an eyebrow. "Honey, I can tell you that he was here for three whole days without going home. And, if I know men, I think he was with another woman Wednesday night before he came here. He had that stink about him."

Jillian straightened. "Three days? You're sure?"

"If he wasn't, it had to be his twin brother."

"And this other woman?"

"No clue." The eyebrow arched higher to accent the knowing blue stare. "Sweetie, we were on the end of a long relationship. We were both feeling out other waters. I know he was chasing new tail. Time for a change, you know what I mean?"

Jillian stared down at her notebook. "Three days?"

How long had that shotgun trap been sitting there, waiting for someone to open that door?

CHAPTER SEVENTEEN

"At least three days, and it could have been more." Jillian whispered under her breath as she sat in the chair across from Bert Wain's chaotic and cluttered desk. She'd stopped on her way back to the hotel to brief Wain on her day. The implications were still crystallizing in her thoughts.

"So who did Charlotte Zypanski think this other woman might be?" Sheriff Wain asked.

"Honestly, she said she didn't know. And I believe her. But if she's right, that's a fricking four-day window when someone could have set that trap. And, worse, everybody and their brother knew the security code to the house. I mean, how easy is it to forget 111222?"

Sheriff Wain leaned back in his chair, hands laced behind his head so that it pushed his hat forward. "I think Ryman Banks had started to think of himself as invincible. We've been looking at the financial data for ICoHR. Yeah, they spent a ton of money on lawsuits, and under the Equal Access to Justice Act, they made it all back and then some. To the tune of millions, win, lose, or draw. And they lost a lot. Didn't matter. One of the biggest ad agencies in New York handles their account. Each time they lost, they'd publicize the hell out of it and the donations would skyrocket."

Jillian nodded, remembering the flashing light on the muted phone. "Carly Joyner said that with news of Ryman Banks' murder, the donations were pouring in."

Something sad had changed behind Wain's eyes. "Figures. Sometimes I don't understand people."

Jillian steered the Durango into the hotel parking lot. Dusk was turning into dark, the last of the winter evening glow fading in the southwest behind cloud-wreathed mountains. Traffic was heavy out on 19th, stop and go, a constant stream of headlights and strobing red brake lights.

She found a parking spot, backed in, and killed the ignition as an older white Ford pickup rolled past before finding a space at the edge of the lot. It, too, backed into the space. As parking lots and spaces got smaller, and pickup trucks got bigger, that trend seemed to be on the rise.

For a moment, she sat, her stomach gurgling in a way that told her the biscuit sandwich she'd had for lunch had worn out.

With a sigh, Jillian opened the Durango's door, collected her purse, and got out. Her heels rapped on the frozen parking lot as she skipped around the icy spots. Inside the lobby, the fire was going, the lounge half-filled with people watching a basketball game on the back-bar TV.

She passed the desk, took the elevator to the 3rd floor, and used the keycard to open her door. She almost missed the envelope on the floor.

Shucking out of her coat and tossing it onto the bed, she picked up the card-sized envelope by its edges. Studied it. The only address was Agent Masterson in block letters.

She retrieved her penknife from a jacket pocket and carefully slit the top of the envelope. Again, holding the envelope by the edges, she shook out the card. It was a standard Hallmark greeting card with the image of a tree on the outside. With the knife blade, Jillian flipped it open. Again, the block letters.

WE NEED TO TALK. MEET ME AT OLD CHICAGO.
BOOTH IN THE BACK. NINE TONIGHT.

Jillian rummaged in her travel bag until she found a pristine quart Ziplock. Then, she carefully slid the envelope and note inside before sealing it.

Seating herself on the bed, she stared at the card. "God, what is this? It's like finding myself in the middle of an old Hitchcock movie."

Jillian retrieved her cell phone, tapping the call icon for Sheriff Wain.

"Yeah? What's up, Jillian?"

"You're not going to believe this."

CHAPTER EIGHTEEN

Jillian checked her phone. Ten to nine. Her heels clicked as she crossed the parking lot from the hotel, darted across the street, and followed the walk to Old Chicago. After her call to Sheriff Wain, she'd found a message from Supervisor Meyer on her phone.

Call me. Now!

Jillian had.

"What the hell are you doing, Jill? I just got my butt chewed by the governor. Did you have a confrontation with Mrs. Jennifer Banks this morning?"

"Yeah, chief. She was trying to lift a copy of the deed from the crime scene. Without authorization. And worse, she had her little kid with her. I threw her out. Told her to go through channels."

"That's it? No threats? No verbal abuse?"

"No, sir. Well, I communicated that she was at risk of being charged for violating a crime scene, but it didn't get nasty or loud. Not even when I wanted to smack her for being a... Well, never mind."

"Jesus. All right. It probably got blown out of proportion going from Jennifer to Tormey to Brewster to me. But, Jill? This is the kind of shit we're dealing with. Lots of guys swinging their... Well, you know."

"Yes, sir."

"Do me a favor. Steer clear of Jennifer Banks if you can. Let poor Bert handle that part of the investigation. Brewster already wants your head on a platter. He's just looking for an excuse."

"Yes, sir."

She'd taken a quick and cold shower. Didn't help. She was still steamed.

Thinking about that look in Jennifer Banks' eyes. Beautiful enough to model for the *Sports Illustrated* swimsuit edition and willing to use her sex to get what she wanted, that woman was pure predator. The smart kind who used all the power and tricks at her disposal. With her resources and brains, not to mention her political connections, she thought she was untouchable.

Unless some piece of evidence turns up that implicates her beyond a doubt.

"So, Jillian, do you think she did it? Or is it because you *want to think* she did?"

Shaking her head, she walked up to the restaurant door and pulled it open. The place was still more than half full, the bar section boisterous as people talked over each other.

The hostess asked, "How many?"

"I'm meeting someone," Jillian told her, stopping long enough to check her phone. The green text message We are here reassured her. That would be the deputies arriving out in the parking lot. Sheriff Wain had detailed them to keep an eye on things. If she needed backup, all she had to do was tap the icon, and the cavalry would come busting through the door.

She started with the bar, walking to the back, finding the booths there crowded, and no one looking as if they were awaiting her arrival.

On the restaurant side, she made her way past the booths. He was sitting in a two-person window booth up front; a lone man in an oversized white cowboy hat, he watched her approach. The guy looked to be in his early fifties, prematurely gray. His face was clean-shaven with a knobby nose, pointy chin, and puffy cheeks. He studied her through medium blue eyes and half rose at her arrival. Turns out he was a short man, barely five foot three if she guessed correctly.

"You're the governor's girl?" he asked, offering a hand.

Governor's girl? Again? Hesitantly, Jillian shook, already pissed off.

Warily slipping into the seat, she pulled out her notebook to write the date, time, place, and subject. "I'm Jillian Masterson, Investigations Bureau, Major Case Section. If the governor has any girls, I'm not one of them. I assume you are the person who left a note under my room door?"

"Yeah." He settled back in the seat, shifted his oversized hat back on his head. His blue gaze dropped to the glass of pale-yellow beer that sat before him. "I'm Dr. Timothy Little. I'm a geneticist. If you're any kind of investigator when it comes to Ryman's murder, I assume you've heard of me?"

"I have. You're attached to some university out in California, but you have your own lab that runs tests on bison genetics. You're listed as an outside expert and consultant for the International Coalition on Habitat Rescue. Your work has been fundamental for a lot of conservation groups working in the Western United States. You've served as an expert witness on bison genetics, especially when it comes to identifying the number of beef genes in modern bison."

Little took a deep breath. "You've done your homework."

"Yes, well, ever since someone murdered Ryman Banks, let's say I've been motivated." She arched an eyebrow. "I suppose you know the Gallatin County Sheriff's Office has been trying to locate you? They have some questions."

Little rubbed his hands together, the soft scrubbing sound of it audible over the laughter from the family seated at the table across from them. "Yeah. I've been on the move. Haven't been home. I had to figure out what to do."

"My suggestion would be to make yourself available to Sheriff Wain's deputies as soon as we're finished here. We know you called Ryman Banks the morning he was killed. What did you talk about?"

Little's expression soured, as if something bitter filled his mouth. "Recent research. Advances in ancient DNA research. That's genetic material recovered from old historic and prehistoric bison bones and teeth. About what it meant for us...for the lawsuit."

Then he leaned forward, a desperation behind his eyes. "Look! I'm not like the rest. It's not about the money. You've got to understand. We're living in an age of global extinction. Maybe a hundred species a day are disappearing across the planet. And the bison? I mean, come on. We almost wiped them out in the 1880s. Maybe five hundred were left after the slaughter."

"I know the figures."

"Do you? Do you know that with just those few

animals left, these asshole ranchers, people like Charlie Goodnight and even the Allards, started trying to cross breed those few poor bison with beef cattle? God, it's like humans fuck up anything they lay their hands on."

"But the buffalo are back. I've been told there are close to half a million in the US and Canada."

"If you call those walking abominations bison. And don't use the word buffalo. To my ears, it's like calling a black man...well, you know." Little almost spat the words, then stopped as if reminded of something. "How many genes? What's the magic number?"

"For what?"

"For when a species is no longer pure? One gene? One hundred? " He pressed his hands to his face, shifting his hat back as he did. "Fucking assholes, wouldn't you know? It's the same damn thing they've been hiding behind for all of these years. But, getting back to the point, that's what I was trying to do. Protect the sanctity of the species. Keep bison as bison. It wasn't about the money."

"But from what I understand, you have made a small fortune selling your test to conservation organizations, to wildlife preserves, and to ranchers who bought into the purity argument." She paused. "How much did you make, Dr. Little?"

He gave her a glare as the family at the table across from them started to stand and put their coats on. "All right. A lot! Why? Is there some law that says you have to be poor to work on a worthy cause? That was just a win-win. The money allowed me to be a better advocate for the conservation of the pure bison genome. Even if... now...it turns out I was...well..."

Little paused, watching the people across from them as the father herded his two kids and wife ahead of him toward the exit. In an absent voice, he said, "I just didn't have the tools at the time to—"

"What kind of relationship did you have with Ryman Banks?"

Little stared at her through weary eyes. "All right, I hated the guy. Him and Joyner, gushing over my work. Joyner? Thought she was different. I really cared for her once. Thought I meant something to her. Turns out she's a cold bitch. A warrior for her cause. But Ryman? God, that guy made me want to puke. He had to be the center of attention. All the lawsuits did was give him a stage to preen."

The vitriol caused Jillian to raise an eyebrow. "Carly Joyner said he made ICoHR."

"Sure." Little fixed her with a hard stare from under the brim of his big hat. "I swear to God, if the cattlemen would have paid him enough, he'd have sold out the bison conservation movement in a heartbeat."

"Did they ever try?"

Little fingered his beer. "Even a bunch of dumb ranchers are smarter than to get in bed with a snake like Ryman."

"To a lot of people in the environmental movement, Ryman Banks was a hero."

"Yeah. To anyone who didn't have to work with him day in and day out. And now? He's a saint who walks on water! You seen the shrine they've built outside the ICoHR offices? Makes my stomach turn."

Little took a sip of beer. "The guy was a showman. Came across bigger than life. I mean he filled a room when he walked into it. Smiling, beaming, shaking hands. He ate that shit up. People would crowd around. It was like throwing gasoline on a fire. And the women, geez.

They flocked around him like minnows around a light. It was disgusting."

"Did you kill Ryman Banks? Set that trap for him?"

"No. But I know why he was killed."

"Why?"

"Because of the research. What it means. We're going to lose it all, now."

"Lose what?"

"The fight. They're going to win."

"Who?"

His gaze had gone absent, as if putting some piece of a puzzle together. "My God, we killed all those beautiful bison for nothing. Maybe it's divine justice."

"What do you mean?"

He leaned forward. In a low voice, he said, "Way back when, we needed a weapon against the ranchers, the exploiters, the people who'd make bison into another fucking kind of beef. We chose introgression. You know what that means?"

"Yes, the influx of one population's genes into another. Carly told me it was beef genes into the bison gene pool."

"Right, so I created a test that would identify certain cattle genes in bison. And it worked. It gave us a way to document purity in bison. The Yellowstone animals didn't have those genes. Hence, purity, right. Untouched by human hands."

"And then?"

"A paper is coming out." Little stared off to the side, as if unwilling to confront the issue. "Researchers just recovered those same genes in ancient DNA from bison bones dating back to long before Europeans brought cattle to North America. Those genes have been here all the time. Just not in the Yellowstone herd."

"So your argument for Yellowstone purity was spurious?"

He nodded. "I've known it was coming for some time now. Should have said something, but when you've invested so much, fought so hard, how do you say, 'Sorry. I was wrong. This new Third Generation Sequencing technology I developed is crap?"

"You knew before the latest lawsuit was filed?"

"I thought, hey, maybe we'll get the ruling before the research is published in a peer-reviewed journal. Listen, everything you think you and the sheriff know about this case is wrong. Just like I was about bison purity. It's not about conservation. And I'm tired of lying, and now that people are being killed over it..." He ended with a shrug of defeat.

"How are we wrong?" Jillian leaned forward, recognizing the conspiratorial expression. From the corner of her eye, she registered movement beyond the window. Probably just someone walking in the distance, but it struck her as oddly familiar...

Little hunched closer on his elbows. "You want to know who's behind setting that trap? Just look—"

The *SNAP-POP* was simultaneous. Two sounds as one in a split instant.

Jillian felt a puff on her cheeks and forehead as the bullet passed and pulverized bits of flying glass sprayed her cheeks. Tim Little's head burst open, the skin rippling on his face. His eyes popped out, hat and hair flying up. Spittle shot from his mouth as his tongue blew out past his lips. Red gore and bits misted from the side of his head in a spurt. His hat was still falling down his back as he toppled over the beer glass and slammed onto the table.

Stunned and hunching, dully aware of the frosted

round hole that had appeared in the window, Jillian scrambled for cover from the next shot. Clawing for her Glock, she watched Tim Little's limp body slide off the cushion, and flop onto the floor beneath the table like some oversized rag doll. As it did, it left a smear of bright red on the table.

But the blood. The bits of tissue, torn skin, and small chunks of bone remained where they'd settled.

In the sudden silence, someone screamed.

CHAPTER NINETEEN

Jillian sat numbly at the table next to the hostess station and watched as the evidence recovery team did its work. The techs hurried about, photographing, measuring, recording the bullet hole in the window, the bloodstains, location of the body, and even the spent bullet where it had lodged in the wall.

One of the techs set up a laser on a tripod. This he used to back-sight from where the bullet stopped, across the blood spatter, and through the bullet hole in the window.

The miracle was that the EMTs had checked and been relieved to find shattered glass had missed her eyes. With tweezers, the EMT in charge dug out the biggest of the splinters before carefully cleaning her face.

Jillian reached for the glass of water, but her hand shook; the ice inside sounded like castanets. Mouth dry, her tongue stuck as she swallowed a gulp and set the glass back on the table.

The replay in her head kept sticking on that fraction of a second when Tim Little's head exploded. The sound, like a meaty dry stick snapping. The freaky way his skin slapped loosely around on his face. And, God. The eyes. The tongue popping out past his lips.

She shuddered, tried to take a breath. Couldn't.

Damn it, closing her eyes did no good. She could see every detail with perfect clarity.

Sheriff Wain left the cluster of techs, walked over, and pulled his hat off. He tossed it onto the table and settled into the chair across from hers. "Hell of a night, huh?"

She knotted a fist to keep him from seeing how it was shaking. "What about the shooter?"

Wain exhaled wearily. "Zip, zero, and nada. The deputies out back didn't have a clue about what had happened. They heard the crack, but inside their car, muffled, it was more of a popping sound. They didn't hear the distinctive report of a gunshot. Best bet? The guy used a suppressed rifle.

"First the deputies knew, people started flooding out, screaming. By then it was too late. By the time they got to the door, it was already chaos. People were in no mood to hang around and be interviewed. Some folks had fender benders in their rush to get away and never even stopped to check the damage. Panic does that." He shrugged. "The shooter would have merged with the rush. We'll check, see if there is surveillance video from the office across the street. Maybe we'll get lucky."

"Anything from the restaurant staff?"

"Not to my knowledge, Bozeman PD is just processing the last of them. They have the perimeter set up and are keeping the Looky Loos away. Media is already on it, lurking out there beyond the tape line and flashing lights."

"God." Another shudder took her.

"Hey, you're doing fine. Most people in your situation would be in tears."

She tried a smile, couldn't.

She closed her eyes, remembering her father. "*I don't care if you are a girl. My girl doesn't cry. Not ever. Not if she wants to be able to look at herself in the mirror with any kind of pride*" The love in his eyes the last time she'd seen him. He'd given her that crooked tough-guy smile as he'd been led away. She dared not think about how long it had been since she'd been to visit him.

Wain leaned back in the chair, something churning behind his gaze. "Yeah, well, guess you'll do fine from here on out."

"Jillian," Wain's voice dropped. "There's something else you need to know. You see that fella there with the laser? That's Kalen Reese. He does all of our ballistics. He was an Army sniper. Didn't see combat, but went through all the training. We've figured out that the shooter was in the appliance store parking lot across the way."

She glanced at the windows. There'd been something, some movement that struck her. Has she seen him lift his rifle? "So he was watching the entire time?"

"Yeah. But you see the window is at an angle from his shooting position. Reese tells me that a bullet hitting glass at an angle doesn't travel in a straight line. Rather the way the glass breaks, it bends the path of the bullet. Deflects it inward."

"I don't understand."

Wain replaced his hat, a hardness in the set of his jaw. "We're left with two possibilities. Either he's a really well-trained military-grade expert who knew just where to place that bullet and how it would deflect for a head shot on Tim Little, or he actually meant to kill you."

CHAPTER TWENTY

An old Sons of the Pioneers song was playing on the truck's sound system when John Cody slowed for the ranch exit. He blinked, feeling as raw as an uncooked sausage. The morning was just breaking; a filtered gray glow shone in the east beyond the Beartooth Front. It lit the high white-capped peaks with a slight pinkish hue, and softened the snow-clad forests of subalpine fir, spruce, and lodgepole pine on the slopes below.

Highway 212 was snow-packed, and Cody could hear the tires crunching on the frozen surface as he turned onto the ranch road. His brain felt hot and muzzy. Through the spears of trees to either side, he could just see the summit of Jim Smith Peak where it blocked the southern horizon.

The thermometer on the Ram's dash told him it was seven below zero outside. Really not bad for this late in January. He yawned, grabbed up his cup from the holder and slugged down the last of the now-cold coffee. It had been a long drive.

"Got to stop doing this," he muttered, wheeling into the yard and pulling up in front of the ranch house. Killing the Cummins diesel, he slumped in the seat, took a moment to enjoy the silence, and stare brain-dead at the historic log ranch house with its full porch. The roof must have had a foot of snow. The modern windows looked out of place against the dark-stained log walls. The corners were neat, all steeple-notched and expertly crafted. The place would have made the perfect Leanin' Tree greeting card. Or maybe the cover of *Western Horseman.*

Opening the Ram's door and stepping out, the cold hit him like a slap in the face. Cody paused long enough to recover his overnight bag from the back seat and shut the door.

Stiff from hours in the cab, he clumped his way across the porch, and opened the door. To his delight, a fire crackled in the fireplace. The desk lamp cast yellow light across the spacious living room. This had been a guest ranch once. Built in 1920, it had served as a jumping off spot for elite tourists visiting Yellowstone, and offered horseback pack trips, tours of the park, and hunting guides for the rich and famous.

That had all come to an end when Cody's parents bought the property nigh on twenty years past. Thought it would provide them with a refuge, a place no one would think to look for them. Especially the Satan's Reapers Motorcycle Club. They'd been Houston-based, most of their operations in Southeast Texas. A world away from the Pilot Creek Ranch where it lay hidden in the Upper Clarks Fork Valley within a couple of miles of Yellowstone.

Maybe it was far enough.

John's parents had been killed in Billings instead of here.

He paused at the door, removed his hat and hung it on the rack just below the old Marlin rifle. Then he shrugged out of his "go to town" parka and hung it next to the thick buffalo coat.

He could hear whistling in the kitchen and left his bag by the door, crossed to the hallway and made his way to the kitchen in rear of the building.

Danny Redweed stood at the big cook stove. The whip-thin woman was wearing Carhartt's and a denim snap shirt. She had a stained white apron tied at the waist. Her long black hair hung down her back in a pony-tail confined by a beaded Shoshoni Rose hair tie. She turned, dark eyes taking in Cody's sleep-puffy face. With her sharp nose, wide cheeks, and broad mouth, Danny looked every inch of what she was: a work-toughened old Eastern Shoshoni horse wrangler and rancher.

"You look like shit, boss," Danny said, before turning back to the buffalo steaks, eggs, and potatoes that sizzled in the frying pan. "Got your text that you'd be in about now. Figured you'd need something hot to fill you up."

Cody crossed to the coffee machine, a Capresso outfit, ultra-modern, and totally out of the place in the old-style ranch kitchen. But so was the big stainless steel Sub-Zero refrigerator hulking in the corner. Cody retrieved his favorite cup and shoved it under the spigots, then pushed the button.

"Yeah, long night." He waited as the machine ground, heated, and brewed the coffee. As he did, Redweed filled two plates and set them on the kitchen table. Retrieving her own half-empty cup, the woman seated himself.

Cody pulled out the other chair, dropping wearily into it. "What's the news?"

He absently picked up his fork, staring at the huge corner-set mirror. The reflection showed him the tree line past the fence. Behind it, the mountain rose in snow-packed majesty toward the cirrus-streaked pale blue sky.

"Elk hit the western fence, snarled it up some and grounded it out. But they didn't get through. From the tracks, it looks like they circled us to the south through the timber. Other than that, everything's fine. All but that new two-year-old heifer you brought home. That 208? She's a mystery. When I'm around, she's calm and sweet as sugar-candy. But all she has to do is lay eyes on you all the way across the pasture, and she starts throwing herself against the corral panels. You sure buying her from that half-assed outfit was such a good idea?"

"You've seen her conformation. Who she's bred to?"

"What does breeding and conformation mean if she ends up stomping you into red goo in an alleyway? Some jackass *taipo* did this to her. Hurt her bad. Scared her. Buffalo are no different than people. They don't forget, and they carry grudges."

"I think she just needs time."

"We'll see. You get killed? Then what do I do? Go back to the rez and get driven crazy by my relatives? You hear me, boy, don't take no chances with her." Redweed took a bite, gestured with her fork. "How'd you do?"

Cody cut off a piece of steak, stabbed it with his fork. "Not sure. I got a couple of hits. Trying to play it smart, you know? Found the casino. Hole in the wall kind of place in Laurel, just off the interstate. So I played the machines, drank for a bit at the bar until just before closing. Asked the bartender, scuzzy kind of guy, if Crank had been around. He said, 'Who?' I look him in the eye, trying to pull my tough-guy act. 'Crank Laumer,' I tell him. 'Used to be in the moving business. We did business about five, six years ago. Wondered if he was still around.'"

"And?" Redweed asked, forking up potatoes.

"The guy said he'd ask some folks if they'd ever heard of him. Told me to check back in a week or two." Cody shrugged, turned his attention to his breakfast.

Danny Redweed studied him through thoughtful black eyes. "John, you sure this is a good idea?"

Cody chuckled wearily. "Hell, no. Did you think it was a good idea when you went after the man that did what he did to your mother?"

Redweed gave him a knowing look, jaw muscles tensing as she chewed. "Sometimes we gotta do what we gotta do."

"Yeah." Cody cut another piece of steak. Danny always cooked 'em just right. Medium rare, lightly spiced with Guajillo chili powder. Eggs over easy, sprinkled with Mexican oregano, and the potatoes thin-sliced and ever so slightly crisped.

"Go get some sleep, chief." Redweed lifted an eyebrow. "I got everything under control. Even if it is the dead of winter and nothing's happening, you'd be as useless as tits on a boar if I needed you for anything important."

"You know, for an old woman, you're pretty full of yourself," Cody muttered, but he couldn't help the smile. He fixed on the trees reflected in the mirror, the branches heavy with snow.

"Yep. And don't you forget it, boy. Somebody around here has to have the brains and good sense." She gave him a ribald wink as she stood and headed down the hallway for her coat, hat, and boots.

The breakfast plates washed, Cody hobbled off to his

bed. But as he lay there, he couldn't sleep. Thinking back to the bartender's face, to that total blank look. Not even a hint of puzzlement. That hesitation as the guy thought it through.

Nope. He knew exactly who Crank Laumer was.

CHAPTER TWENTY-ONE

creams...

Uncle's face...turning blue...eyes popping out wide...

She can see Father's fingers, how they sink deeply into Uncle's throat.

"God damn you, you piece of shit!" Father's voice breaks.

Uncle's tongue looks swollen as it's pushed out passed his lips.

The sound of breaking glass, the banging of Uncle's head against the shelves.

Plates, glasses, cascade down. They explode with a hollow musical sound as they hit the floor. See them? See the pieces? So many pieces. Angular. Dancing as they bounce across the worn tile. Uncle's shoes lift as if he's standing on tiptoe among the shattered plates and slivered glass. Rising...rising...

She awakened on the floor in the little room in the Sheriff's Office complex. Jillian's eyes felt like they were full of sand. On the floor? Hadn't done that in years. When had that happened? Groggy, she sat up, only to bang against the underside of the bed.

She yawned up at the creaky bed's springs, crawled out, and stood. Turning on the light, she checked the featureless small room with its rollaway. Sheriff Wain had insisted that she stay at the SO. That, until the shooter was caught, there was no way to determine if she or Tim Little had been the intended victim. So, he'd put her here, in this oversized closet of a room. A place where staff could catch a couple of hours sleep when things got hectic.

"And I know for a fact that you'll wake up alive," Wain had told her, showing her the room with its uncomfortable-looking bed.

Thank God no one had bothered to check on her. Found her curled under the bed. How would she have explained? What would they think?

In the hall, Jillian made her way to the women's room where she attended to nature. In the mirror, she studied the little gauzy squares that dotted her face. Soaking them off, she checked the cuts. It had been a miracle that the spraying glass had missed her eyes.

An unsettling thought crossed her mind.

So, Jillian, she asked herself, *who was really supposed to die last night? Was Little killed because he was going to rat? Or was it you? Did Tim Little lure you there only to be hit by mistake?*

She washed up, got her hair under control, then hit the break room and poured a cup of coffee. Thus fortified, she made her way down the hall to the offices. Wain, despite it being just after 6:30, sat at his desk. The way his brow furrowed as he stared at his computer, it might have been an oracle that held all the secrets of the universe. This morning he was wearing reading glasses, his mouth puckered into a sour expression.

"Morning," she greeted, her brain stumbling over the uncertainties over whom last night's victim was supposed to be.

"Morning yourself. Sleep well?"

"That's supposed to be a joke, right?" She settled into the chair opposite his desk. "What's the breaking news?"

"Outside of another sensational killing in Bozeman?" Wain let his glasses slip down so he could stare at her over the frames. "Bozeman PD has the lead since this was in town. They've got squat so far, but we're hoping the bullet might shed some light. ERT dug it out of the wall. Looks like a 6.5. Once that would have meant something, but now everyone has a 6.5. Probably a Creedmoor. In the past ten years, it's become the big seller. We might get a clue when the state crime lab looks at the rifling engraved on the bullet, but then again, every major gun maker and all of the custom houses make 6.5s. To confirm a match, we'll have to recover the rifle."

"What about witnesses? Anyone see anything?"

"Nope. The last people out of the restaurant was that family that had been sitting at the table across from you. They saw nothing out of the ordinary.

"Our best guess? When the shooter exfiltrated, he did it professionally. No squealing tires, no reckless dash into traffic. Thought maybe the PD might get lucky with the security cameras in the office building, but they only have intruder alarms. No one was working late. So we're stopped there, too."

Jillian sipped her coffee. Made a face. Police station coffee might even have been worse than the brew in her hotel room, and that was about as bad as she could stand.

"So, what should I do today?" she asked. "Want me to take a crack at the ex-wife or our missing rancher, Dan Butler, from down at Gardiner?"

The look Wain was giving her over his glasses was dark and unforgiving. "Neither. Last night you came within a hand's breadth of a bullet. We still don't know if it was meant for you or if Dr. Little was the target all along. But letting you walk the streets in case the shooter wants to take another shot is out of the question."

Despite his words mirroring her own worries, she said, "Sheriff, you can't just pull me off the streets when I'm—"

"The hell I can't. I've been thinking. Has the thought crossed your mind that maybe Tim Little called that meeting for the express purpose of killing you?"

"Why? I'm no threat."

"Really? Didn't Jenn Banks say you'd get yours?"

"What kind of threat am I to her?"

"How the hell should I know, Jill, but maybe you've stumbled onto something? Some lead you just haven't realized yet."

That stopped her, made her sit back. Had she? But how? What would it have been? Something in the house that day?

He raised his hands imploringly. "And don't pull that 'I don't work for you' crap. I've already been on the horn to your boss, Meyer. He seconds my decision. Wants to talk to you as soon as you're finished here. The idea that someone would take a shot at a DCI agent doesn't sit well back in Helena."

"What could I possible know that's a threat to Ryman Banks' killer?" Jillian asked. "Not that shooting Tim Little makes any sense, either, but killing me makes even less. I'm just an investigator. Taking out a state agent would be incredibly stupid. The whole world would be hunting for this guy's hide."

"That's one of the things that spooks your boss. Maybe that's just what the shooter wants. Celebrity. The Banks murder is front and center on every news show in the state, half the national networks are following the story. Social media is picking up on it, and by the time news of the Little shooting breaks across the wires, we're going to be on every news show in the nation. Taking out the governor's personal agent? That would push his story right over the top. Then, after we finally run him down, every American and half of the world will know his name."

"That would be motive all right," she agreed, a cold shiver running down her back. "But just in case that's not what's behind this, we'd better sit on that hypothesis. No sense in giving him ideas, not to mention scaring the shit of the public."

Wain nodded, eyes vacant. "But why Tim Little? Unless he knew who the killer was."

"I think he did," she told him. "His exact words the moment the bullet hit him were, 'You want to know who was behind setting that trap?' And bang! And there's your motive, Sheriff. That's why I might just as well hit the streets and see if I can interview one of our other persons of interest. I really want to take a crack at Jenn Banks, especially if she's behind this. Catch her off guard. Rattle her by showing up the morning after she tried to—"

"Nope." Wain's lips pursed and he shook his head. "Got another assignment for you, but for the moment, let's consider our other POIs. What would each have to gain? Start with John Cody. According to Carly Joyner, he stands to lose his ranch if the Yellowstone bison are listed as endangered. But then we've got the mysterious Dan Butler, who's already lost his ranch because of ICoHR. He's out there, somewhere. Then there's your ex-wife, Jenn, who avoids a major lawsuit now that Banks is dead, and she's got the money to pay for a hit. But why take out Little?"

"Unless Dr. Little knew she was behind it." Jillian shrugged. "What about Carly Joyner?"

Wain said absently, "We checked her alibi. She can account for just about every hour for the prior three days. Meetings with potential donors, receipts from shopping and buying gas, talks with her neighbors, and phone calls and meetings with her accountant. Plus, she has no motive. Without Banks...not to mention Tim Little and his articles on Yellowstone genetics, she's lost the biggest assets that make ICoHR effective."

"She told me that without Banks, there would be no ICoHR."

Wain nodded, thumbed through some notes on a pad to the side. "Her exact words at the house when Sampson and I interviewed her were 'Ryman is our central pillar. What am I going to do now?' She was pretty shaken." Wain stopped to study one of the pages, adding, "But, yeah, everything she says checks out. Right down to calling her sister moments before finding the body. The sister, Beth, says that Joyner sounded completely normal. Just worried about how their father was doing in Pennsylvania. Not to mention that Joyner's personality is not a gun type. Our evidence guys had to clean up where she puked at the crime scene."

At that moment, Deputy Brody Kielman appeared, rapped his knuckles on the doorframe, and leaned into the room. "Bert? You asked me to check in when we got back."

Kielman was in his fifties, showing more stomach than he'd like over his belt buckle. The guy had wiry steel-gray hair, a jaw that was almost too big for his face, and stubby nose that mocked his wide and thin lips. His tired blue eyes barely masked his interest as he glanced from Bert Wain to Jillian.

"Good morning, Brody. How'd it go?"

"Joyner was pretty shocked. Thought maybe she'd give us an argument, but instead, she just nodded, packed her things, and let the Bozeman PD take her to a safe house. The idea that someone could be taking out ICoHR's big shots, and that she could be next on the list, really freaked her."

Wain looked at Jillian. "First Banks, then Little? What if it's about revenge for something ICoHR has done? We thought it best to get Carly Joyner off the street."

"What about all the people working for her?" Jillian asked.

Sampson said, "They've been told to work from home. Office is closed until further notice. Joyner said she can manage with her laptop until the killer's caught."

Wain said, "Thanks, Brody. You about ready for the road?"

Kielman shot Jillian an irritated look, nodded, and said, "Gotta get some things. Ready in ten." Then he disappeared down the hallway.

Jillian shifted, asking, "So, you said you had another assignment for me."

Wain gave her a bland smile. "You and Deputy Kielman are going to Wyoming."

"God, tell me it's not 'The Train Station.'"

"Might be the next best thing. You are Brody are going to pay John Cody a surprise visit. I've been on the horn to the Park County SO down in Wyoming, and we're just waiting to see if they can detail a deputy to accompany the two of you." He paused. "Uh, you know why we need Wyoming law, right?"

"Jurisdiction," Jillian replied. "If we find evidence, or can determine probable cause, the Park County SO can make the arrest since we'll be out of our jurisdiction. But what makes you think Cody will even talk to us?"

Wain tapped a finger on his notebook before leaning back in his chair. "Turns out that your good friend, the good Governor Brewster, went to law school with Leon Gretz, one of the Park County judges. Given that Cody's hat was found at the scene, Judge Gretz was willing to sign off on a warrant. I'll leave it up to you and Brody as to how hard you want to push. Follow your gut when it comes to this guy. First impressions are that he'll alibi out. But the fact that he and Banks have a history and have tangled in the past? There's a reason why John Cody's hat was found at the scene, and I want to know what it is. How it got there."

CHAPTER TWENTY-TWO

Deputy Brody Kielman weighed in at over one-seventy with a five-foot-seven frame. A veteran of sixteen years on the Gallatin County SO, he'd developed a tough no-bullshit attitude, and his blue eyes could go from chuckling amusement to hard-assed cold at a moment's notice. But then, being on the front lines of law enforcement, Kielman had had a front-row seat when it came to all the flaws vested in human beings.

He slouched in the Durango's passenger seat as Jillian motored south from Belfry, Montana. The route was the long way around given that in mid-winter, the six-mile section of road from the Wyoming line to Cooke City, Montana was unplowed. The locals called it "The Plug" and it made travelers from Cooke City and the Lamar Valley who needed to travel east to Sunlight Basin endure a long three-hundred-and-seventy mile circle around to Gardiner, north through Livingston, east on I-90 to Laurel, then south through Bridger and Belfry almost to Cody, Wyoming. From there they took the Chief Joseph Scenic Highway over the tortuous Dead Indian Pass.

After that, they'd have another forty miles just to reach John Cody's ranch.

For Jillian and Kielman, traveling from Bozeman, it was only a measly two hundred and fifty miles. That was the thing about the West. "As a crow flies" was rarely an option.

Finally approaching the junction, Jillian shot Deputy Kielman a sidelong glance. In the three hours they'd been on the road, she'd barely come to know the man. You could say this about Brody Kielman: he was anything but talkative. His attitude had been dismissive, almost bordering on contempt. Something about the short way Kielman answered her attempts at making small talk, evaded any references to himself, his family, or history.

Since they'd stopped in Bridger for fuel and a bathroom break, Kielman had been hunched in the seat, sucking on one of those huge thirty-two ounce soda drinks. The man kept his eyes fixed ahead, had only grunted when Jillian had pointed at the blue sign with a bucking horse, and remarked, "Well, there it is. We just crossed the Wyoming line."

Jillian couldn't stand it any longer. She gave the man another hard look. "Is there something bothering you?"

"Like what?" Kielman didn't take his eyes off the road.

"Is there a problem between us? Have I done something?"

Kielman chuckled under her breath. "You ask me, you haven't done dick. Well, maybe got yourself shot at. What the hell are you, anyway? Fresh graduate from Missoula. Hired right off by the Montana DOJ for the Investigations Bureau and detailed to the Billings Major Case Section? Then, bam! Bigwig Ryman Banks gets blown away, and suddenly, here you are. What, twenty-six, twenty-seven—"

"Twenty-nine."

"Right. Twenty-nine. All bright, young, and beautiful, looking like an Indian maiden from a Leanin'Tree card with those perfect dark eyes and that gleaming black hair. And boy, do you make an impression, or what? You prance into the crime scene and wrap good old Bert right around your little finger. Granted, I'm used to men thinking with their dicks, but what did you do, throw in a little magical smile and bat those big brown eyes to seal the deal?"

Jillian ground her teeth, bit her lip, and tightened her grip on the wheel. That old burning anger flickered to life down in her belly. "Just doing my job, Deputy. Following the direction provided by my supervisor. Sheriff Wain has been nothing but professional."

Kielman failed to stifle bitter laughter. "You that blind? You don't see the way he watches you? That lost puppy look in his eyes? Hell, he's got his boxers in such a tight knot his balls are turning blue. Why? Just because you dodged a bullet last night? Put you up in the office so you'd be safe?" He raised a finger and wiggled it. "As if he'd have lifted so much as a pinky for any of the rest of us. 'All in the line of duty,' he'd say and send us straight home. Figure we were capable officers of the law and that we could take care of ourselves." A pause. "Now I'm on a babysitting mission while the hunt goes on for the shooter."

"Oh, fuck off. That's what you think this is? Babysitting?"

Kielman's lips bent into a hard smile, his eyes still fixed on the road.

Though tight jaws, Jillian said, "John Cody's hat was

found inside the door not six feet from that shotgun. Doesn't matter that he's trying to alibi-out for the night of the murder. Fact is, that shotgun trap could have been set anytime. Maybe before Cody claims he left for Denver. We don't know how long it had been since Banks was home last. Charlotte Zypanski said she thought Banks had been with another woman the before he showed up at her place."

"What woman?"

"We don't know yet. But she'll turn up. Maybe in a credit card receipt, hotel register, but somewhere along the line of evidence."

"Wow! Smoking hot investigative work there. Bet that came right out of the 'How to be a Cop' textbook back at the university."

Jillian rolled her eyes. "Forget it. This is going nowhere."

They rode in silence, Jillian glaring at the long straight section of Highway 120 as they headed south across Chapman Bench, Kielman staring out the window at the cloud-covered Beartooth Range off to the West.

Finally, Kielman broke the impasse. "Sorry." He made a gesture. "Shouldn't have bitten your head off."

"It's okay. I can see where you're coming from. It's not like I asked for this assignment. My butt's on the line, too. Since I got that call from Supervisor Meyer, I've been terrified I'd screw this up." A chuckle. "I feel like I've been thrown in the deep end, and I'm not sure I know how to swim. Then to be there, see Dr. Little's head explode." She slapped the wheel with her hands. "Still puts a quaver in the pit of my stomach. I spent half the night wondering if I should call it a day, go home, and turn in my resignation."

"Not like they show it in the movies, huh?"

"The way I expected this to work, my training, is that I'd be on the team sifting through the evidence, doing interviews, putting the pieces together to find the bad guy." She shook her head. "I'll leave the busting down doors and making the collar to officers like you."

Kielman actually smiled. "Okay, rookie, maybe you're not the self-aggrandizing cunt I thought you were. I'll give you a break." A pause. "Till you prove me wrong."

Dropping down into the Pat O'Hara Creek bottoms Jillian saw the sign for Wyoming 296 and the Chief Joseph Scenic Highway. A Park County Sheriff's Office pickup and an explorer could be seen at the pull off.

"There's our warrant and escort." Kielman sat straighter as Jillian pulled in next to the pickup. She shifted into Park and stepped out into the cold morning. A breeze chilled her cheeks and nose, trying to toss her hair.

Kielman alit from the passenger side as the deputy—a young man dressed in an olive nylon jacket with badge and patches, duty belt, and dark-brown western hat—descended from the pickup. He held a manilla envelope in one hand. Doors on the Explorer opened and two other deputies, a man and woman, emerged.

"Agent Jillian Masterson," she said, offering her hand. "And this is Deputy Brody Kielman."

"Jim Cosgrove." He took her hand.

She was looking into soft brown eyes; and the guy had a nice smile. Good cheeks, a straight nose and firm jaw. Just the sort of iconic Wyoming deputy that would grace a recruitment poster. Jillian stepped back as the Cosgrove shook Deputy Kielman's hand and welcomed him to Wyoming.

Cosgrove indicated the others. Pointing to the tall blond guy in his twenties, he said, "Deputy Shane Brock.

He's part of our team. And finally this is Madison Wade. She's been on the force since dirt was young."

Handshakes went all the way around.

"Appreciate your cooperation on this," Kielman said. "We're not sure that Cody is our man, and we're not anticipating any problem." He glanced off to the west toward the mountains. "But a back country ranch? This far from town? No telling what we'll run into."

"Yeah," Cosgrove said, following Kielman's gaze. "We've never had any interaction with Cody. Nothing on his record. But some of these guys still think it's 1880 out here when it comes to property rights, the law, and who's in charge. We'll do our best to keep it low key until we know what we're dealing with."

"That's the warrant?" Jillian asked, tucking hair behind her ears where the wind kept pulling it loose.

"Hot off the press," he told her, handing the envelope over.

Jillian removed the document, scanning it as the wind kept trying to fold it over her fingers. Proof by affidavit having been made, assuming the address was correct on Highway 212, Deputy Cosgrove had the right to search the Pilot Creek Ranch premises for evidence related to the Ryman Banks homicide. There followed a description of buildings, out buildings, a barn, and sheds. Probable cause being John Cody's hat at the murder scene and Cody's having had a history of antagonism with the victim. Any evidence discovered to be brought forthwith before the judge. All signed by the judge's scrawled signature.

"What specifically are we looking for?" Wade asked, skepticism behind her gray eyes. She had her thumbs stuck in her duty belt.

"Anything that might tie John Cody to Ryman Banks'

murder." Kielman gave the woman a shrug. "You read the documentation of the crime scene. Cody has a history with Banks. So we're looking for literature, books, letters, and anything on his computer that might tie to ICoHR, rightwing conspiracy, or any militant anti-government group. It's not like Wyoming doesn't have a history of that kind of thing going clear back beyond the Johnson Country war."

Wade turned to the others. "So, if this John Cody is into that sort of thing, we could be walking into an armed camp. Maybe a weapons stash, explosives, and if he's into booby traps like were used in Montana, we'll take him into custody and let the ATF and FBI sort it out."

Jillian noted the sober nods, the tightening of jaws. God, what kind of trouble was she headed into?

The image played in her mind: The loud pop! Tim Little's head exploding. His skin rippling as gore blew out the side of his head.

Uncle's facial skin is rippling with each impact. The broken china cabinet banging against the wall as Father smashes Uncle's head into it.

She screams, "No, Daddy! No!"

"Hey?" A hand touched her shoulder. "You with us?" Kielman asked.

Jillian came aware of the others, watching her with curious eyes. How long had she been out?

"Lead the way, Deputy," she told Cosgrove. "Let's see what we find."

"You got it, Agent Masterson," Cosgrove said. "Um, it's our jurisdiction, but given that it's your case and the warrant's wide-ranging, don't be afraid to point us in any direction."

As Jillian opened the driver's door on her Durango,

she could feel Kielman's gaze. Shifting into Drive, she followed Deputy Cosgrove's pickup out onto the narrow strip of blacktop. The Explorer pulled out behind her.

"What happened back there?" Kielman asked. "It was like you totally zoned out."

Jillian ground her teeth, bucked her seat belt. "Flashback to last night. Seeing that man's head blown apart." She shook it off. "I'll be all right."

She just couldn't be sure that the storm clouds hanging in the high country were any less threatening than the renewed uncertainty she saw in Kielman's eyes.

CHAPTER TWENTY-THREE

"Where the hell are we going?" Jillian asked as they descended the switchbacks on the west slope of Dead Indian Pass. Below and to all sides, she swore this was one of the most spectacular high-country vistas she'd ever seen. Towering mountains, topped by ragged peaks, all snow-capped, rugged, and shrouded by misty streamers of cloud that looked as if they'd been torn out of the sky itself. Below the snow-drifted crags and cresta-ridged alpine heights, steep slopes were carpeted with spruce and fir forests rimed in white where snow hung heavy in the branches. Mixed in were dark green conifers that had been swept free by the wind, leaving mottled patterns across the mountain sides.

This was wilderness as God had intended, high country broken by cliffs that thrust out like the very bones of the earth, while talus slopes cascaded below bedrock outcrops in fountains of jumbled rock. In the valleys, clad in mosaics of lodgepole pine and fir she could see rounded humps of bedrock worn smooth by countless millennia of glaciers. Threaded through it all were ice-capped streams and rivers that had eaten deeply into the bedrock.

Kielman shot her a curious look as Jillian slowed to gape. The Explorer behind crowded her bumper, no doubt wondering what was wrong.

"Where are you from? Missoula, you say? You've never seen mountains? Like the ones surrounding the city?"

"Not like this," Jillian admitted. "Sure, I got up in the Bitterroots a time or two. Somehow, I mean, like, they're softer, you know? This? Damn, it's just raw wilderness."

"Yeah, well, while you're feasting your eyes, our deputy lead dog is half way down the mountain."

Jillian forced herself to accelerate and pay attention to the road. Challenging as that was, she still managed to steal gaga-eyed glimpses of the stunning scenery. The good news was that they were the only ones on the road.

It just got better as they followed Cosgrove west through the Clarks Fork Valley.

"One hell of a place for a buffalo ranch," Kielman muttered, then adopted a quizzical look. "According to the file, Cody is just thirty. No wife or kids. How does a guy that young afford a ranch in the Upper Clarks' Fork? Inheritance? Rich family back East? Oil money or tech?"

"No clue." Jillian started as a herd of elk burst from the timber. Apparently spooked by Cosgrove's patrol truck, they split, a half dozen racing across the road in front of Jillian's Durango. She panic-braked, slowed enough that the last of the tan animals clattered to safety. Behind her, the Explorer was on her bumper again.

"Shit!" she breathed.

"Yeah, Agent," Kielman told her smugly. "Total your state vehicle on a back road in Wyoming? You'll be filling out forms in paperwork hell for the next three centuries."

Shaken, Jillian accelerated, anxious to keep Cosgrove in sight, trying to use X-ray vision to see through the trees lining the right-of-way for any other wildlife that might try and commit suicide on her grill. It was a no-go on the X-ray superpower, so she settled for eyestrain and edge-of-the-seat adrenaline instead.

Passing the 212 Junction, Cosgrove slowed, and they could see him studying the south side of the road. After a couple of miles, he pulled to a stop before a turn off. The small wooden sign looked hand-carved.

PILOT CREEK RANCH
TROPHY NORTH AMERICAN BISON

A county address was posted to one side of the snow-covered road that vanished down into the thick screening of trees.

Jillian pulled in behind Cosgrove as he stopped and got out. The Explorer followed suit.

As they all stepped out, it was to wave as a pickup loaded with snowmobiles passed them, headed for "the Plug" snow machine trail that led to Cooke City. Outside of a couple of pickups and a Subaru topped by a rack of cross-country skis, since leaving the 120 Junction they'd seen no other traffic.

Cosgrove stuck his thumbs into his front pockets as they gathered around, studying the road. "Doesn't look like much. Most of the traffic through here, like those snowmobilers, they'd miss it unless looking closely. Can't see anything of the property from the highway. No telling what we're getting into. We're on the ragged edge of WyoLink Service. That's our statewide network of interagency radio. Highway Patrol, Highway Department, emergency services, we all use it. I think the SO picked up my call in. Couldn't make out the response, but I think it was a 10-4."

It added to Jillian's unease that Deputy Bock carried an AR15 in the low-mount position, and a pump shotgun hung from Madison Wade's right hand. Both deputies were warily scanning the thick belt of trees stretching off to either side. Jillian reflexively patted her holstered Glock where it was hidden by her suit jacket.

Jillian followed Deputy Wade's gaze as she inspected the road. Tire tracks could be seen in the freshly fallen inch of snow. "Somebody drove out this morning."

"Yeah," Kielman said, shifting his duty belt. "Hope that's not our perp."

"Pray he didn't get wise and run." Jillian couldn't help but note.

Cosgrove bent down, studied the tire tracks.

"What do you see master tracker?" Wade crouched beside him.

Cosgrove pointed with a finger. "See how the little ridges of snow are standing straight up in the middle of the tread imprints? These are tracks from a dually pickup, and the vehicle was headed downhill. It went in, not out of the ranch."

"How do you know that?" Jillian asked, bending down to study the snow.

Cosgrove told her, "Even in four-wheel-drive, the tires displace the snow when the truck accelerates, like he'd be doing if he was coming up from below and turning onto the highway. Nope. Someone drove into the ranch sometime this morning, and no one has been out since it snowed last night."

Jillian already had her phone out, taking photos.

"Well, what the hell?" Kielman said, standing. "Let's go see if it was the neighbors coming over for a cup of coffee, or John B. Cody barely beating us home after killing his latest victim in Bozeman last night."

Jillian flinched. Stared at the man, flash-backs—again—of Little's head exploding leaving her shaken.

That hollow crawling feeling began to tickle her insides.

CHAPTER TWENTY-FOUR

The sound of the John Deere's diesel and the rattling of the implements and tire chains filled John Cody's hearing as he drove across the winter pasture. One last blue mineral tub remained on the pallet riding the loader forks; it was tucked tight as he rocked and rolled across the snow-covered buffalo pies. The things froze as hard as river rocks and could jounce a man's innards sideways or tip a top-loaded tractor on its side if he drove too fast.

After his nap, Cody had dressed in his cold weather gear, checked with Redweed, and dove headlong into his chores.

The bison were still occupied with the new bales at the feeders. The dominant cows had eaten and wandered off to lay down, jaws working placidly as they chewed cud. Now the low-ranked cows were taking their turn, the newly weaned calves and yearlings rousting each other as they waited their chance.

Cody stopped in the corner of the pasture where the

slope rose to meet the tree line, lowered the forks, and climbed down from the cab. Grabbing the mineral tub, he rolled it off the pallet and onto the snow. Then pulled off and folded the plastic sealant that kept the molasses-sweetened mineral mix fresh.

He was climbing back into the cab when he saw the three vehicles emerge from the trees and pull up as if in a protective formation before his house. Across the distance, Cody could see deputies emerging, looking around warily. Given the long guns they carried, this wasn't anything like a social call.

The barn blocked part of his view, but from the way the deputies shifted their attention, Danny Redweed had probably just walked out into the yard.

"Son of a bitch," Cody muttered under his breath before opening the cab door and seating himself behind the wheel. Lifting the forks and angling them back, he shifted into high range and started back across the pasture. The loader and blade in back kept banging and clanging in accompaniment to the musical jingle of the tire chains as the diesel grumbled and he bounced over the frozen buffalo chips.

At the gate, he slowed to a stop. Could see the deputies fanned out. Danny standing by the Park County Sheriff's office pickup, her arms crossed, looking irritated. The other officers watched as Cody climbed down, opened the gate, drove through, and closed it again. Then he got back in the cab and drove the big John Deere into the yard. While he lowered the implements and throttled down, he studied the invaders: five of them. The Park County sheriff's office pickup and Explorer were self-explanatory. The black Durango with Montana state plates was not. Nor was the single woman not in uniform. She wore a black wool coat more suited to a city, had long midnight hair confined in a ponytail, and wore what he considered to be city dress boots. The kind with blocky heels and that zipped up the sides of her legs.

Killing the engine, he released the pressure on the hydraulic system and climbed down.

Damn if they weren't fingering their weapons, standing in a half crouch, as if in anticipation that he was Ike Clanton and this was the OK Corral.

Cody raised his gloved hands, calling, "Hey, stand down. No one is resisting here. What's this all about?"

The older female deputy, her tag read Wade, stepped forward, offering a manila envelope. "You are John Bernard Cody?"

"I am."

"I have here a legal warrant to search the premises for any evidence relating to the murder of Ryman Banks the Third on Sunday last."

Cody took the envelope, was opening it when Deputy Wade added, "Having been so served, sir, you are advised not to interfere with or in any manner hinder or obstruct our search of the structures and premises. Please comply with any requests made by the attending officers. Do you have any questions?"

"Yeah," Cody said, scanning the lines of text. "Are you people out of your god damned minds?"

"Sir, that warrant—"

"Yeah, yeah." Cody waved a hand. "Search all you want. Danny and I aren't going to get in the way." He paused. Looked Wade in the eye. "Anything in particular you're looking for?"

The attractive woman in black stepped forward, an intensity in her dark eyes. "Who drove into your ranch this morning?"

Cody shot a glance at Danny, saw her jaw muscles clamp, gaze dropping. As if to make a point, she spit a stream of brown Copenhagen juice onto the snow.

Cody took a deep breath. "I did."

"Where were you last night?"

"Billings." He fixed on her, and damn, what was it with those half-haunted eyes? Who in the hell was she?

"Billings? Doing what?"

He felt his stomach pull into a knot. Damn. How much did he tell them? Meeting her stare-for-stare, he said, "I was at a casino. The Red Thunderbird if you really need to know."

"All night?"

"Until they closed."

"And then?"

"I drove home. Got in about six this morning."

He noted the slight quiver at the corner of her lips. "Mr. Cody? Do you own a 6.5 caliber rifle?"

Cody arched an eyebrow. "Nope. Never had much use for the caliber to tell you the truth."

As he said it, something flickered behind her eyes, a slight shiver playing down her body. Or was that just his imagination?

Over the woman's shoulder, he could see the deputies as they crossed his porch and entered his house. "This is going to be a pain in the ass, isn't it?"

"Depends," she told him. "Did you kill Ryman Banks the Third?"

"Nope. Like I said, I was on the way home from the national bison show in Denver. If you'll follow me to my office, I'll dig out the receipts."

"We will attend to your office, Mr. Cody. Please avoid any possible interference with our officers."

"Uh, what about me?" Danny asked. "I'm just the hired help."

She gave the older woman a measuring glance. "Mrs. Redweed, you indicated that you live in the small cabin behind the barn. If you will be so kind as to confine yourself to your lodging, we'd like to ask you some questions before we leave."

"John?" Danny asked, and he could see the devil brewing behind her dark eyes. Danny never knew when to keep her mouth shut. The fact that she had so far was a miracle.

"Do as they say." Cody tried to grin reassuringly. "Guess in the meantime you can read that CJ Box book you've been itching to start."

Danny nodded curtly, shot a wary glance at the woman, and headed off for her cozy little house. Cody her heard her muttering something about a nasty *taipo gwidahpe ta'ih* as she went. Good thing the cops didn't understand Shoshoni.

"Who are you?" Cody asked, facing the woman.

"Special Agent Jillian Masterson. Montana Investigations Bureau, Major Cases Division. We spoke on the phone when you called Sheriff Wain."

"Ah, yeah." Cody pulled his gloves off. "You guys searching my kitchen?"

"I assume so." She kept watching him with such intensity. Like she was trying to see down right down to his core.

"Nothing there," he told her. "Not in my kitchen, and while you're trying to see into my soul, there's nothing there that's linked to murdering that snake, Banks. So, that being the case, I'm going to go in and make coffee for you and the deputies. Something tells me this is going to be a really long day."

"After you, Mr. Cody." She indicated with a graceful gesture. "Would you mind answering some questions while you make coffee?"

"Ask away." She was probably a voracious man-killing predator, but at least if you were going to be interrogated, it was nice to be grilled by a nice-looking one.

CHAPTER TWENTY-FIVE

The situation struck her as surreal. She was sitting at a table—her notebook open before her, pen in hand—in a kitchen, across from a man who might have murdered two human beings. At the same time, she was feeling completely at ease. It came from the way he looked at her. Not with longing or that intent male-predator look. But something honest in his eyes.

Pay attention, Jillian. Psychopaths are experts at faking empathy.

Her nose could still detect the delicious scents of breakfast; that was barely overlaid by the rich smell of freshly brewed coffee.

Periodic patches of sunlight appeared as the broken clouds cleared outside. They filled the south-facing kitchen windows with light. Most unique, however, was the mirror that had been set in the corner behind the small table. Who would put a big mirror in a kitchen of all places? Where she sat, she could look at the reflection and see the tree line a couple of hundred yards up the valley. But, then, it added light and an illusion of space.

Beyond that, taking stock, the kitchen would not have been what she would have expected from a single man. The place was neat and organized, the counters clean, the dishes all stacked in the drying rack next to the sink. While the white-painted cabinets looked old, perhaps even original, the oversized Sub-Zero refrigerator and the fancy Wolf stove with all of its burners came across as anachronistic. Especially when compared to the worn vinyl floor.

So, was he a murderer?

She studied the man across from her. Tried to see who or what was lurking behind those tan eyes. His thick brown beard and mustache had been trimmed. They gave him a self-sufficient outdoors look, and his full head of dark hair bore the line where his hat had mashed it down flat against his skull. Broad shoulders, like she would have attributed to a rancher, filled his red-checked flannel shirt, and when he'd peeled off his brown Carhartt insulated overalls, he'd been wearing faded jeans held up by a worn leather belt with a shiny buckle with raised bronze lettering that read CLASSIC PRODUCER AWARD over DAKOTA TERRITORY.

So far, nothing had tripped her triggers, or cried "Danger" in her subconscious. And that was most curious.

Also curious, he remained unflappable as Deputies Cosgrove and Wade oversaw the invasion of his privacy as they poked through his office and files, bedrooms, inspected his firearms, and counted his ammunition. They pawed through his drawers, looked in his cabinets, and inspected all of his books, even holding them open and ruffling the pages lest anything fall out.

She noted, "Most people would be really put out by this."

He lifted his coffee, smiled, and studied her. "Maybe it's worth it."

"Worth it? How? You're a suspect in a murder investigation. Not only that, each time a victim dies, you're" —she mimicked quotations—"on the road. Sure, maybe you've got the receipts, but given the time frame during which Banks' shotgun trap could have been set and the shooting last night took place?" She shook her head. "You're not cleared Mr. Cody."

His expression pinched as he sipped his coffee, frown lines deepening in his forehead. "What shooting?"

"You haven't seen the news?"

"Nope. After I got in, Danny and I had breakfast. Then I took a nap and went to work. Who got shot?"

"Last night in Bozeman. Another person related to Ryman Banks was killed. Another of your enemies, by the way." She hesitated, pen in hand. "Want to take a guess?"

His eyes narrowed as he thought. "Logic says it would be Carly Joyner. She was the other half of the ICoHR fraud. Those people bilked millions out of donors, the government, maybe even school children for all I know."

"Why do you call it fraud? They're trying to protect the last remaining wild and pure bison in the country. Surely, you, as a bison rancher, don't take issue with their suit to have Yellowstone bison listed as endangered?"

"You bought that?" For fleeting second, she saw irritation flash behind his expression, then he chuckled. "Of course, you did. You and the rest of the world. That's how a good scam works. Okay, here's how the science lines out. There's no such thing as a"—it was his turn to hook his fingers in quotation—"wild and pure bison."

"But as I understand, history is full of people breeding bison to beef cows."

"Uh-huh. Granted. But the *bovini* tribe has been hybridizing for millions of years. What's called 'gene flow.' Not enough to stop speciation, but enough to leave what you'd call beef genes in the bison gene pool. And don't forget the yak. It's a sister species to bison. They all share genes. Purity is a myth."

"Yak? Like in Tibet? That's a joke right?"

"Bison, yaks, and beef cattle all have a common ancestor."

"That's all well and fine, but we're talking about murder, not extinct animals."

"It's all related."

"Really? How?"

"Money," he told her. "How do you convince people that bison are endangered, so they keep donating their hard-earned cash to protect them, when there are close to a half a million bison in the US and Canada? Where's the threat to survival if buffalo are thriving? ICoHR had to turn commercial bison into pariahs. Profane because they'd been touched by the hand of man. The conservation movement staked everything on purity."

She thought back to Tim Little's confession that his research had been wrong. "You're saying the Yellowstone bison aren't pure?"

Cody leaned forward, a gleam in his eyes. "What's about to kick ICoHR in the balls is the latest research on ancient bison DNA taken from paleontological digs in the US and Asia. The final paper has been written and is going to be published soon. Oxford University ran the DNA samples through seven different TGS techs to see how they compared and—"

"If it hasn't been published, how do you know that?" Would he tell her the same thing Tim Little had?

"I know the archaeologists working on the sites. The upshot is that Little's Third Generation Sequencing technology is garbage. They—"

"Could you explain third generation sequencing?" she asked, and saw Cody take a deep breath as though preparing to give her a lecture. "The short version, please."

"Well…" He made an airy gesture with is hand. "Okay. So. Existing second-generation DNA sequencing methods have drawbacks, things like PCR amplification biases, but more importantly, they break lengthy DNA strands into short segments, called short-reads, and then infer nucleotide sequences—"

"Infer? You mean they guess?"

"Correct. And the guesses are often wrong. That's why there was a vital need to develop better technology. Third Generation Technology. TGS works with long-reads, and the resolution is stunning. There are a lot of companies developing Third Generation Sequencing technology for the human genome. Little was the first person to develop a TGS technology for bison, and he claimed it could sequence the bison genome with unprecedented accuracy. He published articles in every scientific journal saying that, despite earlier studies, his new testing of Yellowstone bison proved they did not have cattle genes. He said they were the only wild and pure bison left in the world. Therefore, they had to be declared endangered. You know what my archaeologist friends say?"

"He was wrong?" She flipped her pen in her hand.

"Bingo. Bison all have ancient and modern cattle genes." He cradled his coffee cup, something in his gaze causing her to shift uneasily. "The ancient genes go back thousands of years, but bison also have genes from attempts to cross modern beef cattle and bison. Keep in mind," he heaved a breath. "Yellowstone bison are punching bags, used and misused by ranchers, conservation groups, and every scientist with some new theory to prove. The poor animals just want to be left alone, but—"

"Are ranchers still tainting the bison genome?" She deliberately taunted him to see where it would go.

"Tainting? Do we still encounter the occasional lunatic trying to breed white Charolaise cattle with bison to make so-called sacred white buffalo? Sure. But so what?"

"So what? What about saving the species as they were before human beings screwed them up? Isn't that what ICoHR is trying to do? Stop the damage?"

"Damage? What damage? Species survive by pulling the genes they need from closely related species through interbreeding, and bison are masters of survival. Most crosses are deleterious, but the ones that aren't bring new genes into the population. It's called adaptation. New genes allow a species to adapt to changing climate or new diseases. Evolution doesn't stop. Get the notion of damage out of your head and think adaptation and survival. If bison were 'pure' they'd certainly be on a fast road to extinction."

"Explain."

"If you step back to my library and pull down my range management manual, you'll see that there's over two thousand five hundred introduced invasive and sometimes noxious species of plants living on the Northern Plains. And that's just the botany. Compared to before the white guys came, the air's different. Soil's different. Climate's changing. All those introduced grasses, bushes, trees, forbs, animals and insects can't be rounded up, eliminated, or sent back to where they came from. Not to mention fungus species and birds like starlings. And there's a slew of introduced European diseases including varieties of H_5N_1 bird flu, Texas splenic fever, West Nile, blue tongue, and introduced strains of bovine tuberculosis, malignant catarrhal fever, and a shitload of others."

"I'm not following you." She drew a doodle in the notebook margin.

"You ever take a course in evolutionary biology?"

"No."

He sighed, looking up as Brody Kielman walked out of his office, what had to be his computer encased in a plastic sack. "They need my computer, too?"

"What if there's an email on it from you to that old Indian woman, Danny, saying, 'Not going to make it home tonight. Gotta rig a shotgun to blow Ryman Banks away?"

"That's my herd records. My accounts and payroll."

"And who knows what else?" Jillian arched a challenging eyebrow.

"Just because someone blew slime-ball Banks away, why should I have someone going through my personal business?"

"That's what being a suspect is all about. Get back to evolutionary biology and why that clears you of guilt in the Banks case."

"Right. It's not the same world anymore. Hotter. Different environment. Different diseases. You know what almost wiped out the buffalo?"

"Sure. White hide hunters."

"Wrong."

"Huh?"

"From sixty million bison in 1800 to one-thousand-five-hundred in 1880? Assume that only half the adult cows are reproducing every year, which would be a really low reproductive rate. That's still at least twenty million new bison being born each year—year after year. What could kill that many bison? You couldn't mine enough lead, mill enough powder, build enough rifles, or bows and arrows, or hire enough hunters to wipe them out. Do the math."

"I'll bite. If it wasn't hunting, what was it?"

"European diseases devastated the bison herds just like smallpox, measles, and influenza wiped out the Native Peoples. Introduced Old World pathogens like splenic fever and malignant catarrhal fever, plus new European mutations for mycoplasma bovis and brucellosis and tuberculosis. Stuff our bison had never been exposed to."

"What does that have to do with ICoHR and Banks' murder?"

"Everything, if my guess is correct. It's basic biology: When a species is under stress and the environment is changing, it can move, adapt, or die. We know that hybridizing, like between beef and bison, adds new genes. That's adaptation. You can't predict what genes will be beneficial, neutral, or deleterious. So what if a buffalo's got some beef genes? In a thousand years, those may be the very genes that allow bison to survive. Nothing's pure, Jill. Nothing. Not even human beings. We all have Neandertal, Denisovan, and *antecessor* genes."

"What?"

He seemed lost in his head. "God, what I'd give to see the look on Tiny Tim Little's face when he reads the latest research comparing the accuracy of his TGS tech to that of other TGS companies. Or should I say, inaccuracy. Bet the little puke turns beet-red and chokes on his own tongue."

She studied his expression, seeing the anticipation.

Cody's expression lit up. "The 'Purists' can't stop it now. Bison have, and have always had, cattle, yak, and other bovid genes. Buffalo 'purity' was made up by conservationists to generate money. That means that thousands of bison were slaughtered because of bad science and greed, and now Tim Little and the rest are going to have face the music."

"Well, Tim Little won't." She swallowed hard, remembering the man's head blowing apart. Shutting her eyes, she said, "He was shot to death last night. Sitting in a booth. Right across from me."

CHAPTER TWENTY-SIX

Cody straightened in his chair, watched the woman's expression. Her eyes—suddenly huge—reminded him of glassy dark pools. Bottomless, reflecting of an endless depth of horror. Her lips parted, jaw gone slack.

"Hey, Jillian. You here?"

He placed his cup on the table, reached across, and took her hand where it held her pen. The skin was warm, smooth, her fingers delicate and soft.

She blinked, started, jerked her hand back.

He could see her struggle. How the little muscles in her face were straining, the half-panic behind her eyes. She'd gone ridged, muscles tensed as if on the verge of bolting.

"Ease down," he told her softly. "It's all right. You're at Pilot Creek Ranch. You're safe."

Her breath caught. She placed a hand to her throat, and he could see the pulse racing in her neck. "Sorry." It came out half-whispered.

"I got it," he told her. "Sometimes things set us off.

Got my own demons. But, my God, woman. You tell me that Tim Little was shot? That you were there? That's what you just saw in your head, wasn't it? What the hell are you doing down here today? Jesus, that's insane."

She forced a swallow down what sounded like a dry throat. "My job."

He handed her the cup of coffee. She absently drank, and he could see the tremble in her hand.

"You're a tougher person than I am, Agent Masterson. I think I'd need a month and a couple of bottles of ninety proof to get over that."

"Yeah, well, Sheriff Wain wasn't sure if it was me or Little that the shooter was after. Wanted me out of town."

Cody felt the pieces falling in place. "And then you find out I was gone all night. No wonder you and the rest are so damn sure I did it."

She was back in control, those large dark eyes fixed on his. He could see her uncertainty and suspicion.

He spread his hands wide. "All right, no. I didn't kill him. I'm too much of a vindictive bastard. I'd prefer that the sawed-off little son of a bitch spent the rest of his life thinking about how many innocent bison he condemned to death. Conservationists value genetics? Really? How many rare bison genetic lines were lost because Little's TGS technology said the animal had a single cattle gene? Maybe the same gene its ancestors brought across the Bering Land Bridge two hundred thousand years ago. A gene that helped them survive in a new world?"

Her gaze sharpened.

Cody shrugged slightly. "And you can bet your ass, I sure as hell wouldn't have been gunning for you. That's nuts. I don't even know you."

But there was something about her. He shook it off.

Jillian stared down at her notebook, the page half filled. "So, where were you last night?"

"I told you. The Red Thunderbird casino."

"Doing what?"

He hesitated, eyes locked with hers. Could see her suspicion growing again. "Looking for a man named Jerry Laumer. Calls himself Crank. I need to talk to him about something that happened long ago."

Just saying it felt like a dam giving way, a weird mix of panic and relief surging through him. Only Danny knew. And now he'd spilled his guts to a fricking cop? What the hell was wrong with him?

"What happened?"

Cody chuckled softly to himself. "Well…I guess you're going to run across this once you start digging into my past, so I'll tell you right out. I think he may know something about my parents' murder. But that was almost ten years ago."

He saw when the investigator mask fell away and the woman beneath was exposed. It was in the dilation of her pupils, the parting of her lips. "How did they die?"

"Badly. In a basement in South Billings. At least that's where the bodies were discovered. I wasn't told all the details. Not sure I want to know. According to Danny, they'd gone to Billings to buy supplies for the ranch. When they weren't back two days later, she called. Asked if they'd been in touch. I was in the middle of genetics classes down in Texas A&M. Figured they'd gone off on one of their excursions. They did that. Disappeared for a week or so without explanation. Then, gosh, it was about a week after, I got a call from the Billings PD. They'd been found in that basement."

"And they never caught the perpetrators?"

"Not a clue. I suppose you'll check, but it's still an

open case." He looked down at his hands. "So, there it is. My big ugly secret that you, the Park County Sheriff's Office, and your people up in Bozeman were going to uncover."

"Did you tell the Billings PD about this Crank Laumer?"

"Not yet. Figure I'd better get my sorry ass clear of this case first." He gave her a reassuring smile. "But I think if you can figure out who left my hat at crime scene, you'll have your murderer."

She gave him a faint nod, gaze distant. "Sheriff Wain figures the same thing."

CHAPTER TWENTY-SEVEN

A s Jillian shifted the Durango into Drive, she glanced out at the bison beyond the pasture fence. The effect was like she might have been seeing them for the first time. Black forms, humped, some standing, others lying like curious wedges in the snow. Should she feel an ancestral connection? Her Shoshoni ancestors had been living with bison, hunting them, depending on them for tens of thousands of years. Wasn't that in her blood? Maybe somewhere down in her soul?

Then she glanced back at John Cody, standing on his porch, watching as the procession of vehicles pulled out. In his hand he had the list and receipt for the evidence they'd taken. The guy looked like rock, permanent, invincible, and across the distance, his gaze met hers. Somehow, it felt challenging. A weird connection. Part of her hated to go.

What was it about him?

"What do you think?" Kielman asked as Jillian steered

up the narrow road that led through the line of timber to the highway.

Jillian slapped her hands to the wheel. "I don't think he's our guy. What's your take?"

"He's into something," Kielman mused, leaning his elbow on the windowsill. "There's calls, too many fuel receipts, and hotel bills. The guy's been on the move more than a good-old-boy buffalo rancher from Wyoming should be."

"He told me he was looking for a guy. Jerry Laumer calls himself Crank. You ever heard of him?"

"No. Should I have?"

Jillian turned onto the highway, the Park County units following. She was aware of her tires scrubbing as she accelerated onto the snow-packed pavement. Funny, the things you learned in an investigation.

"Did you know his parents were killed? Cody told me about them. William Bernard and Samantha Grey. About ten years ago in Billings. Case was never solved. Cody says he's been looking ever since."

"No shit?" Kielman turned his thoughtful eyes on Jillian. "Wait a minute. Yeah. I think I remember something about that. If what I remember is right, it was pretty gruesome. And now their kid is a suspect in another couple of homicides?"

"When I got the story out of him, he said he was away in college. Majoring in Ag at the university in College Station, Texas. I'd expect that Billings PD would have checked out his alibi. But according to Cody, that's what all the suspicious activity is about. That's why he was in Billings last night. I'll follow up on that, but I suspect he's telling the truth."

Kielman was studying her from the side, those knowing cop eyes peeling away the layers.

"Like him, huh?"

"He's a suspect." She felt the flush, wondered where in the hell it had come from. And even more bothering, why in the hell she was feeling it?

To turn the tables, Jillian asked, "So, what did you get out of Danielle Redweed?"

"Salty old broad. Had the feeling that it took all of her will to keep from telling me to fuck off. She's been on the ranch for years. Cody's folks hired her way back when. Been there ever since. She said he loves living there and working with the buffalo. Knows that Cody has issues with what she calls the 'the conservation weenies' and that there's no love lost. Says if anything, she'd have figured that Banks and Joyner would have had Cody killed for all the trouble he's cost them. I guess that each time Cody testified about bison genetics, or made appearances at public meetings, he made ICoHR look like idiots. According to old lady Redweed, ICoHR would show up with slick videos of bison, fancy hand-outs, and lots of gruesome photos of buffalo being shot and butchered outside the park. Then they'd make this really emotional presentation, drawing tears and sniffles, and Cody would stand up and say, 'Excuse me, but your facts are in error.' And then there'd be a brawl. Like, the guy just didn't back down. The way Redweed told it to me, you could see pride in her eyes. She thinks Cody is a hero fighting to save buffalo."

Jillian said, "According to Cody, the whole bison purity thing is a scam."

"How can it be a scam if there's only a couple thousand bison left?" Brody raised a grizzled eyebrow.

"Cody says there's close to a half million. That the conservation lobby propaganda has created the notion that all but the Yellowstone herd are beef-buffalo half-breeds. And now, if we can believe Cody, it's going to turn out that all buffalo have some cattle genes dating way back to the Pleistocene."

"What's the Pleistocene?"

"Um, the Ice Age." Jillian frowned as she thought it through. "Maybe that's what Dr. Little was trying to tell me last night. He said, 'Because of the research. What it means. We're going to lose it all, now.'"

"Lose what?" Brody asked.

Jillian shot him a side glance. "The lawsuit to have bison declared a distinct population segment is based on genetics, correct? Dr. Little's new TGS tech? He started to tell me who'd killed Banks and...and..."

The darkness was closing in...

The skin on Little's face slaps back and forth at the impact of the bullet, his eyes and tongue popping from his...

"Hey! Watch the road!" Brody screamed.

Jillian blinked, caught the drift over the centerline, and almost over-corrected getting back in her lane.

"Damn!"

Brody was clutching the "Oh Shit" handle on the dash, wide-eyed gaze darting back and forth from the road to Jillian. "What the fuck was that?"

"Nothing. Thinking. Seeing it all in my head," she lied.

"Well, see the road instead. You want me to drive?"

"No. I got this." Jillian swallowed hard. "Okay. It was a flashback. I've just never seen or heard anyone shot before. It's not like in the movies."

For a time, darkness falling to obscure the scenery, they drove in silence.

They were on the east side of Dead Indian Pass when Kielman finally said, "I don't like it."

"Like what?"

"Call it close to twenty years on the job, but my gut says something's not right." Kielman turned to face her, ticking off a finger. "Cody's got motive. Not only does he have a history of conflict with both of the vics, if they do manage to get the Yellowstone bison listed, Cody's ranch, just like Dan Butler's, would become critical habitat under Federal law. Cody will lose the use of that big beautiful ranch we were just at. He'll have to slaughter or sell all of his supposedly impure buffalo to cleanse the land for incoming pure Yellowstone bison."

He ticked off a second finger. "Cody always has too good an alibi. He was in Denver when the shotgun trap was set. But we don't know when the last time Banks was home. Maybe Cody set the trap and left for Denver? He was there for what? Supposedly four days? But we've been making phone calls. People are sure he was there, but when we ask which days, they're not sure. When it comes to Wednesday and Thursday, we hear a lot 'I think so' and 'He must have been around somewhere.'"

Tapping a third finger, Kielman said, "Tim Little was the science guy. ICoHR built their entire case against Cody on Little's genetic test. Little told you, 'Because of the research. What it means. We're going to lose it all now.' But what exactly did he mean by that? Not to mention, Cody claims he was in Billings last night, and I'll bet he was. But Little was shot just after nine. Want to bet the Red Thunderbird doesn't close until two am? It's two hours drive from Bozeman to Billings. What time did Cody show up at the casino? Like, maybe, eleven fifteen?"

"That's plenty of time to shoot Little and arrive at Red Thunderbird," Jillian agreed, an uncomfortable tickle at the base of her spine.

Kielman ticked off his pinky finger. "And, finally,

there's the enigmatic O'Farrell hat. Right there next to the shotgun. Was it really stolen out from under Cody's chair? Did he really wear it into that banquet? Or did he have to think up a story after driving away from Ryman Banks' house, realizing he'd left his hat behind?"

At which point Deputy Kielman clapped his hands together. "And now, on top of all that, we learn that John Cody's the son of William and Samantha, who were killed in a grisly Billings double murder almost a decade ago. Cody, the only son, inherits the Pilot Creek Ranch." A pause. "In the business, we call that Occam's Razor. The simplest explanation is the most likely one. And too many things point to Cody."

"He said he was attending classes at Texas A&M when his parents were killed."

Kielman shifted uneasily in the seat. "My memory's sketchy. But, as I recall, it was some time before the bodies were discovered. Maybe a week? And, again, if memory serves, the investigators thought they'd been killed elsewhere and dumped."

"So, you're thinking he could have...what? Caught a flight up from Texas, killed them, dropped them in that basement, and flown back to the university? Then he went off to class as if nothing had happened?"

"Wouldn't be the first time." Kielman waited while Jillian slowed for the stop sign at the Highway 120 junction, waved goodbye to the Park County contingent, and headed north toward Montana, before adding, "And, if you ask me, I think John Cody is a really smart guy. Did you see his library? Smart enough to argue convincingly against a PhD geneticist. And he's self-possessed and persuasive enough to sideline and sway most of the people in a public meeting."

"Got a point there, Brody. He sounded pretty convincing to me."

"And another thing," Kielman was now tapping a staccato on the armrest with the fingers he'd been counting. "The guy didn't even flinch when we showed up out of the blue, served him with a warrant, and started taking his house apart. What did he do? Wandered into the kitchen, made a cup of coffee, and didn't even ask for a lawyer."

"Maybe he figured that, being innocent, he had nothing to fear."

Again that scathing look from Kielman. "Jillian, I don't care how fricking innocent you are. Anyone who doesn't freak when cops are searching their house is either an idiot, a moron, psychologically challenged, or he knew the search was coming."

Kielman slapped the armrest. "And we all know about high-functioning psychopaths and murder, don't we? They're the smart charming ones. The ones who, when they're finally caught, everyone says, 'But he was such a nice guy!'"

CHAPTER TWENTY-EIGHT

The good thing about technology was that it saved so much legwork. Seeley Atherton, in the comfort of his hotel room, had been able to trace the airtag he'd placed on Jillian Masterson's Durango. Had watched with interest as the map function on his computer tracked her journey.

That she'd headed east on I-90 toward Billings hadn't bothered him. But when she'd turned abruptly south at Laurel and pursued a path into Wyoming that led not ten miles from his front door at the foot of the Beartooth Range, he'd experienced growing alarm. She couldn't know it was him who had taken that shot, could she?

But as she'd driven past the road that would have taken her to his front door, he'd relaxed. Then watched with growing curiosity as she'd taken the Chief Joseph Highway into the Sunlight Basin, and, ultimately to John Cody's ranch. That had brought a smile to his lips. It was working, just like the client had said it would.

"Two birds with one stone," Seeley told himself as he

typed in his latest update to the client. "She's locked on Cody. Now, it's just a matter of time."

The die was cast. It had been essential that Agent Masterson and Cody meet face-to-face. "Got you now, you son of a bitch. Police will be looking for motive when she gets capped. And there you'll be. The prime suspect. Just removing another potential threat. And that'll be three in a row, Cody. That makes you a serial killer."

Cops loved bringing in serial killers. It made for such good press they tended to overlook little details that might otherwise create doubt. God, this was a great game! And he was just getting started.

The airtag had given Seeley plenty of notice as she drove back from Wyoming. Enough so that Seeley had finished a fine supper at Open Range steakhouse before going back to his computer. To no one's surprise, she'd driven straight to the sheriff's office, where she'd lingered for maybe a half an hour before driving back to her hotel.

Seeley was waiting, he picked a parking space at the edge of the lot where he had a good view of the main entrance. First, it allowed him to scope out shooting positions. Determine how long the target would be in sight as she walked from her vehicle to the door. Second, his Ford pickup would be familiar to any of the hotel staff who might notice. There was always someone who stepped outside to smoke or maybe make a phone call. When it came time to make the shot, no one would look twice at his F-150.

The black Durango wheeled in right on time, slowed as Masterson searched for a parking space and backed into an empty spot at the edge of the lot.

Seeley watched as Masterson stepped out, slipped her arms into her coat, and slammed the door. The lights flashed as she set the security system. She had her head down, looking tired as she walked across the pavement. Seeley counted sixteen seconds under his breath before she reached the glass doors. They slid open, and Masterson could be seen crossing the lobby.

"Well and good." He rolled the driver's window down and used his laser rangefinder. The distance to the front door was seventy-two yards. "Call that the perfect shot," he told himself as he hit the ignition, shifted the Ford into gear, and motored quietly out of the lot.

CHAPTER TWENTY-NINE

"*Well?*" the governor asked, his expression brooding on the computer screen.

Jillian sat forward in the chair, staring at her laptop where it rested on the hotel room's desk. She felt wooden, sodden with fatigue. Didn't matter that she and Kielman had stopped at the truck stop in Columbus, downed a burger, and coffeed up; Jillian had even torpedoed a large can of Red Bull. That last thirty miles over the pass had left her blinking, yawning, and fuzz-headed. And she'd let Kielman do most of the talking as they'd debriefed Sheriff Wain.

Now, she tried to keep from nodding off as Governor Brewster and Gaylen Meyer split her computer screen, each anxious for the latest update.

"I'll write up a full report in the morning," she told them. "But for now, the Park County Wyoming SO has the evidence seized from Cody's ranch bagged and tagged. They've already informed Sheriff Wain that, as a courtesy, they'd be happy to have one of our investigators present to look over their shoulders as they process the bags."

"*That wasn't what I meant,*" the governor said sharply. "*Is he the killer? And when are you going to make an arrest down there?*"

Jillian fought the urge to yawn in his face. "Can't say. So far everything's circumstantial. Could John Cody have pulled it off? I suppose so. Deputy Kielman thinks he could. But we both agree, and so does Sheriff Wain, that we don't have anything that nails the case. Unless we can turn up something that sticks, the DA would tell us there's insufficient evidence. A jury would see reasonable doubt written all over this."

Brewster's dark gaze literally was burning through the computer. "*Supervisor Meyer? I thought you said you and your people had this under control. We're almost a week into this thing, another person is dead, and it sounds like we're no closer to nailing the bit of two-footed vermin that killed Ryman than we were. Maybe you'd better delegate some more capable people to the hunt?*"

"Governor, *sir!*" Jillian snapped. "There's more to this than just a random act of violence. Not with Dr. Little's murder in the mix. The man was shot across the table from me when he was on the verge of naming the perp. My gut tells me that no matter what we're led to believe, it wasn't Cody who shot him. His only motive would have been vengeance, and I don't buy it. Not when—assuming this new bison genetics research stands up—the whole purity argument is dead. Cody himself said he'd rather watch Little squirm over being wrong."

That fire of anger had begun to flicker down in her stomach, as she added, "No, sir There's something else going on here. Another layer, if you will. Something deeper."

Brewster was fuming, sucking a breath to respond when Meyer cut him off. *"Jill? So, from what you're saying, could there be two different killers? Whoever left the trap for Banks and someone else who shot Dr. Little?"*

Smooth move, Jillian thought, given the governor's sudden distraction at the thought.

"Could be. Yes, sir," she said, stilling her own emotions. "Nothing precludes it. Honestly, we don't have evidence either way."

Again, Meyer preempted the governor, saying, *"You look like you're asleep on your feet. Given that you were within inches of being dead last night, not to mention on the road all day, get some shuteye. We'll tackle this in the morning."*

"I have more—"

"In the morning," Supervisor Meyer insisted. To the governor, he added, *"Talk to you then, sir."*

And the screen went dead.

Jillian shut her computer down and closed the lid.

She pushed back from the desk, rubbed the back of her neck and made three steps toward the bathroom. That's when she saw it. The envelope hadn't been there when she'd entered the room. Or had it? Could she have stepped over it, her mind so fixed on other things?

Walking over, she used the tips of her fingers to pick it up. Nothing special about it. Just a plain old ordinary No. 10 regular envelope.

Crossing to the bed, she fished out her penknife. The envelope hadn't been sealed, just folded with the flap inside. With the knife blade, she jiggered the flap open. Sliding the contents out, she found a newspaper article clipped from the Billings Gazette. The headline read:

CONTROVERSIAL YELLOWSTONE RANCH UNDER CONTRACT

The gist of the article was that Daniel Butler, a fifth generation descendent of the original homesteader, had recently placed the historic five-thousand-acre ranch on the market. Located at the edge of Yellowstone National Park outside of Gardiner, the ranch had been the center of a controversial lawsuit brought by the International Coalition on Habitat Rescue that culminated in the property being declared critical wildlife habitat. Within hours of the listing, the property had been placed under contract with a scheduled closing three days away. According to papers filed, the buyer was an asset management firm with headquarters registered in Delaware. No other details on the purchase were available at the time.

Jillian used the knife tip to ease the article back into the envelope, placed it safely on the desk and undressed. Another note? Just like Tim Little had done? But who? And how freaking eerie was that?

Turning off the light, she asked herself, "What in hell could a ranch sale outside of Gardiner have to do with Ryman Banks' murder?"

CHAPTER THIRTY

Cody used a shovel to break the thin skifter of ice. He lifted the floating pieces out and tossed them clear of the big tank. This was the major source of water in the large pen at the end of the corrals, and the edges around the tank were slick enough where buffalo dribbled water from their beards.

From her pen, #208, the bred heifer, watched him with fixed attention. From the way she stood, tension in her body, the position of her head, he could tell she was thinking about how to stomp him. Danny might be right. He might have to send her down the road. He just wasn't ready to give up on her yet. Wounded people could be healed.

The corral design was called a "modified Bintner system." A beef rancher would have looked at the way the pens were laid out and scratched his head. Unlike a cattle operation where a central alley ran down between contiguous square pens, the design at Pilot Creek Ranch had an additional alley that ran around the circumference, enclosing the two rows of pens in a big O. But then, bison were different from cattle. Handling them required a low-stress environment with a host of different options for penning and sorting animals. The Pilot Creek corrals were designed so that the bison could be worked at a walk. No running, shouting, or waving arms. High pressure areas, where the buffalo were crowded, were lined with catwalks to ensure safety for the animals and the people who worked them.

The problem with bison was that they were smart and had very long memories. A buffalo that had been put through the system might refuse to go through the same gate a second time around. So, the smart operator had another gate or a backup alleyway that would lead the bison to the required destination. Nor could different ages of bison be penned together in confinement. The older animals would take it out on the younger, sometimes savagely. Calves, yearlings, and two-year-olds had to be penned separately based on their ages. That meant that any system of buffalo corrals had to be adaptable and provide the operator with multiple options.

Bracing the shovel over his shoulder, Cody walked to the main gate that led out into the winter pasture. Leaning on it, he stared out at the herd. Most were bedded down in the snow, chewing cud, tails flipping.

He hadn't slept. Images kept replaying in his head from the day before. He couldn't get the memory of Jillian Masterson's eyes out of his head. Dark brown and haunted. When the beams of sunlight caught in her hair, it had gleamed with a bluish hue, lustrous as a raven's wing.

That brief moment when she'd gone silent, vacant, spoke of something terrible inside. Now, there was a fascination. How did a young woman become an agent of the Montana Department of Justice, tough as that had to be, and still hide a vulnerability like that?

Through an act of will, he told himself.

"Hey! *Taipo,* wake up!" the sharp words from behind brought him back to the corral.

Cody turned, found Danny Redweed no more than an arms' length behind him. "Didn't hear you come up."

"No shit?" Danny walked over, draping an arm over the Powder River gate. "I was asking if you'd put fuel in the snow machine. Wondering if I needed to fill it up before we check the fence line. Oh, and if we do, did you remember to fill the gas cans last time you went to town?"

Cody squinted out at the snowy pasture where it was dotted by bison, trying to think back past images of Jillian's face. "I think so. But you'd better kick the cans. See if any are empty."

Danny's gaze sharpened as he studied Cody's face. "Huh? Did you hear what I said? Did you fill them while you were on that last midnight gallivant to Billings?"

Cody shook his head. "Don't think I took them with me. Had other things on my mind."

"Yeah, I can tell. So, what is it today? Crank Laumer or Jillian Masterson?" She raised a hand. "Don't deny it. You've had that look. Last time you had it was when Tami Tillotson showed up at the nationals in Denver and wrapped you around her little finger. Even then, you didn't look this moon-eyed."

"There's just something about her."

"Yeah. She's a special investigator who wants to lock your skinny white ass away in the penitentiary. What part of that don't you find terrifying as all hell?"

"She doesn't terrify me."

"Then you're dumber than those first two husbands I

divorced. Dumber than rocks, they was. And, boy, there's been times when I thought you been a bohunkus kind of idiot. More so of late."

Cody gave the old woman an irritated look. Said sarcastically, "Glad you always mince your words carefully so that you don't hurt my sensitive and delicate feelings."

Danny grinned. "Yeah. Honest talk is so rare between us. But, seriously, John, that lady's trouble. This whole damn thing's trouble. I watch TV. I know. They don't show up with a search warrant unless they think you done it."

"I kind of wish I had," John admitted, gesturing out at the bison. "You know who pays the price every time some jackass academic writes an article on bison for *Frontiers in Conservation Science* or *The Society for Conservation Biology*? Or publishes another buffalo book on the plight of the vanishing American icon? Buffalo pay the price."

"Yeah, boss. I know. And don't launch into what happens if the conservation loonies win this latest court case in Washington." Danny looked around at the surrounding mountains, the heights and forested slopes snow-clad and stunning. "We lose all this."

"Not you and me. We get to stay for as long as we can make enough to pay the taxes and keep the property up. We're just outside Yellowstone, and this was built as a guest ranch. We bring in some saddle horses, build a couple more cabins, and cook steak and beans for the 'real Western' experience. We get to live here." Again he gestured at the bison. "They don't. Suddenly, if this is declared critical habitat, in that instant, our impure bison are a threat and have to be removed lest they mix with the suddenly rare and priceless pure bison that trickle out of the park."

"For all you know, she's got a boyfriend. Maybe she's

LGBTQ. Or is she married and just don't wear the ring when she's on duty? A lot of cops don't."

"Damn you're sour. Who shit in your Post Toasties this morning?"

"It was the nightmares I had after being interrogated by that Deputy Kielman yesterday. I mean, damn. Took all of my self-control to keep from tellin' him just what a *yuni we'an* he was. He's from Montana, you know. Maybe he had run ins with some Crow or Blackfeet. Them people ain't normal."

"And the Shoshoni and Arapaho are? Probably shouldn't go around calling cops limp dicks, not in any language. One of these days, you'll get found out." Cody shot her an appraising look. Redweed often said the reason she didn't go back to the Rez was because of her mixed ancestry. Being half and half, she figured either one of her families would make her go to war with herself.

Danny made her usual disgusted-with-the-world face, shook her head. "Don't matter, boss. Not if you're in jail for killing Banks."

"There's no way they can prove I wired that shotgun to the door. Could have been anybody." He was thinking of Jillian Masterson's fleeting smile. What was it about her?

Danny slapped gloved hands to her sides, walking off in a huff. "There you go again. I tell you, John Cody. You got a death wish, and that woman will be the cause of it."

CHAPTER THIRTY-ONE

Jillian hadn't slept well; her dreams had been full of John Cody when they weren't about bison. And there had been mountains. Tall, forested, snow-covered. Sometimes the mountains were intertwined with her and John Cody, walking through fir trees, their branches rimed with fluffy white. Bison, the animals looking magnificent as they stepped through the freshly fallen powder, had surrounded them. Cody had given her that smile, his beard gleaming in the winter light.

She remembered him telling her, "They're going to take the ranch, Jillian. It's condemned. There's nowhere for the bison to go. They'll kill them all. Shoot them down and leave them to rot."

Even as he'd said it, the skies had darkened. Around them, in the increasing gloom of the forest, the bison began to fade, sinking into the blackness until only their ghostly memory remained.

Losing the ranch. The pain in his words had wounded her souls.

As a result, she'd awakened feeling irritable and sour.

And, of course, fixed on the envelope containing the ranch-sale article where it rested at the edge of her desk.

"Just like Dan Butler lost his," she had whispered as she went about showering and dressing. The envelope and its contents, of course, would be turned over to Sheriff Wain.

But all through breakfast, something had been nibbling at the back of her thoughts and continued to nag at her as she wrote her report to Supervisor Meyer and sent it flying off with a press of the Send button.

Was Cody telling the truth? When she called Wain's office, she'd been surprised to learn that Carly Joyner had turned down additional protection. Declared herself safe and could be found at her office.

Jillian pulled into the same space just around the corner from the ICoHR headquarters as she had the first time. Call it serendipity.

Closing the driver's door, she locked the Durango with the fob and started down the sidewalk. The white and red older Ford F-250 with tinted windows and a missing tailgate caused her a double take. Was it the same truck? Déjà vu? Or, by whatever happenstance, just two of the same models? This time, she noted the license plate. Saw the 49. Park County...the one in Montana, with Livingston as a county seat.

The tinted windows came across as dark and opaque as the truck signaled, made a right onto Main, and rumbled off up the street. The tailgate was missing. Had to be the same truck.

A curious flutter went down Jillian's spine. What the hell?

Is someone stalking Carly Joyner? Is the woman a fool? Will she be the next target?

Or was it just a local? Someone who lived or worked

in the neighborhood? Now that was more likely. God, she was getting paranoid.

Jillian rounded the corner. The pile of flowers, vases, and placards two doors down at the ICoHR office door had to be twice as big as it had been two days ago.

Jillian stopped at the door and studied the cardboard signs. Some read Not In Vain! And Ryman Died So They Will Live with a photo of bison in a sage-filled valley. RYMAN GAVE HIS LIFE! I'LL GIVE $1000 with a photo of Banks smiling out at the world. List Yellowstone Bison! Donate Today!! One of the posters decried Tim Little Died for Their Sins! And there were others mixed in with the flowers and candles.

Jillian pushed through the door, and where the office had been tomblike the last time, it was now a bustling hive of activity. She counted six people, two young men, bearded and longhaired—one with dreadlocks—wore heavy sweatshirts and ripped-and-faded blue jeans. The three women, barely in their twenties, had that look of youthful outdoorsy activism right down to the cargo pants, hiking boots, and flannel shirts. They all looked up from the desks and tables cluttered with stacks of fliers. Two had phones to their ears, and even as Jillian entered, the phone at the third desk rang, the guy in dreadlocks answering, "International Coalition on Habitat Rescue, how can I help you?"

At her desk in the rear, Carley Joyner sat with her head bowed over her computer, tapping away at the keyboard. Frown lines incised her forehead, her lips pursed. Something about her posture gave her a harried look.

"Can I help you?" the blonde woman wearing glasses asked.

"I need to see Ms. Joyner."

"*Carly!*" the blonde called in a way-too-shrill voice.

As Jillian walked back through the obstacle course of tables and desks, the blonde was already back to stuffing envelopes with fliers that sported the slogan Did They Die In Vain? Below were photos of Banks and Tim Little, then Donate Today!

Carly Joyner fixed her pale green eyes on Jillian as she approached. "Have a seat, Agent Masterson."

Jillian dropped into the chair across the desk from Joyner, indicated the chaos of voices in the background. "But for the shrine outside, I might think I was in the wrong place."

Joyner's smile spoke of satisfaction as she looked around at the hubbub. "They're all volunteers. Asked what they could do to help. I just wish Ryman and Tim could see. Know how much their work meant to so many. Sometimes it takes something like this to make us appreciate."

"You sure this is smart?" Jillian indicated the room with its large plate-glass windows. "Two of your partners are dead."

"At this very moment the police department has this place under surveillance. An officer brings me to work in the morning, and he'll take me back to the safe house tonight. It's like they've got a protective net around me."

"Must be unnerving to live like that."

Joyner's eyes tightened. "Yeah. Creepy as all hell. But you'd know since you were there when Tim died. Makes your insides feel runny when you take the time to think about it. So, I don't. Or at least try not to. Work will see me through."

Then Joyner leaned back and massaged her neck. "So, how's the investigation going? I hear that you're about to arrest John Cody."

"How would you hear that?" Jillian dug her notebook out of her jacket pocket.

Joyner reached for the folded newspaper on the far corner of her desk, tossing it toward Jillian. "You seen today's paper? You made front page, above the fold."

Jillian picked up it, reading, Wyoming Rancher Person of Interest in Dual Murder. She scanned the article, gleaning that, according to an anonymous source, a search warrant had been served and conducted on John B. Cody's Wyoming ranch in a joint effort by the Gallatin and Wyoming Park County sheriff's offices and the Montana Department of Justice. There were photos of Ryman Banks and Tim Little, along with a description of their backgrounds and murders. Included was speculation about why the two had been targeted and the stakes behind the latest lawsuit to have Yellowstone bison listed as a distinct population segment.

Jillian laid the paper down and sighed. "How the hell did they get that?"

"It's the press. Nothing's secret." Joyner leaned forward, a keen gleam in her green eyes. "So, you're closing in, huh? Couldn't wish it on a more worthless piece of shit than Cody. Well, I could. I could include every cattle, sheep, and horse rancher in Montana. Them and their fences and overgrazing."

"Tell me about Tim Little's research. Before he died, he was telling me that there's some new information coming out. Something that's still in peer review."

Joyner hesitated. "Oh, that. Look, Agent Masterson, there's a lot of resistance out there. Like all of those ranchers I just mentioned? They jump on any chance of discrediting Tim's work and the environmental cause. Why? Because they've got a lot to lose. Like our good buddy John Cody does. But here's the takeaway: it's science. And genetics, especially ancient DNA studies, are a dicey business. DNA doesn't preserve well when it's in the ground for a couple thousand years, freezing, thawing, surrounded by soil organisms. And then, there's the recovery. Fragments of DNA are tiny. And there's a gajillion ways it can get contaminated in a world where it's literally drenched in DNA from everything living around it. Not to mention on the very clothes of the people who recover it."

"I thought they had protocols for that?"

"Sure." Joyner leaned forward again. "But here's the thing you need to understand: Tim Little's test has been around for almost ten years. That's called withstanding the test of time. And, yes, someday we may find some genes shared in common between bison and beef cattle. They're related, you know, like we are to chimpanzees. And, if we do, so what?"

"Then all bison may have beef genes?"

Joyner was tapping her long fingernails on the desk. "It's not rocket science, Agent Masterson. Um, can I call you Jillian?"

"Sure."

"Okay, the bison were here before the Europeans brought cattle to the New World. Maybe fifty or sixty million bison roaming around North America. Today, we have only a few thousand left. Got it?"

"What about the five hundred thousand in private herds?"

"They're hybrids, Jillian. Half-breeds. Not to mention they're domesticated. Tame. Same as a sheep. A human creation. Like a labradoodle or a cockapoo dog. They are even listed by most states as livestock. And ranchers raise them, breed them, and work them just like cattle. Put tags in their ears. Then they put them on trucks and send them off to the feedlots and processing plants. And I tell you, *that* is not a bison."

"But, genetically—"

"They have been interbred with cattle." Joyner slapped a hand to the desk. "Look, think it through. In Yellowstone, we have the last herd of free-running unfenced bison in the United States. Just a few thousand of them. Untainted by human contamination. But they're overrunning the park. Is it too damned much to ask that they be allowed to access just a sliver of their historical range? What are a handful of white cattle ranchers compared to the last pure free-roaming wild bison in the world? Is that so much to ask?"

Jillian shrugged. "What do you know about the Butler Ranch sale over by Gardiner?"

Joyner blinked. Something flickered behind her eyes. "How did you get to that?"

"What do you know about it?"

Joyner's lips twitched, and she seemed to be thinking. "Not sure who's buying it. But here's the thing, whoever it is, is going to be highly restricted in what they can do with the place. They're going to have to share it with the annual migration of deer, elk, bison, and other species migrating out of the park. No development, no ranching, no fences, no plowing. Just keeping it as pristine habitat. In essence, it's a conservation property."

Joyner smiled in reminiscence. "That was our first victory, you know? Suing the Butler Ranch, forcing him to take down those fences. Ryman was so proud of that."

And look what it got him, Jillian thought.

The phones continued to jangle in the background, the heady volunteers answering.

Joyner's distant look didn't match the smile on her lips.

CHAPTER THIRTY-TWO

The restaurant was one of the trendy steak houses on Main Street. The historic building had an Avant-guard atmosphere with its bare brick walls, the ceiling joists painted black, with large stainless-steel fans slowly pushing warm air down from the overhead ducting. Her booth was backed against the wall, and she perched on an elevated bench. Across from her, two young women worked the bar, pouring drinks and tapping beer. Lights gleamed on the bottles lining the backbar.

Jillian cut a piece of bison tenderloin. Raising the fork she considered the piece of meat. No less an authority than the media mogul, Ted Turner, had said, "If you want to save the buffalo, eat them." And here she was, having bison for her evening meal. Despite an offer from Sheriff Wain, she'd chosen to eat by herself. On a whim, she'd picked a restaurant that specialized in bison meat.

Around her, the young-and-affluent evening crowd was clinking silverware, talking over each other in a babble, and periodically laughing. Just normal everyday folks going on about their lives. Socializing. Eating. Drinking. Doing what people do.

And none of them was preoccupied by murder.

Or Sheriff Wain.

Ever since her conversation with Brody Kielman, Jillian had been more aware. Though she wasn't sure that Wain himself knew, he was indeed more attentive around her. It was his posture, the eye contact, what bordered on too much familiarity. The guy was married with two almost-grown daughters. Old enough to be her father.

So, was that it? He was just being paternalistic? Protective of the younger woman under his care? Or was it something more intrinsically sexual? The Alpha male preening before a younger female, driven by that ancient instinct hidden down in the limbic system. The one that was constantly looking for a...

Her phone rang.

Jillian reached it out of her inside pocket, glanced at the number, and froze.

"I'll be damned."

She pressed the green button to accept the call. "Agent Masterson."

"*Uh...hi, Jillian.*"

"And a good evening to you, too, Mr. Cody. What can I do for you?" Her heart was flip-flopping. Uncertain of what she wanted him to say next as she reached down, fishing in her jacket pocket for her notebook.

"*Um...I was wondering. What's the status of my stuff? I mean, how long's it going to take for those guys to figure out I really was on the road home from Denver when Banks was killed?*"

"I can't speak for the crime lab. I'm sure that they'll—"

"*So, what are you doing?*"

"Having supper."

"What's on the menu?"

"Bison tenderloin, actually. Maybe you piqued my interest."

"You ordered it medium rare, didn't you?"

"I did." She wrote the location, date, and time as she prepared to take notes.

"Good. That's the thing with bison. It's got half the fat that a beefsteak has, so it's got to be cooked at a lower temperature for longer. Otherwise, you can burn all the moisture out of it."

"I guess I like all of my meat medium rare." Then she cringed. "Is there another reason you called, John?"

She endured a five second silence.

"Maybe I... Oh, I don't know. This is crazy. But, well, I wanted you to know that I really enjoyed talking to you. Haven't had anyone sitting at my table over coffee but Danny. And, well, this being a murder suspect is all new, and maybe I don't understand the ropes, but I kind of wanted to see what you were doing."

She rubbed her face, thinking, *Is he fricking insane?*

"You're a suspect in a murder investigation. Talking to one of the lead investigators. Now, I'm delighted that you enjoyed my company. I actually enjoyed yours. And the coffee was great. But I'm hoping the reason you called is to finally confess that you killed Banks or Little, and I get to bring you in. Am I right?"

"It would almost be worth it. But there's something I need to find out. Um, I wouldn't want to confess to anyone who's in a relationship. Especially if she was married or really attached to someone else. But, if she was single and might be interested in maybe having a cup of coffee in a very public place and just talking...? You know, I mean after I'm no longer a suspect."

Jillian couldn't help it, she burst out laughing. "Are you for real?"

"I hope so. I'm way too solid to be imaginary."

"So, if it turns out that I'm not in a relationship, but free and single, you'll confess to the murder of Ryman Banks III and Tim Little?"

"So, like, are you seeing anyone?"

"No. Are you confessing to the murders of Ryman and Little?"

"I didn't kill anyone. That means I'd get what? Maybe a day or two in your company being processed before I spent life in prison for something I didn't do? Hmm. I'm thinking. Might be worth it."

She stared at her phone in puzzlement. Was he serious?

"Tough call, but no. I think I'd rather spend time in your company doing something besides being booked in a police station and taking the chance that I might get a glimpse when you testified. Doubt they'd let us talk much. And there's another concern. Whoever killed Banks and Little, used my hat. As much as I'd give for a chance to see you again, that means whoever the piece of shit is who tried to pin this on me would get away with it. And, Jillian, I'd really like to know who that asshole is."

She nodded at the conviction in his voice. "John, you do know that anything you say can and will be used against you, right?"

"I'm not stupid. But neither is whoever put Banks and Little down. I mean, think about it. Taking my hat a couple of weeks back so they can leave it at the scene? Whoever did this has been working out the kinks for a long time. Planning. It's not like they woke up one morning, said, 'I'm killing Banks and Little because they're pricks' and did it on a whim."

"Okay, I'm with you there. But we can't find a motive that sticks for anyone else."

"What about Dan Butler? I ran into him a couple of times. I mean, if there's a man who hated Ryman Banks, it was him.

That ranch he lost outside of Gardiner had been in his family since the eighteen eighties."

"It's been put on the market, the new buyer is closing on it at the end of the week."

Silence.

"John?"

"I'm thinking."

She toyed with her steak.

"Doesn't make sense. He loved that place. His great grandparents are buried there. What did he say when you interviewed him?"

"No one has seen or heard from him since the murders. He hasn't responded to our phone calls or requests."

"Now, that's an interesting turn of events. Given his record, he'd know he was a prime suspect. You'd think he'd have shown up front and center, screaming 'I didn't do it!'" A pause. *"Assuming he's still around to scream."*

"Elaborate on that." She was writing furiously.

"Call it a gut feeling. Not that I know Dan that well, but he's kind of an intense fella, especially after what ICoHR has put him through. You guys check it out, but something tells me his ranch being put up for sale changes the whole interpretation of your case."

"How would that be?" God, she shouldn't be talking to him. Where in the hell was the professional divide between the chance of telling him too much versus gleaning information from a suspect?

"If Dan's selling out, it's because he's given up. That's one way of looking at it. And, if he has, maybe he's lost any reason for living. So, who cares if he puts a bullet in his tormentors? He's got nothing left to lose."

"That would be motive, all right."

"Second way to look at it: Someone forced him to sell, and as

soon as he signed the listing agreement, whoever forced the sale, took care of good old Dan. And... Give me a second. Let me think this through."

Intrigued, Jillian took another bite of the excellent steak. What if Cody was right? What if whoever was behind this was setting him up to cover for something else? What did the ranch have to do with the murders?

"Yeah, that makes sense."

"What does?"

"What if this whole thing is a distraction? What if Dan's already dead? Maybe he didn't play ball? Said he'd take it to the police. So, they killed him. Closing on a property can always be done remotely. Through computer-signed documents at the title agency. Dan never has to appear in person anymore."

"But why kill Banks and Little?"

"Distraction? Maybe they were part of it? Knew of it? Were going to spill the beans?"

"God, John, don't you think you're grasping for straws?"

"Nope. Like I said, when this is all figured out, it's going to have something to do with Dan Butler's ranch. That's the hinge on which this whole thing turns. The only thing they didn't plan on was me being out of town that week. And why would they? It's the end of January when most ranchers are home feeding their stock and keeping water open."

"You have a very active imagination."

"Hey, it's a kind of curse, huh? Sort of like imagining seeing you here in the kitchen, drinking coffee in the morning light. But I'll settle for a couple of hours at someplace like Starbucks. I could meet you half way. Like up in Billings? There's this great coffee shop in the Northern Hotel—"

"You are a murder suspect."

"Yeah. We're going to have to do something about that. Like solve the case first. Deal?"

"Deal? Hell no. I don't make deals." She smiled grimly. "I leave that up to the district attorney."

Cody might not have heard. *"Find Dan Butler, Jillian. He's the key."*

"So...you think he's behind stealing your hat? Setting all of this up?"

"Maybe, but I doubt it. Sure, I think Dan's got it in him to kill the people who tormented him. But he's not that complicated. Think old-school rancher. Walk up and shoot them dead while you look them in the eyes. This other stuff? He's not wired that way."

"I'll take that under advisement."

"Okay." A pause. *"You know, it's as nice talking to you on the phone as it is in person. I think I'm going to sleep well tonight. 'Till next time."*

"Good night, John." She pressed the button, laid her phone down and scowled at the scrawled notes.

"So, what the hell are you up to, John Cody?" Either he really was onto something, or he was doing his best to misdirect her investigation. Deputy Kielman had said he was clever.

She smiled as she remembered the morning light reflected by the mirror in his kitchen, how it had glistened as it caught stray hairs in his beard, and how his tan eyes had twinkled as he poured coffee.

"Find Dan Butler, huh?"

Who, exactly, had slipped that envelope under the door? Cody? Or was there another party involved in this?

The laughter took her by surprise. What kind of lunatic called up an investigating officer and tried to set up a date?

"Cody, you're either an idiot or a cunning psychopathic killer."

CHAPTER THIRTY-THREE

Time to bring this all to a head. The final act. Everything was now in place. Here was the last nail in John Cody's coffin.

Seeley Atherton lay on his sleeping bag in the bed of his pickup; the Ruger American 6.5 Creedmoor rested on the cushion of his pack. Through the open topper shell window, he had an unimpeded line of sight to the hotel's front door. In the parking lot lights, the rows of vehicles gleamed, windows and chrome reflecting. Through the hotel windows, the lobby was ablaze, and a steady stream of people were checking in.

With an exhale, Seeley watched his breath fog in the cold night air.

It wouldn't be long now.

He froze as headlights from an entering car bathed his truck, then veered away as the SUV drove into an open space. Not that anyone could see into the shadowed shell's interior. Even if they could, Seeley's profile was low, mostly hidden by the pickup's box. If they'd see anything it might a reflection from the scope lens.

Busy night for the hotel, the parking lot was filling up. Good. She'd have to park farther away, take a longer walk. He'd have time to track her the entire distance. Tag her right before she stepped into the entrance as the automatic doors slid open.

He cleared his mind, embracing the chill on his nose and cheeks. He'd never minded the cold. His favorite time to pack into the backcountry was late fall. The leaves were falling from the aspens, the bull elk bugling, the sounds of the geese and blue herons flying in Vees overhead. At those times, the forest had a different smell, crisper, clean. Even the black timber seemed to sigh, the only sounds those of birds and chickarees as they scolded each other while harvesting cones for winter.

Sometimes he'd get the drop on elk, catching them totally unawares. He'd set himself up for a shot, lay the crosshairs on whichever animal he'd chosen. Rest his finger on the trigger, breathing, settling the shot. Let the clueless elk graze, the stadia lines on the animal's heart, neck, or ear. Then he'd whisper, "Bang."

Seeley would lift his finger from the trigger, the gun unfired. And away the great elk would graze, never knowing it had been no more than two-and-a-half pounds away from dead.

So much power—the feeling of it would surge through his chest. Death or life. His to dispense at will. The knowledge there that—but for Seeley's God-like munificence—the elk would have been dead. Sprawled in the grass, its life evaporating from each cell in its body.

"No choice this time, though," he told himself. The reality warmed him inside. Made him smile.

Lights played on the side of his truck again. He kept his gaze lowered, unwilling to night-blind his retinas. But as the vehicle slowed at the other side of the lot, then backed into a space, he could see it was a black Durango.

"Bingo," he hissed under his breath and settled the Ruger's stock into the pocket of his shoulder.

In the parking lot lights, he found her in the scope. Watched her climb out of the driver's side and slam the door. She must have pressed the lock function on the key fob, for the lights flashed on the Durango. Then she started across the asphalt for the entrance, heels rapping on the hard surface.

Seeley liked a woman who walked with confidence like that. Made tagging her more satisfying than if she'd slouched and scurried. Dropping the proud ones—like not shooting the elk—fed his sense of power. Where was the glory in taking out a sniveling fearful wretch?

Following her in the scope, he wished for an illuminated reticle, but for the plan to work, it had to be the Ruger with its cheap scope. Against her black coat, he couldn't make out the stadia, couldn't tell when the crosshairs were aligned perfectly. Didn't really need to. Bullet placement might not be with his usual precision; at this distance, and with the 6.5 Creedmoor's energy at impact, it would be enough.

"Five, four, three, two, one," Seeley counted as Jillian Masterson crossed the concrete apron to the entrance. The automatic doors slipped open. Seeley exhaled, took up the slack, and triggered the rifle.

The night split with the supersonic crack, muzzle flash and report muffled by the suppressor. In the scope, he saw the woman's body take the impact, her long ponytail flapping as her head jerked. She hit the ground limp as a pile of rags.

As quickly, Seeley flipped around, crawling through the sliding window, across the back seat, and behind the wheel. Even as he slid into place, he'd punched the start button. As the engine came to life, he shifted into Drive and pulled out of the space.

Casting a quick glance back, it was to see the woman's body sprawled, one arm out, legs bent. She just lay there looking pathetic. Broken. The doors had closed on their own, as if in a final insult. To his joy, no one seemed to have noticed. Even as he turned onto 19th, glancing over his shoulder, he could see no activity in front of the hotel.

"Clean and crisp!" he called, whooping his delight.

Pulling up his phone, he typed in his password. One eye on traffic, he thumbed through the menus to the client's address. With one thumb, he texted:

> The wild west show just lost their queen.

He was turning onto I-90 when the phone buzzed and he glanced down.

> If you get a chance tomorrow afternoon

> I think something's blocking the culvert.

That was the thing about the client. There was never any bullshit about payment.

He thought about the Ruger rifle in the back. So, just one job left. Then he could kiss the big city of Bozeman goodbye and slip off to his property and chill. All the while, knowing he'd made a difference.

CHAPTER THIRTY-FOUR

ody's phone rang where it hung on the kitchen wall. He was sitting by the fire in the living room, sock feet up on the ottoman. He was in the middle of a Chris Mullen Western about a Texas rancher down on the border. Good stuff. Tossing the novel to the side, he climbed to his feet, stretched against the kink in his back and padded into the kitchen.

Pulling down the handset, he said, "Hello."

"John Cody?"

"The very same."

A short silence.

Then he heard a weary exhale. *"Shit!"*

"I've been called worse, but generally I know why and by whom."

"This is Deputy Kielman, Gallatin County Sheriff's Office. This is your land line, correct?"

"Yes, it is. Mind telling me what's got you calling me at this time of night?"

"You had a conversation with Agent Masterson this evening?"

"I did. She was eating a buffalo steak. Tried to talk me into making a confession. Got to say, she's dedicated."   .

"Is Danny Redweed also at the ranch?"

"Yeah. She's out in her cabin."

"What did you and Agent Masterson talk about?"

"I told her that this whole case was tied to the Butler Ranch sale. That if she could find Dan Butler, she could probably figure out who's behind it. I got the feeling that she's still keeping all of her options open, but that she'd consider that."

"Jesus! What are you trying to do? Get yourself arrested for interfering with a—"

"Hey! I'm trying to get my ass cleared of suspicion. Like I told Jill, if I didn't do it—and I know I didn't do it—I want the son of a bitch who did to get what he fricking deserves! And I'm really ticked that the piece of shit is trying to pin it on me. So, yeah, I'm going to pitch in and help in any way I can. Just ask Jill. I think the Butler Ranch sale's got something to do with this."

Silence.

Then: *"Mr. Cody, Agent Masterson was shot fifteen minutes ago in front of her hotel. The ambulance just drove off with her. You were the last person she talked to on her phone. Did she say anything? Like maybe she had an appointment? A meeting? Expected to see someone at the hotel?"*

Cody sank into his kitchen chair, blinked. His voice softened. "What? Shot? Is she okay?"

"Damn it, I don't know! When I got here, they had her on the gurney, ventilating her. She was groaning, alive, but looking really bad, you know?"

"Son of a bitch!" He knotted a fist. "Why her? What's the point? I mean it isn't like she's close to nailing the bad guy. She's as much in the dark as I am."

"Are you, Mr. Cody?"

"Am I what?"

"In the dark?"

"I don't follow."

"Maybe Jillian is close to nailing the bad guy. It wouldn't be the first time that a perp hired someone to take out a cop who was closing in. Do their dirty work. Now, why don't you do me a favor and go get Danny Redweed. I'd like to establish that she, too, is present on your ranch. I want to talk to her on this same phone. And I want to be sure she sounds as good as you do. Like, she's not talking through a cell phone from somewhere here in Bozeman."

"Yeah, yeah, I'll go get her. It'll be about five minutes. You'll have to hold. And, damn you, last time I checked, you'd have to teleport to get from Bozeman to here that fast."

He put the handset down, made a face. Walking to the door for his coat, he muttered, "Please, God, tell me she's going to be all right."

CHAPTER THIRTY-FIVE

Whispers of black shadows...
        Hands, like serpent heads on arms...
        The insidious whispers of the man's voice...
"Shhh! Don't make a sound."

Jillian can only cower under the blanket, huddle her body into a tight ball. Pull her legs up and hug them close to her chest. She prays. With all of her heart and soul, she wills every bit of her into making the blanket magic. That it will protect her. Act as a shield. Impenetrable.

The man's soft voice insists, "Shhh. We're going to play our special little game."

Jillian tries to squeeze herself out of her body. Make her soul float away into the wind. Like the little puffs of cottonwood down. Light, drifting, rising and falling in the...

A cry strangles in her throat as the blanket is pulled away. She feels it sliding off over her skin and jammies. The chill comes, seeping in as the warmth and safety vanish into the dark.

She shivers, still clutching her thin legs to her chest. Her heart hammers as his weight compresses the springs and mattress.

She flinches as the hand settles on her shoulder, strokes down *her arm. It pulls at her jammies, and she can feel the calluses as it finds her bare wrist.*

"Shhh! You're a good little girl."

She tries to breathe, but her lungs are hot and starving as her arms are pulled away from her legs.

"You be a good little girl now and maybe I'll give you a treat later. You'd like that, wouldn't you...."

But Jillian has drifted away, turned herself into the cottonwood down. She floats, rising and falling with the breeze. So light. Her soul twirls and dances...twirls and dances...

"Jillian?" The voice is distant.

Jillian gasps, tenses, expecting to feel the blanket being pulled away. She blinks her eyes open. Not to blackness, but to bright lights. She's muzzy. Can't seem to think. And she's cold. So cold. She shivers, staring up at the blinding light.

A nurse...yes, a nurse, leans over her. She's in scrubs, a facemask hanging by one strap to free her face. Blue eyes are looking down. An older woman. "Jillian? Can you hear me?"

Her mouth is dry, like being hung over. She tries to swallow. Blinks, and nods. "Cold," she whispers. "Why am I so cold?"

"You've been in surgery. You're all right. Lucky as all hell, actually. What's your name?"

"Jillian Masterson."

"Birthday?"

Jillian rattles it off.

"Where are you?"

"I...uh?" She tries to glance around.

"Who do you work for?"

"Montana Department of Justice, Investigations Bureau. I'm...I'm in Bozeman. I was at the hotel." She blinked again, feeling like half her brain was missing. "Where am I?"

"Recovery room, Jillian. You were shot. Do you remember?"

She shook her head, trying to think through the haze. God, if she could just stop shivering. "No. Shot?"

"Are you in any pain?"

"No. God, why am I so cold?"

"You just came out of surgery. I'll get you a heated blanket. You're going to be fine."

The nurse turned, walking across the room. Looking around, orienting herself, Jillian counted another five people, all in scrubs, some working on notes, others talking as they attended to tasks.

She looked up to see the saline drip on its high stand. A monitor was recording her heart rate and oxygen ratio. And then the cuff on her arm tightened until she thought her fingers were going pop as the machine took her blood pressure.

The shivers kept wracking the length of her body.

Somehow, the blanket the nurse put over her only seemed warm for a couple of seconds.

Shit! What's worse? Being awake in this torture chamber or the soul-numbing nightmares in the dark?

She wasn't sure she ever made the choice, drifting back into the gray haze to become a bit of cottonwood down dancing on the breeze.

CHAPTER THIRTY-SIX

Seeley Atherton's phone buzzed. He was driving through the Best Western parking lot, eyes peeled for an older Ford F250. According to Seeley's information, Dan Butler was driving such a vehicle. Supposedly it was white and red, but Seeley would know when he found it by the 49 county plates with Butler's license number. Seeley had been through three other motels in the area.

He squinted in the parking lot lights, staring at the lines of parked vehicles, and pulled out his phone. Scrolling to messages, he tapped the screen and read:

> She's alive. Check KBZK for nightly news.

> What happened?

Seeley let his pickup roll to a stop.
What? How?
He thumbed his way to the browser, typed in the

streaming feed for the station, and flicked through the choices to news. There it was, the lead story.

Breaking News!

Montana DOJ Agent shot outside local hotel.
Reported in stable but serious condition.

Seeley played the segment, seeing the familiar entrance to the Hilton Garden Inn, now awash in flashing red and blue lights and swarming with police. He listened incredulously as the reporter—an attractive blonde woman—talked into the microphone. Using that serious-reporter voice, the woman was explaining that the female agent had been gunned down by an unknown assailant and was reportedly in surgery. That preliminary reports were that Agent Masterson was expected to make a full recovery.

Seeley's jaw dropped when the reporter added, *"Apparently, the agent's life was spared when the bullet struck the agent's sidearm in her shoulder holster."*

"I'll be go to hell," Seeley muttered softly.

"This is reportedly the second attempt on Agent Masterson's life. She may have been the intended victim when well-known geneticist, Dr. Timothy Little, was murdered just across the street two nights ago."

The camera turned to focus on the Old Chicago restaurant across from the Hilton.

His phone buzzed again, and Seeley scrolled to messages.

Your thoughts?

Seeley typed,

Wait and see.

Same effect.

Might be for the best

And it might be. Poor old John Cody would still be the prime suspect in the shooting, and surely Masterson would be taken off the case. Put on administrative leave, not to mention that if she was in surgery, she'd have a long recovery.

"John Cody," he chuckled, "all the shit in the universe is about to fall on your head. You poor son of a bitch. Hope you're looking up with an open mouth when it hits you full in the face."

Seeley had never met John Cody up close and personal. He'd just studied him from across the room. What mattered was that the guy bought and sold and perpetrated the trade in domestic half-breed bison. Cody represented and personified the continued corruption of a magnificent iconic species. To make matters worse, his ranch sat like a fucked-up toad right on the migration corridor for Yellowstone bison. The guy had to go.

The best-case scenario was that Cody would take the fall for Banks, Little, and Masterson. Not only was the piece-of-shit eliminated but his very existence would be another black eye for the buffalo industry. They'd all be tarnished by association. Discredited.

Someone flashed bright lights from behind and brought him back to the present. He shot a glance into the mirror, realized he was stopped dead in the middle of the aisle. He accelerated, letting his gaze scan for Butler's Ford. Didn't matter what happened to Masterson for the moment, there was still good old Dan Butler to deal with.

CHAPTER THIRTY-SEVEN

Jillian stared dully at the acoustical panels in the ceiling. She felt tired and irritable. It didn't matter if she drifted off and finally fell into a deep sleep. Every hour, on the hour, the blood pressure cuff tightened to the point she thought her hand was going to explode.

No sooner did that happen, then the nurse on duty came in to ask her name, what her birthday was, where she was and why she was there. Not only was it boring, but it was pissing her off.

Grousing, she glared at the IV stuck in her forearm and the tube running up to the drip bag. Tried to shift and felt the bandage wrapping her ribcage tighten as she struggled to take a deep breath. She had managed a glance at the wrapping when one of the nurses came in to check the bandage. Said that she had broken ribs and that the doctor would be in to talk to her about the surgery.

All she knew was that she'd been shot.

Why the hell am I alive?

Jillian tried to remember.

At that juncture, a man in scrubs entered, stetho-scope draped over his shoulders. An ID card was clipped to a lanyard around his neck. One of those surgical caps covered his close-shaved head. The guy looked to be in his fifties.

"How you doing, Jillian? I'm Doctor Francis Quinard."

"Bored stiff, Doctor."

"Are you feeling any pain?" He lifted the sheet and pulled her gown back, fingering the dressing.

"No. And it doesn't make sense. They say I was shot. It should hurt like a son of a bitch."

He gave her a winning smile. "It's the drugs. And you were shot. Your gun took the impact. Saved your life. But you've got broken ribs and one hell of bruise. Trust me, you don't want to see what your left breast and side look like. Call it black and Technicolor."

"They said surgery?"

He put her gown back in place, checking the readouts on the machines. "Yeah. Fragments of the bullet jacket penetrated into your chest. Nothing life threatening, but we took them out. Crime lab's got them for ballistic comparison. While we were in, we made sure that no bone slivers from your broken ribs had penetrated into your lungs."

He seated himself on the edge of the bed. "Any dizzi-ness, nausea, disorientation? Anything like that?"

"No. Head's a little thick. Throat's sore. They said I was intubated."

"That will pass. Follow my fingers."

Quinard raised his index fingers, moving them in a square as Jillian followed them with her eyes.

"Good to go. I heard they had you up walking?"

"Yeah. To the bathroom and back after they took out the catheter. Um, was that really necessary?"

"Any time we're in a patient's chest. Yeah. Sorry about that."

He shone a flashlight in her eyes, flicked it off, and stood. "I think you'll be out of here tomorrow."

"What's wrong with today?"

He gave her that grin again. "You have bruising in your left lung and your heart took a wallop. We've got you on drugs that keep things from swelling and act to counter any fluid buildup in the pericardium. That's the sack around the heart. If that were to happen—"

"I know. It would squeeze the blood out of my heart. We had to take an EMS course as part of the degree."

"Then you know why we're going to keep an eye on you for another day or so." He rose. "I'm clearing you for visitors. In the meantime, don't do anything dumb. Take it easy. Rest. No lifting, straining, or walking by yourself. Catch my drift?"

"Yeah, Doc. Thanks."

Jillian watched him walk out, saw the deputy on duty outside, and a moment later Gaylen Meyer strode in. He was dressed in a tan jacket and tie, slacks looking neatly pressed. Meeting her eyes, he smiled and shook his head.

"My God, Jill. You are a sight. And to think I just wanted a report on a homicide. What the hell are you doing? Playing Rambo?"

"Hi, Boss. What are you doing down here? Thought they had you chained to a desk up in Helena?"

He plopped himself in the easy chair recliner across from her bed and clasped his hands as he leaned forward. "It isn't every day that one of my agents gets shot. You're big news. They're even holding press conferences in the lobby."

"Shit." Jillian closed her eyes.

Meyer's voice dropped. "What are you into, Jill? Why did someone try to kill you?"

She sighed, hating the restriction around her chest. "Sir, whatever this is about, I keep finding layer after layer. Like an onion. It occurred to me that we're all being played. One of those half-dream images that pop into your head when you're on the verge of sleep. Me, dangling from strings, my arms and legs being made to move."

"Interesting, but not something I can take to the attorney general."

"It's bigger than it's supposed to look, sir. I'm not sure I get the whole picture, but I think it has to do with the sale of the Butler Ranch outside of Gardiner. Or maybe it's just Jennifer Banks playing everyone for fools, giving us hints that it might be more than a final fuck you to her piece-of-shit husband. But, if that's it, why kill Dr. Little? Why kill me? Why try and frame John Cody?"

"You think Cody's being framed?"

"Yeah. And don't ask me why. It's a gut feeling kind of thing."

"Deputy Kielman thinks Cody's our doer, but the guy has a solid alibi for being at his ranch. And he still has the best motive. If ICoHR wins this latest lawsuit, he'll lose his ranch."

"Dan Butler still missing?"

"He is. We had an agent at the title company in Livingston for the closing. Butler didn't show up. Just signed the papers remotely." Meyer shook his head. "So much for technology. It wasn't like there was anything we could do to stop the sale until he came in."

"Why'd he put it on the market?"

"Best guess is that he couldn't make the taxes. As his

profile as a person of interest in this case grew, I had one of our people check his finances. Without his agricultural exemption, the property taxes on that ranch went through the roof. No way he could pay, and in fact he was delinquent. The buyer paid all back taxes and fees. Butler even sold his pickup and bought a clunker to replace it. From his credit card receipts, he's staying in cheap motels every couple of nights. Sleeping in his truck the rest of the time for all we know."

"An old clunker," she thought. "Wait, you said Cody had a solid alibi?"

Meyer nodded. "Deputy Kielman called him while you were still enroute to the hospital. His number was the last call on your phone. Not that I'm complaining, mind you, but you need to be more careful about who's watching when you type in your phone password. Fortunately, Brody had seen you type it in. Accessed your phone and called Cody. He confirms Cody and his sidekick were on the landline. No place he could have been but his ranch."

"He called me," she whispered, remembering the conversation at the restaurant.

"Is that important? He still could have an accomplice, and the call was to verify your location."

She shook her head. "No. My take on Cody? He's a look-'em-in-the-eyes-when-you-face-them kind of guy."

"Then who shot you? The lab has established it was a 6.5 mm high-velocity rifle bullet. Jill, but for your Glock, it would have killed you on the spot. Your shoulder holster saved your life."

"Like I said, boss. Every time you peel a layer, you find another layer. Wonder what I'll find when we reach the middle?"

"You're out of the game, Agent Masterson."

She shot him a hard glance. "Why's that? The Doc said I'd be cut loose tomorrow if there are no complications."

"I'm informing you now. You're officially on administrative leave for the next month."

"Hey! I'm right in the middle of an investigation. You can't—"

"You've been shot! It's now more likely Tim Little was collateral damage, and it was you they were gunning for the last time. No. We've got your notes, and we'll call if we need your input. You did good work up to this point. Above and beyond what was expected. And I'm writing you up for a commendation."

"This isn't finished, sir."

He shook his head. "No, it's not. But you've done your part, and we'd never have made it this far without you. Now let us take it from here."

"There're still things I have to do. There was a box missing from Ryman Banks' safe. We still can't explain John Cody's hat. Tim Little said the killings aren't about conservation. Dan Butler's ranch sale, the Banks divorce settlement, it's all tied together. We still don't know who gains from shooting either Banks, Little, or me."

"But we'll find out, Jill. My word on that."

"Let me at least—"

"Governor's orders, Jill. He signed off on your administrative leave. In person. Never seen that before."

For the moment, all she could do was stare, seeing the discomfort behind his tired gray eyes.

CHAPTER THIRTY-EIGHT

T he kind-faced sixtyish lady wearing the frumpy blue dress at the front desk told Cody that they couldn't give him the room number. So, he found it the old-fashioned way, he just walked the halls. He had anticipated that the search would have been a bit more difficult, that he'd have to explain that he was lost trying to take coffee to his sister or some such fib.

For camouflage, he carried the two cups of coffee in the little cardboard tray, wisps of steam periodically ghosting from the small holes in the plastic lids. He smiled at the nurses and doctors and other staff, figuring the different colors of scrubs they wore were some kind of insignias of rank or responsibility. To the patients ambling past in their gowns and sticky socks, sometimes pushing IV stands on wheels, he just nodded. Tried to look like he shared their concern.

Having exhausted one floor, he took the elevator to the next. Stepping out, he rounded a corner, and there, at the end of the hall, a deputy in uniform sat on a plastic chair outside one of the rooms. Hmm. Deputy.

He passed the centrally located nurses' station where they all sat peering at computer screens. Just beyond, he stopped, placing the coffee on a handy tray, and took out his cell phone. That was the thing about cell phones. No one looked twice at anyone talking into one.

The room door was closed so he couldn't see inside.

Then God smiled. One of the nurses stood and exited the nurses' station. Passing Cody, the man tapped at one of the tablets they now used to record patient information. The guy proceeded down the hall, said something to the deputy, and entered the room.

Cody grinned, pulled his hat down tight, and picked up his coffee. No one got into the buffalo business who wasn't an optimist, willing to take a little risk, and more than a half a bubble off plumb.

Walking up to the door, he called, "Jillian? Got that coffee."

Like a shot, the deputy was on his feet, hand out. "Excuse me, sir. You'll need to step back."

"Coffee for Jill," Cody explained seeing the surprise in Jillian's eyes as she gaped from the bed. The nurse had turned.

The deputy was reaching for the handcuffs as Cody called, "Jill, this deputy is going to make a scene. And you agreed to the coffee."

"Hey!" Jill called. "Clark! He's okay! Let him in."

Where he blocked the door, Deputy Clark peered around Cody "You sure? My orders—"

"Yeah," Jill called. "He's on our side. It's all right."

Deputy Clark looked anything but friendly as he dropped his cuffs back into their belt pouch. "Your name, sir?"

"William Bernard," Cody told him as he beamed his friendliest smile. "Old friend of the family. What? You mean Jill hasn't mentioned me?" He shot a glance into the room. "Jill! And to think you used to obsess over me."

She raised both eyebrows and shook her head. "Seriously, Clark, I take full responsibility."

"Right." Clark was noting something in the little notebook he pulled from his pocket. "Leave the door open."

"Yes, sir." Cody walked in, nodded to the nurse who was scanning Jillian's wristband with the laser on the handheld computer.

Cody carefully placed one of the coffee cups on the tray table, waited for the nurse to leave, and rolled the tray over so Jill could reach it. Then he lowered himself to the recliner, cuddling his own cup of coffee. Jillian was giving him the most incredible "Why are you here?" look from her dark eyes. She looked oddly vulnerable and fragile in her hospital gown and with all the tubes and monitor wires.

He sighed. "God, I was worried when I heard. How are you feeling?"

"Like I've been shot. What the hell are you doing here?"

"Well, that's a story. Mostly I came to see you. We were going to have that cup of coffee, remember? The idea that someone shot you really pisses me off. From the news, they said it was a miracle you made it. How bad is it?"

"Mostly a bruise, caught some bullet jacket and lead fragments. Some broken ribs. Bullet hit my gun." She stared thoughtfully at the coffee she cupped her fingers around. "Guess that poor Glock looks like someone took a hammer to it."

He sighed, a sense of relief welling. He'd been terrified of what he'd find. "Yeah, well, we both owe our lives that single miracle."

She glanced up. "How's that?"

"It didn't make sense at first. I lay there all night, thinking about it. Then everything fell into place. Elaborate, almost choreographed. You are shot dead. Why? Because you are closing in on the suspect. That's me. They'd think I was panicked. So I drive up and shoot you from ambush. It's perfect. I'm on the ranch with no witnesses. I have no alibi except that Redweed says I was there."

"Why wouldn't they believe Danny?"

"Because she's a felon."

"Huh?"

"It was a long time ago. The folks hired her as terms of her parole. She was just a dumb kid back then. Got in a shooting scrape down on the Wind River Res. Shot her first husband when he sorta got way out of line. But that's her story, and she tells it a lot better than I can. Anyway, the point of all this is that you're supposed to be dead, and I'm supposed to have killed you. And there's supposed to be no way I can prove that I didn't. And, if you want to ask me how certain I am, go no farther than Deputy Kielman. He called while they were..."

"...Still driving me away. I know." Jillian used the control to elevate her bed. Sipped the coffee. "That's good."

"Large black coffee with two shots. You cleared for caffeine? I forgot to ask."

"Yeah. Just no lifting, straining, or strenuous activity. So if I decide I have to beat the crap out of you, I'm calling on Deputy Clark to stand in for me."

She might have said it lightly, but he could see her gears turning, thinking.

"Now the clue to breaking this wide open is why pick me?"

She shot him an unkind look. "No egotism there, huh?"

He shook his head. "There's a whole slew of people who were in Banks' life who would have fit the bill better than me. Say, Jennifer Banks is behind all this. She'd be more likely to pick one of Banks' girlfriends to take the fall. Maybe that gal he was shacking up with before he was shot? What's her name?"

"Charlotte Zypanski. I interviewed her a couple of days after the murder. In my youth they had a word for that kind of woman." Jillian frowned. "And then I met Jennifer. What was it about Banks and tall stacked women who look like cover models for Victoria's Secret?"

"Can't say stacked anymore. Not even when you're a woman. That's called body shaming."

She gave him that "you can't be serious" glance again. Then said, "Jennifer told me that I was too shabby and plain, but that Banks would screw me anyway just for the hell of it. Made me feel just peachy."

He stopped short. Met her dark eyes and saw the question there. "Haven't I told you that he was an asshole? But that's my point. Any of the people Banks has screwed, male or female, sexually or financially, would have worked for the fall guy."

She pointed a finger. "Did he ever screw you?"

"Nope. But with this latest suit, he was trying to. I'm not saying I won every round, but I ended up on top more than he did." He made a face. "Ooh. Don't take those words out of context."

She stifled a chuckled, winced, and placed a hand to her side. "Don't make me laugh."

"Got it. No laughter." A quizzical pause. "But they say that's the best medicine."

"Not with broken ribs."

"No argument there. Thought I'd die." He made a face.

"When did you have broken ribs?"

" Buffalo ran over me in the alley one time."

"Did they tape you up like a mummy? That's what I feel like."

"No tape. That would have meant emergency room, doctors, X-rays, medical bills, and cost me two days of missed chores. I just ground my teeth and worked my way through it."

"Tough guy, huh?'

"Naw. I'm just a crème puff. All pudgy and squishy by nature."

That measuring look was back. Like she was really seeing him for who he was. "Sure you are." A pause. "Did you know that Jennifer gets the house and all of Ryman Banks' assets? Can't divorce a dead husband."

"And the deal on the Butler Ranch closed today. I read that in the Livingston paper when I stopped for coffee and a pee break. They didn't report who bought it. Only that it was an investment group from back east and the ranch sold for a million six. I mean that's ridiculous for that acreage. Granted, the house is a historic fixer-upper relic, and the out buildings are falling down, but for just shy of six thousand acres with more than a mile of river front and bordering the Park, it should have sold for twenty or thirty million. The article noted that most of the property was listed as critical wildlife habitat and that without a conservation easement, it would be taxed at recreational property rates. So whomever bought it is going to be shelling out as much in property taxes as most people make in a year."

He watched her take another swig of coffee, liked how her throat worked as she swallowed. Then she said, "That's the operating hypothesis. Butler couldn't make his taxes. I heard he was so destitute he sold his pickup for a junker."

"Yeah, I've seen it. An old red and white beat-up Ford ranch truck that—"

"With tinted windows?" she asked suddenly. "No tailgate?"

"Yeah. Just like that."

"Son of a bitch," Jillian whispered. "I keep seeing that truck. It's been following me all around town." She raised her voice, shouting, "Hey, Clark! Get in here."

Cody heard the chair screech, and Deputy Clark burst into the room, one hand on his holstered pistol, fierce eyes pinning Cody as if in anticipation of mayhem. "What's up, Jill?"

"Get on the horn to Bert. Tell him I've got a description of Dan Butler's truck. BOLO for older model Ford F-250. White with red accent panels on the cab and box sides. Missing its tailgate. Ball hitch for a gooseneck in the bed. Tinted windows. That Butler is spending every other night in a cheap motel."

Clark was scribbling in his little book. "Got it."

"And one other thing," Jillian told him. "I think Butler was following me around. I mean I saw that truck in the hotel parking lot. Several times. It might even have been there the night I was shot. I'm not sure."

Cody closed his eyes. "God, Dan, tell me it's not you." But he had a sinking feeling down deep in his gut.

CHAPTER THIRTY-NINE

J illian didn't remember falling off to sleep. If anything, the caffeine should have jolted her wide awake. Or maybe it was the trauma her body had survived. One of the deputies had taken great pleasure in telling her that a 6.5 millimeter one-hundred-forty grain bullet travelling at twenty-eight hundred feet per second would have expended about a ton and a quarter of energy when it hit her pistol.

She wasn't sure she really needed to know that. Or that, but for a quarter inch in either direction, instead of fragmenting on her Glock the bullet would set up into a mushroom as it smashed through her ribs and took out her left lung. After it blew a quarter-size hole through her heart, and exploded her right lung, it would have blasted out the right side of her chest.

Maybe that led to the fantastic shades of her dreams. Like torn bits of cotton cloth, they floated, rippled flaglike, carried by currents of dark and smoke-charred air. Among them, she saw her father's face, that twist of fury that had so frightened her. How he'd grabbed Uncle by the throat, shoved him hard into the antique china cabinet. Heard the glass break, the shelves buckle, *watched the mismatched plates as they tumbled out around Uncle's shoulders to smash on the floor.*

Heard herself scream as Daddy bellowed and roared, his face inches from Uncle's. How the veins had stood out on his neck. The way his spittle had spattered Uncle's face.

And she'd stood there, screaming...screaming...

"Jillian?" the soft voice was accompanied by a hand on her shoulder. "You all right?"

She stifled a gasp, jerked, and spear of pain transfixed her. She felt the tightness in her chest and clawed her way back to the world. Opening her eyes, the familiar hospital room came into focus. The same acoustic tile ceiling, the monitors, the big white board with its list of on-duty nurses and explicit instructions, like No Walking Alone.

John Cody was leaned over, his hand still on her shoulder. Something reserved lay behind his tan eyes, but it faded into a twinkle. A smile bent his beard and mustache. "Whatever dream that was, it sounded like it was no fun. Not like you and me riding old Mitch and Betsy up into the high country, or maybe enjoying a picnic on a beach somewhere with real surf."

She shifted. "What makes you think I'd go riding with you, let alone have a picnic?"

"Well, you had a cup of coffee with me today and it didn't go too badly, did it?"

"God, being around you is surreal." But she smiled. Winced as she sat up. "I've got to pee." She swung her legs over the side of the bed, pulled the IV stand around. "Where's the damn nurse's button."

"I've got you," he said, rounding the bed. "Here. Take my arm."

She gave him her most evil glare. "No. I'm not letting you walk me to bathroom."

It was his turn to give her the elevated eyebrow look. "You just spent the last two hours sleeping like a baby with your prime murder suspect in the chair across from you. Now, if that don't make me trustworthy, I don't know what does."

"I shouldn't be doing this."

His smile did wonderful things for his beard. It reminded her of the kind of smile Tom Selleck had when he was young. That same kind of fun lighting up his eyes.

"Well, Jillian there's a lot of things we shouldn't do. Maybe finding myself dazzled by a woman who could still have me thrown in jail for murder isn't smart either. But, hey. How will I ever figure out if she's a fantastic as I think she is without a little risk?"

What the hell was it about him? If he was a rogue, he was the most charming one she'd ever run into.

She took his arm and towed the IV stand along. Let him help her into the bathroom and turned as he closed the door behind him. She stared at the *DON'T FALL* sign on the wall. Considered the call button on its string next to the john. When she'd flushed, she stood, straightened her gown, and called, "I'm finished."

He was still smiling as he helped her back to bed.

She eased onto the mattress, and damned if he didn't help her with the blankets. God, he was like the perfect companion.

Considering that, she heard voices in the hall. Clark talking to someone. And a moment later, Sheriff Wain stepped in. Saw Cody and stopped. His brow knit as Cody picked up his hat from where he'd laid it.

"I'll give you two time to talk," Cody said. To Jillian, he added. "I'll check in with you later." Then he gave Bert Wain that winning smile. "Sheriff. Good day to you."

Amazed, she caught herself grinning, watched as he clapped his hat onto his head and walked out.

Wain turned, pointed, "Is that who I think that is?"

"Yeah, Sheriff. We just had coffee. Long story. Either he's crazy, or I am."

CHAPTER FORTY

S eeley kept his eyes down as Sheriff Wain passed him in the hall. Scouting out the hospital was risky. They had cameras everywhere. But finding Jillian Masterson's room hadn't been hard. It was the only one with a deputy sitting in front of the door.

He made a couple of passes up and down the hall, got a glimpse through the open door. Could see Masterson in her bed. Both times she'd been asleep. Vulnerable.

He'd considered maybe trying to distract the deputy, but each time, there'd been that damn cowboy in there, sitting in the visitor's chair. Then he got a solid look at the guy: *John Cody?* What the fuck?

The deputy was one thing: The man was bored, just doing his job. He'd have to pee. Get a cup of coffee. Who knew? But Cody? He was supposed to be at his ranch in Wyoming, ready to take the fall. And, instead, he's sitting like a fucking guard dog at Masterson's bedside? The last place on the planet Cody was supposed to be?

But what did it all mean?

If Masterson was to die, Cody was perfectly placed to

be the culprit. Sitting right there, less than a foot away. On the spot with plenty of opportunity. Seeley fingered the syringe in his coat pocket.

All it would take would be seconds. Long enough to walk in, empty the syringe into the IV line, and walk out. Fifteen ccs of the cattle sedative, Rompun, would put Masterson down for good. It was the kind of drug a buffalo rancher would know of and use. Tailored to blame Cody.

Seeley waited. Nodded to a nurse as he lounged by the coffee machine. After fifteen minutes, the deputy stood, said something to the people inside, and walked off toward the men's room. Seeley ambled leisurely forward, glanced in. Masterson was asleep. Cody was seated with his legs crossed, leaned back, and his arms were laced behind his head.

The guy looked up, met Seeley's eyes in the instant before he passed out of sight. That rattled him. Something about those tan eyes, almost burning over that hard nose and full dark beard. With those bulky shoulders, the guy had a Western wolfish look to him Seeley hadn't seen before. Not the sort to be fooled with.

Seeley pondered as he strolled the hall. He'd just passed the same nurse he'd already seen and nodded to three times. Glancing up, he was painfully aware of the cameras. The tingle began to run along his spine.

Damn it, this was taking too long. Even if he could get to Masterson, it would be too easy for them to pick him out from the security footage.

Come on, Seeley. Something's not right here. Somehow, Cody's managed to turn the tables.

What in hell had Masterson figured out? Somehow, she'd determined that Cody was innocent. But how? And if she had, that meant the entire plan was in jeopardy.

Without a fall guy, the cops would keep looking. Might trip over a bit of evidence that would lead them right to the client. Or worse, to him.

"Nope. Got to wrap this up. Give them a perp."

As he headed for the exit, Seeley pulled out his phone, hit the message icon and accessed the client.

> Girl knows Buffalo Bill is innocent.

> Plan A compromised.

> Plan B only option.

He had just reached his pickup when his phone buzzed. Settling himself behind the wheel, he read,

> If true.

> Reluctantly agree.

"Right," Seeley agreed, starting the F150. "Now, all I have to do is find the poor son of a bitch."

CHAPTER FORTY-ONE

C ody had raided the various waiting rooms and lobbies and carted off any reading material that looked in the slightest bit engaging. He'd gone through most of it. Seated in the easy chair across from Jillian's bed, he squinted at the article, reading it aloud. Not that he was really that much into *Cosmopolitan*, but Jillian had appeared much more interested in the article entitled "Ten Ways to Tell if He's Really the Right Guy" than she'd been in the *Guns & Ammo* article entitled "Great-Grandpa's Round Still Has Merit: Why the 30-30 Shines."

"Number eight," Cody continued to read. "He's more invested in you than himself. We all know guys who talk the talk, smile the smile, and pay perfect attention on that first date, but where are they when you really need them? Do you get the feeling that you're only interesting because you're the latest model to come down the line? Or is it that he's just amusing himself until the score is made? If you're looking for just that right guy, he'll be there when the chips are down. Not sure he will be? Test him!"

Cody looked over where Jillian was watching him through dark eyes, her expression thoughtful. He asked, "Is that why you allowed yourself to get shot? Make sure I wasn't just after the latest model?"

A slim eyebrow arched. "Believe me, I can think of a whole lot of ways to figure that out. Ways that don't necessitate surgery, broken ribs, and a hospital stay." She hesitated. "I still haven't figured out what you're after."

Cody tapped a hard finger on the magazine page. "Yeah, well, I'm not reading number nine on the list."

"What's number nine?"

Cody screwed up his face, took a deep breath. "I'm just reading this verbatim, mind you. The title is, 'You're three months into the relationship, and the sex is still ringing all of your bells.'" He paused. "Um, I'm not going into all the details about all the details that I'm not going to go into."

"That makes you a first." He heard the weariness.

Placing the magazine aside, he studied her pinched expression, the absent look behind her eyes. The words had opened some door down inside the woman. Must have been bad, and it must have involved a man who'd really hurt her. Attractive woman like her? He could guess.

"Jillian, the thing about living is that it's full of people. Most of them are just basically mediocre. Some are really good folks. But sprinkled into the mix are a bunch of monsters who are at a minimum callous or heartless, or all about stroking their egos. And then you have the purely evil. The ones who break, debase, and abuse others in order to glut their most sadistic appetites. Sometimes the mere act of living leaves you with scars."

"Which one are you?"

"Don't know," he told her softly. "I've got my own issues. They hinge around justice, I guess. I know the monsters are out there. I learned that when my parents... Well, by the way they were tortured and killed. Some really sadistic monster...or monsters had to be behind that. For the moment, I've had to put that on hold. But once this Banks thing is taken care of, I've got to pursue it. You understand?"

The look she was giving him through her dark eyes drilled right through him, as if seeing right down to his core. Nevertheless, she gave him a slight nod.

To change the subject, he said, "I took a pistol class once. The instructor said, 'There are three kinds of people: sheep, wolves, and sheepdogs. Decide now, which will you be.'"

She said, "I heard something like that in one of my classes. I guess it's true. I chose to be a sheepdog."

Cody leaned forward, meeting her eyes. "Yeah, well, there's a fourth kind."

"What?"

"Buffalo."

"Explain."

He set the magazine aside. "I'm a buffalo. When the wolves come, figuring they're going to kill and eat me, I'm going to kick the shit out of them, and maybe die trying. The difference between a buffalo and sheep is that bison don't depend on anyone else to keep them safe. And let me ask you this: If you were a wolf, who would you attack? A defenseless sheep? Or a buffalo who's going to kick, stomp, gore, and fight you to the end?"

"The sheep," she said simply. "But why are you here?"

He chuckled to himself. "Well, hell, I guess someone

needed to read you this article so that when the right guy comes along, you'll know he's a keeper."

"Have I ever told you that you're a lunatic?"

"Time or two. You see, the thing about a lunatic? You'll never be bored."

"That's something to think about, John." She yawned. "Maybe I'll close my eyes for a bit."

He waited. Fifteen minutes later, she was out, breathing evenly.

Cody stood, stretched, and tried to ease the cramps from his back and legs. Walking to the door, he found Clark's relief, Deputy Jones, perched uncomfortably in the plastic chair.

"Jillian's asleep," Cody told him. "Gonna hit the cafeteria for whatever kind of choke-and-puke they're serving today."

Cody made it to the elevator, surprised to see Sheriff Bert Wain when the doors opened.

"Hi, Sheriff."

Wain stopped short, an eyebrow lifted. "So...you're still here?"

Cody stepped into the elevator, Wain not moving as the doors closed. "Jillian's asleep. Thought I'd get something to eat."

Wain pushed the button that would drop them at the cafeteria floor. "Why don't you and I have a little chat while you're at it, okay?"

The tone in his voice sent the alarm bells ringing. Cody just nodded, smiling pleasantly. "I'd enjoy the company."

Stepping off, Cody led the way, Wain walking along, hard eyes seeking to burn holes in the side of Cody's head.

"What's your game here?" Wain asked as they entered the cafeteria.

Cody turned. "Look, Sheriff, since the beginning, someone's gone way out of their way to set me up for Banks' murder. But for the fact that I talked to Jill the night she was shot, and Kielman called me at home, I'd be behind bars right now. You'd have a pretty airtight case, wouldn't you?"

Wain worked his jaws, nodded.

Cody continued, "So, here's the thing: I like Jillian. But for a tiny bit of luck, that bullet would have killed her dead. They're going to try again. Probably to cover their trail. I'm not sure how or why that may be the case, but they're way ahead of us in this game."

"Us?" Wain asked.

"Outside of me, who else stands to gain here?"

Wain's frown tightened. "I'm not at liberty to discuss the details of an on-going investigation."

"Yeah," Cody said, starting for the serving line. "But let's think about that. Banks' heirs, for sure. You'd know more about that than I would. ICoHR? Can't see what Carly would gain, especially with Little's death. And but for you putting her under protective custody, she might be a victim, too. Not to mention that she's just lost two of the three pillars that hold ICoHR up." He paused, cocked his head. "Unless it's someone else in the conservation scam trying to horn in on their action."

"Doesn't work," Wain told him. "All of the other conservation organizations have different spheres of influence and interest but losing ICoHR weakens the entire movement."

"You checked out Dan Butler's ranch sale?" Cody asked.

"Turns out it's an investment corporation made up of

a bunch of LLC's with a Delaware address. But, outside of Dan Butler looking for revenge, we can't see how the ranch sale would tie into the murder. We..." Wain stopped, chuckled. "And that's all I'm going to say."

Cody nodded. "Keep thinking. The answer's there somewhere. And, hell, maybe it is Dan. I know how he feels. If this latest lawsuit leads to Yellowstone bison being listed? Yeah, it'll be a government taking, and I'll lose my bison herd and the use of my land. Maybe, unlike Dan, I can continue to pay the taxes, turn it into a dude ranch, but I'm not sure I'd want to without the buffalo. I'd resent the hell out of it, especially knowing it was a con and a lie that led my having to send my entire herd off to slaughter. That sort of thing could really fester."

Wain's grin went thin. "And that's what we call motive, Mr. Cody. Which is why I don't want you hanging around Jillian. In fact, I'd have 86'd your ass out of here already, except that Jill asked me not to. See, I like the woman, too. And I damned sure won't let anything happen to her on my watch."

"Then, we're agreed on that."

Wain tapped a hard finger into Cody's chest. "Just watch your ass, cowboy, 'cause I'd like nothing better than to lock you up on the charge of obstructing an investigation and send you off to Deer Lodge."

Cody narrowed a tan eye. "If I watch my ass, I can't see where I'm going, and I'll run into things. And, just for the record, Sheriff, I'm not a cowboy. They do beef, I do bison. Different beast. That makes me a buffalero."

"Don't get smart with me."

"And don't think I'm going to allow so much as a hair get hurt on Jill's head." Cody raised his finger to poke back. Stopped himself before he could commit such a foolish error. "Now, I'm on your side in this. Like you, I want to see the guilty party brought to justice. 'Cause, honestly, Sheriff, something's really rotten behind all of this."

Wain's brown eyes flickered, his lips twitched, and his face grew even more florid. A slow nod barely inclined his white Stetson. "All right, Cody. You think you're so smart. Maybe I'm buying it. But, so help me God, if you so much as sneeze wrong, I'll have your ass."

Cody took a deep breath. "Yeah, well, Sheriff, if I was so smart, I'd have the bad guy figured out, and I wouldn't be in this mess to start with."

CHAPTER FORTY-TWO

When the nurse came with Jillian's discharge orders. Cody had given her a salute and left, telling her he'd see her later. She'd watched him leave the room with a sinking sensation in her chest. What was it about him? Why in hell did the guy think there was any chance of a relationship? And, more to the point, what did he see in her? If he only knew what a screwed-up wreck she was, about the baggage...the nightmares and flashbacks.

She shook it off, trying not to think about it.

Dressing, she took the list of instructions from the nurse and signed the papers. They made her ride out in a wheelchair to the curb where Deputy Barbara Sampson waited. She was knocking on fifty, maybe 5 foot 5 and close to one hundred and seventy pounds. The woman kept her hair cut short, and had the kind of blue eyes that could go glacial cold in an instant. After twenty-some years in the SO, she'd grown hard as rock. Barb held the passenger door open on a sheriff's office cruiser.

Jillian hadn't expected a police escort on her release.

After the nurse locked the wheels and folded up the footrests, Jillian carefully rose. Still slightly wobbly, she stepped over to the cruiser. Tenderly, she settled herself in the passenger seat, then winced as she fumbled for the seatbelt and clicked it in place. To her irritation, a TV camera crew had been filming the entire thing.

After Sampson slid into the driver's seat, Jillian pointed. "What the hell is that all about?"

"You're the big celebrity. The whole state...hell, the whole country is talking about you."

Sampson shifted into gear and motored out of the pick-up area, making a "rolling stop" at the corner. After a left onto Highland, she added, "Me, I think you're the luckiest bitch on two feet. I've seen your gun. Talk of the department. Looks like someone smashed it with a sledgehammer. Slide and barrel's bent, plastic frame's cracked, but not as bad as you'd think. Glock makes a pretty tough pistol."

"Yeah, you ought to see my side."

Sampson smothered a smile. "Thanks, but no thanks. It might scare me off of tenderized meat."

Jillian started to laugh, regretted it immediately.

Sampson slapped fingers on the steering wheel. "I don't know how you talked Bert into letting you stay at the Hilton Garden Inn again. I'm not sure it's anything like a smart move."

Jillian was careful to keep her breathing shallow. The drugs helped, but she'd started to feel the pain. How the hell had John Cody kept working after being run over by that bull? Must have been a tough son of a bitch. Jillian, drug-numbed, felt like someone had drained all of her get-up-and-go. All she could think about was getting back to bed.

Sampson signaled, making a left on Main.

"Barb, my stuff is there. The room's paid for until the end of the week. Not to mention that I can't climb the steps to my apartment in Billings, and they don't want me to drive for another three or four days. Besides, if there's a chance the shooter's going to make another run at me, we'll be waiting. Bert and the Bozeman PD are staking out the parking lots. If he tries again, we've got him."

"So, you're happy being bait?"

"Hell, no!" Jillian shot her a narrow-lidded glance. "Talk about putting a chilling tingle down your spine? A quarter of an inch in either direction and I'd be dead. As it stands, I'm looking at months of recovery before I'm back to anything resembling normal. Happy? I'm scared half shitless. But if it brings the guy who did this in? I'll tough it out."

Again, that veiled look from Sampson.

"What, Barb?"

"I owe you an apology. You'll do to ride the river with."

"Like...rafting the Gallatin?"

"Old cowboy saying. You've got a place on my team any day." Sampson took the right onto 19th.

Jillian smiled at that.

"So, you're on administrative leave, but you're staying at the hotel? How's that supposed to work?"

Jillian stared at the passing houses. "Paid leave. I'm off the case. Not that I'm physically able. Doctor's orders. No bending or lifting anything for a week, and then I'm limited to ten pounds. No straining. Not even on the can. But I'm encouraged to walk as much as I want so long as I don't overdo it."

At the turn off, Sampson wheeled into the hotel parking lot and pulled up in front of the entrance. Jillian glanced out at the familiar doors, the lobby behind. A sudden thumping let her know her heart was battering at her breastbone. Images surfaced of that night, the hotel lights, the automatic doors sliding open.

"Yeah"—Sampson read her expression—"this is the exact spot. Think of it as finishing that walk you started that night. Just be thankful for each step you take."

"Amen, sister." Jillian reached for the door handle, opening it. By the time she swung her legs out, Sampson was there to offer a hand. Rising from the seat brought a stitch through Jillian's chest. Getting to her feet, she stared off across the parking lot. Thought about where the bullet hit her, how she'd been facing.

"He had to be right there," she said softly. "Edge of the lot."

"Pulls your pucker-string tight, doesn't it?" Sampson had her eyes on the now-empty parking spaces.

"Yeah," Jillian told her dryly. "If I never have another encounter with a bullet, I'll call it a life well lived."

"Come on," Sampson took her arm, steadying her. "Let's get you inside and out of the line of fire."

Going through the doors, Jillian glanced back at the parking lot, cold and pale gray in the afternoon winter sun. But she could feel him, out there, waiting...

CHAPTER FORTY-THREE

The throbbing ache in her chest brought Jillian awake. She opened her eyes; the bedside clock let her know it was almost six. A look at the windows where the last rays of sunset were dying in the southwest told her it was time to get up. Not only did her chest hurt, but her stomach was growling. She hadn't had lunch, waiting as she'd been for her discharge.

She gasped as she eased herself upright and swung her legs over the edge of the bed. Taking her time, she stood. Tried not to aggravate the pain in her chest. Made her way cautiously to the bathroom. She might have moved like a ninety-year-old lady, but she attended to her needs, brushed her teeth, and got a comb through her hair. The sponge bath at the hospital that morning hadn't left her feeling clean. With a wistful glance at the shower, she shook her head. She was going to have to rely on washcloths until the stitches were removed.

Dressing was a real chore, but she managed with only a few grunts, groans, and a couple of "Shit that hurts!" outbursts. Ordered not to bend, her shoes were a challenge until she figured out how to pick them up with her toes so that she could slip them on while sitting upright.

Headed for the door, she picked up her phone. Saw the list of messages from Supervisor Meyer, Sheriff Wain, and there was text from Cody. She wondered what it meant that she opened his first.

> Jillian. I'm in Room 306 just two doors
> down.

> Put my number on speed dial.

> One press of the button, and I'll be there
> in ten seconds.

My knight in shining Levis' and a buffalo-snot-stained Stetson?

The other messages were from her boss and Sheriff Wain. Both offered the same "if you need anything" messages, but Wain stressed that the hotel was under 24-hour surveillance.

Jillian considered Cody's number, then thought better of it. It would be good to be alone. To think. To try and put the events of the last week in some sort of perspective. Opening the door, she slipped out, tip-toeing down the hall past room 306 on her way to the elevator.

Making her way to the lobby, she took in the dining room and attached lounge. With her newfound wariness, she chose a table back and away from the windows. A total of six men and two women were seated in the lounge over drinks and meals. Only one—the gray-haired guy in the back wearing the western shirt and faded gray cowboy hat—seemed aware of her. He studied her thoughtfully through fatigued-looking gray eyes. Might have been in his late sixties, tall, lanky and looking hard-used.

God, Jillian, you've been all over the TV. Doesn't mean he's a threat.

She studied the menu, opting for the steak and potatoes *au gratin*.

She'd just picked up her glass of water when the old gray-eyed cowboy slid onto the bench at the next table to hers. She tensed, a sudden spear of terror like an electrical shock went through her. Instinctively, she reached for her shoulder holster. Another chill filled her as she realized she was unarmed. Totally defenseless. Her body too traumatized to even attempt the defensive moves she'd learned in academy.

Instead, she frantically pawed for her phone, fumbled it, was tapping the security code furiously when the man said, "Please. Don't. I'm not here to hurt you. I just want to talk." A pleading note in his voice, he added, "Please?"

She hesitated, shot him a look. "Who are you?"

"Dan Butler," he told her, lowering his gaze to the beer he'd carried over. His weathered and calloused hands were clasping it like a prayer. Head down, his shoulders had slumped. "I mean it, I'm not a threat."

"How'd you get here? The parking lot is under surveillance. We've got a BOLO out on your pickup. The old beat-up Ford? White with red panels? Missing the tailgate?"

"Yeah," he told her. "Parked it out back over at Lowes' and walked over here. Had my coat over my shoulder as I walked in so the cops on stake out could see I wasn't packing. Thought I might be able to get a chance like this. To tell you about the ranch."

"Why shouldn't I just hit the button on my phone? Sheriff Wain and the Bozeman PD all want a chance to put you in the chair for a little talking to."

"The guy who shot you was in a dark blue Ford F150.

Not sure of the year, but it's about five, maybe six years old. Has a fiberglass topper on it. Wyoming plates, but I couldn't tell what number. Dusty, you know. Covered with grime. Looked completely stock. I mean nothing about that truck stands out. Looks like a hundred others."

She met those intense gray eyes, felt the tickle of fear around her heart. "How do you know that?"

"Because I seen it. Was watching the night Tim Little was shot. Been following you. Wanting to see if you'd figure this case out. It's the ranch that's at the bottom of it. Maybe it's more than that, I don't know."

"Was that you who put that article under my door?"

"Yep." His jaw clenched, eyes narrowing. "Not sure why they had to kill Banks and Little. But it's got something to do with this latest lawsuit. And that might be why they started putting so much pressure on me to sell."

"I heard that you were behind on taxes."

He shot her a sidelong glance. "Without cattle, I couldn't make income. Takes a lot of money to run a ranch. That's just upkeep. Got to keep the fields watered, the noxious weeds sprayed, the pipelines and ditches up. And there's the house needing a new roof, the panels blowing loose on the pole barn. Keeping the tractor in fuel. Making sure the baler has new tires. Blading the road. Would have had fence added to that, but I was ordered to tear 'em down."

"So you went broke?"

"Yep. And the taxes just kept going up." Again, that wire-thin glance. "Lost the agricultural exemption. County reclassified it as recreational property. My bet is that my tax bill on the place is more than you make in an entire year. Tried talking to some of the realtors, they said that with it being designated as critical wildlife habitat, they couldn't sell it for anywhere near the value it should have commanded. Said no one would want it unless they could build where they wanted, subdivide, manage the property as an investment. Couldn't do any of that with the US Fish and Wildlife Service as a de-facto co-owner. Fish and Wildlife have to sign off on any kind of disturbance or potential impact."

"So, why did this investment firm want the property if it has all these restrictions on it?"

A grim smile crossed his lips. "Now, there's the question, don't you think?"

"We've looked into it. It's an investment firm registered in Delaware. Not much information on them but for the officers. None of them were names that came up on the NICS search."

"They wouldn't." Butler leaned forward over his beer. "My bet? They're a cut out."

"Why?"

"Whoever's behind this doesn't want anyone to know. But figure this. Real estate people tell me the Butler ranch could have sold for between fifteen and twenty million given the river front and timbered acreage, not to mention the water rights and irrigated land right there adjacent to the park. After closing and paying off the liens, I got out with a little more than six hundred thousand. Someone made a killing on that property. And if ICoHR wins this latest lawsuit? That same thing that happened to me is going to happen to every rancher, developer, and mineral rights holder bordering the park. They're using Yellowstone buffalo as the excuse to devalue private land. The way the ESA is written? Anyplace that bison might roam outside of the park becomes critical habitat. Read the language in the law."

"But how can anyone who buys any of that property make money off of it?"

"Figure that out, Agent Masterson, and you've figured out this entire case."

She studied him, frowning, feeling some big piece of the puzzle out there just beyond her reach. "Tell me, would you have killed Ryman Banks if you could have?"

Odd that she hadn't asked straight out if he'd done it.

Butler's lips pursed, the brim of his hat pulling down as he frowned. "That day I went to the ICoHR offices, I might have. I was crazy enough. That was when it was just sinking in that I'd been taken for everything. It wasn't just the land, but everything that was me. My family. My heritage. All of my cows. You understand that? We grow up out here taking care of the land and the animals. Passing it down. All that work. Everything my family endured through droughts, floods, fires, the times we had to kill cattle infected with brucellosis, the winterkill, the endless work. Just...gone."

"I can understand."

He gave her a thin smile. "No, you can't. Not unless you've lived it."

"So, assuming you have nothing to do with these murders, what are you going to do?"

"Take off. I'm sixty-eight with arthritis, aches in my bones, and a family history of prostate cancer. Maybe I'll rent an apartment in San Diego or Austin. Someplace warm. What I got out of the ranch ought to be enough to see me through till I die. If that's sooner rather than later, it'll be enough to leave something to the kids."

"What about the ranch? What do you think's going to happen to it?"

He worked his jaws as he shrugged. "It's dying, Agent Masterson. When I left, the main house was in need of repair. Weeds are growing thick in the corrals, and I haven't been able to water the irrigated land for the last year and a half 'cause the main ditch needs cleaned. In just that time, leafy spurge, spotted knapweed, tumbling mustard, kochia, and Russian thistle got a start. Even if I could afford it, you think Fish and Wildlife would give me permission to spray? The cheat grass and Japanese brome is taking over in the pastures. These environmentalists, they think if you just leave land fallow, it will grow into paradise. They don't realize we can't go back to that mythical Eden before the white man got here." A pause. "Hell, even the Indians burned the prairie every fifteen years or so."

"Those plants you talk about, is that so bad?"

He pushed his hat back with a finger, studied her. "Agent Masterson, they have rules about taking only weed-free certified hay into Yellowstone and the surrounding national forests, and now somebody owns a ranch right next door where those same weeds are growing wild, shedding seeds and pollen and spreading like wildfire. My cows wouldn't eat that stuff. I can promise you the bison, elk, deer, and moose won't touch it either. You tell me if it won't turn into a cluster fuck."

"Then why have it declared as critical habitat in the first place?"

"Because I kept those pastures healthy and productive for my cows. And when the elk and buffalo came out of the park in November, they grazed it, too. So, what's supposed to be critical habitat will now become a dead zone."

And with that he stood, touched the brim of his hat. "Excuse me for a minute. Have to hit the men's room. Be right back."

As the waiter placed her supper on the table, she

watched Dan Butler disappear down the hall toward the rest rooms. She waited, figuring that older men from a family with prostate issues probably took longer to get the job done.

But that was the last she saw of Dan Butler, even after she alerted the Bozeman police officers. They even went so far as to check the men's room. Somehow, the old rancher had slipped out and vanished into the night.

CHAPTER FORTY-FOUR

The hot water coursed down Dan Butler's skin. But not much of it. The showerhead just didn't have enough spray, and the water pressure wasn't that great to start with. He'd become used to such things in the days since he left the ranch. Somehow, knowing that in a matter of days it would no longer be his, he just couldn't stay there until closing. It had hurt too much.

In the days prior to leaving, he'd made two long-haul trips to the county dump with full stock-trailer loads of furniture, family belongings, fixtures, and household goods. Dishes, clothing, saddles, tack, the ancient oaken file cabinets, the books he'd grown up with from the living room bookcase, he tossed them onto the piles of garbage. The same with the family photos going back to the 1870s. Even the old worn steamer trunk with its big brass hinges and lock. The trunk his great grandparents had hauled by wagon from the railhead at Livingston. Should have brought him to tears, but he'd worked mindlessly, his heart like a cold stone in his chest.

Thrown it all out.

The guns, including his great-grandfather's 1874 Sharps, Uncle Mathew's Winchester Model 71, his father's 1911 Colt, the .22 Dan had grown up with, all went to the pawn shop. Probably for half of what he could have made in the collector market. His other guns had been confiscated by the police that day he'd made a fool of himself in Bozeman.

None of it mattered.

The ranch was gone.

So, Dan had done his best. Given that cute little Agent Masterson his best guess on the reasons for that son-of-a-bitch Banks' murder.

Now, he was finished. Tonight he'd spend here, in the Bit O' Rest Motel, listening to the traffic on the Interstate. Tomorrow morning, early, he'd head south. Take Highway 191 down to West Yellowstone, then catch US 20 to Idaho Falls, then I-15. Maybe see if there was a cheap rental in St. George, Utah. Or Mesquite, Nevada. Someplace where no on knew him.

The shower was symbolic. Standing there, letting the feeble stream run, using up the thin little bar of soap. Wash. That's it. Scrub the last of your life away. As if the sacrifice of all those ancestors, all that hard work, battling the weather, the droughts, the ever-falling beef prices, and barbed wire scars, could be scrubbed off to sluice down his old hide and swirl on the plastic shower floor before vanishing down past that drain where the cheap chrome was flaking off.

In the end, the soap bar was gone.

Reluctantly, Dan reached up and turned off the water, hearing the faucet squeak as he did so.

He dried off with the too-small and scratchy towel. Didn't bother to clear the condensation from the excuse of a mirror on the tin medicine cabinet hanging over the sink.

Stepping into the motel room, he almost missed the figure sitting in the worn, 50ish red armchair by the window. Dan started, stared. Fought the urge to flee back into the bathroom for the towel to cover himself. But the figure seated in the chair was too bizarre. Covered in a hazmat suit, hair bonnet, and wearing gloves, the intruder looked like something out of a science fiction movie. Swallowing hard, Dan plucked his pants from where he'd tossed them on the bed.

Stopped short at the sight of the rifle. It lay on the spread, the bolt open.

"What the hell? I mean...who...?" Dan ended on a high note, almost shrill. "What the fuck are you doing in my room!"

As Dan pulled on his pants, the seated caricature smiled. Looked to be a man in his thirties? But Dan couldn't be sure given the baggy hazmat suit and scrub hat. Then Dan fixed on the large black semiautomatic the man held low on his lap. The damn thing was fitted with a cylindrical suppressor. The black hole in the end was pointed right at Dan's middle. That eerie shiver down in his guts tickled him. As if he could anticipate the bullet.

"I'm here because we need you, Mr. Butler."

Dan snapped his pants, feeling better, but still scared as hell. "Need me for what?" He shot a quick look at the rifle lying on the bed. Hunting rifle, scoped, the bolt open to expose the empty magazine. Did he dare make a grab for it?

Nope. Empty magazine. It was unloaded. And that big black pistol was aimed right at his gut. Couldn't miss.

"First off," the man said, "I want you to take a look at the rifle."

"Why?"

"Maybe you might want it? Go ahead. Pick it up. It won't bite. Check it out. Make sure it's in good order."

Dan choked a swallow down his tight throat. Almost shook as he reached out and lifted the gun. Saw the maker's mark: Ruger. The barrel imprint listed it as being a 6.5 Creedmoor. Looking into the action, he could see that nothing was in the chamber. All in all, the thing looked brand new.

"Looks all right to me."

"No, go ahead. Work the bolt. Dry fire it."

Dan did so, a prickling like a thousand ant feet running up and down his spine. All the time, he kept his eyes on the intruder. "Who are you? What do you want from me?"

"I want you to shoulder that rifle, Dan. Check out the scope. Go on. Yes, that's it. Change the magnification. Run it all the way up to nine power. Good. Now, cock it. Work it just like you were shooting coyotes. Run it through a whole magazine. Fast as you can."

Fighting the urge to throw up, Dan cycled the bolt and dry-fired as quick as he could. Five times. Then he lowered the rifle, almost panting from fear. "There. You happy?"

The man was smiling, seemed to be enjoying himself. "Very good. But you'd better pull the bolt, made sure it's in good condition. You know how to do that?"

Dan studied the receiver. Found the release and removed the bolt. He looked it over, licked his dry lips. "Looks all right."

"Now, a good rifleman would check the bore." The

intruder gestured with the pistol. "You know, hold it up and made sure there's no rust. That the rifling is crisp."

Dan tucked the bolt under his armpit, lifted the rifle until he could see through the receiver and down the bore. Pointing it at the light, he said, "Looks like there's some fouling. Not bad."

He nerved himself, lowered the Ruger. "What the hell do you want from me?"

The intruder smiled wider, looked as if he was choking back laughter. "I want you to slide that bolt back into the gun. Then you can toss it over to this side of the bed."

Dan struggled to take a breath, slid the bolt home and into battery. Then he hesitated, wondering if he could sling it at the intruder, buy enough time to burst out the door and...

"Nope." The intruder raised the pistol, holding it steady on Dan's chest. "Toss it easy-like. You'll never make it."

Dan nodded, exhaled, and did as he was told. Then, to his surprise, the intruder reached into a pocket and tossed a box of cartridges to Dan's side of the bed. "Go ahead. Pick 'em up. Tell me what you see."

Dan worked his fingers, fought the trembling, and plucked up the box. "Hornady 6.5 Creedmoor 140 gr bullets."

"Are they all there?"

Dan opened the box. "Looks like two are missing."

"One by one, I want you to take the cartridges out, inspect them, and put them back in the box."

"Are you crazy?"

Dan stopped short as the pistol raised, the man taking aim at Dan's face. "You can do it, or the housekeeping lady can spend hours washing your brains off the wall. Your choice."

Shaking now, Dan upended the box, carefully inspecting each bullet before putting them back in the slots in the ammo box. "I...I can't find anything wrong."

"That's good, Dan. That's really good." The man stood, the pistol raised. "We're almost done here. Now, I need you to lay down on the floor beside the bed. On your stomach. Hands clasped behind your back."

As Dan dropped to his knees, he pleaded, "Please? Just tell me what you want. I...I'll do anything. I just need to know what you want? Money? You can have it. Take it. I—"

"Shut up, Dan. Just lay there and keep still. If you get up before I'm gone, I'll have to kill you. What I want? I want you to lay there, quiet, for fifteen minutes. Do you understand? I don't want to hurt you. Don't have to."

Dan, face down on the dirty carpet, his nostrils filled the odor of must and mildew, nodded. Felt the tears leak past his eyelids. "I won't move."

"Good."

Dan could hear the man's hazard suit rustling. Realized the intruder wore booties. The familiar sound of the bolt being worked on the Ruger could be heard.

God, just let this be over with!

"Dan? You can roll over on your back now."

Dan fought the shivers, nerved himself, and flipped over on his back. To his horror, the intruder was standing over him, the Ruger in his arms.

"But, you..."

There was no time to react. The man thrust the gun downward. The Ruger's thin barrel speared hard into the soft flesh under Dan's jaw. His tongue jammed painfully against the top of his mouth.

He got his hands on the barrel, tried to push back.

The explosion happened so fast Dan Butler never felt a thing...

CHAPTER FORTY-FIVE

Back in her room, Jillian stared into her computer screen. Supervisor Meyer stared back, his expression pinched. He slowly shook his head, lips making a tsking sound.

Jillian told him, "I was on the phone the minute Mr. Butler was out the door. Told Sheriff Wain that Butler was on his way to his truck behind Lowe's. To get someone there."

"I don't like it, Jillian. What if the guy hadn't just wanted to talk?"

She lifted her phone high enough Meyer could see it. "I was in the middle of the dining room, sir. Surrounded by potential witnesses. You can damn well bet I made sure the table was where no one could have seen me through the window."

Meyer ran a hand over his face. *"I wish to hell you were someplace else. My inclination is to send in the local team to pull you out of there, haul your butt to Billings, and put you in the safe house."*

"We went over this, sir. If there's any chance to tag

the shooter, it's worth it. Bert Wain reluctantly agrees. And, besides, I'm on leave, right? Officially off the case."

"Damn right, and I can see that you're doing such a good job of staying out of it. Good thing that interviewing prime suspects isn't a normal part of the job, huh?"

"The sarcasm doesn't help, sir. And it wasn't like I went out of my way to snag Mr. Butler. He just walked over and sat down. What was I supposed to do?" She arched an eyebrow. "Tell him to leave?"

Meyer was rubbing his face again. Was that a new tick he'd developed? *"No, you did fine. I just reviewed your report. You don't think he did it. Okay. You're welcome to your own opinion. But we'd really like to have a sit-down so we can wring this guy out."*

"Like I reported, I immediately sent a text to Bert. Told him about the shooter supposedly driving an F150 with a topper and Wyoming plates. He texted back that he'd pinged Bozeman PD and they were on it and would put out a BOLO. Said they would try to intercept Butler. Haven't heard back if they got to Butler before he could get his truck out of the Lowe's parking lot."

"Let me know if they pick him up."

"Sir?" Jillian shifted, winced at the stitch of pain in her ribs. "Dan Butler's ranch? The way he describes it? Is it really a problem if all these weeds take over? I mean, they're plants, right? Was Butler shining me on when he said that wildlife won't eat them?"

Meyer's forehead lined as he raised his eyebrows. *"Do I look like a wildlife biologist? How do I know?"*

"But if that's the case, it flies in the face of all the arguments the conservation lobby has been making for years. I mean, if they drove Butler off his land to protect it for critical habitat, but then, doing so ruined the land, who'd be responsible?"

"Can't answer that either, Jillian." Meyer pursed his lips. *"All I can tell you is that the governor is scorching my butt with every call. He really wants this thing solved. So far, the only thing he's taken as good news was when I told him you'd been put on administrative leave."*

She couldn't stop herself. "Good to know it took getting shot to make his day."

"Sorry. You got thrown into the deep end of the pool when you shouldn't have. My call, which is the one that counts, is that you've handled this in an exemplary fashion. You've taken this investigation in directions no one thought to go. Now, sit back, rest and recover, and let the rest of us bring in the shooter. I've got a team headed down there to work with Sheriff Wain. When we wrap this up, your name will be prominent."

"Thank you, sir."

"Anything else, Agent Masterson?"

"No, sir."

"Good. Now, get some rest...and stay out of trouble."

Supervisor Meyer's face was replaced by the Montana Department of Justice shield against a blue background.

Jillian closed the window, staring hollow-eyed at the screen. "Something...something's not right here."

CHAPTER FORTY-SIX

Seeley Atherton stepped out of the motel room, glanced up and down in the darkness. No one moved. There were only six vehicles in the parking lot. Stuffed under Dan Butler's chin, the rifle's report had been muffled. No lights were on in the motel rooms.

The chill in the air nipped at Seeley's nose and lungs. The temperature had to be down in the single digits. His breath curled around his face as he stripped the cloth-covered nitril gloves from his hands and stuffed them into the pockets of his thick coat. The hazard suit was rolled into a plastic-wrapped bundle that was tucked under his left arm. Changing out of the suit inside the room might have been a risk, but it beat stepping outside still clad in plastic. Anyone who might have observed him would have paid attention.

Looking back, he could see Dan Butler's white-and-red F250, it's windows and hood frosted white. Well and good. Poor old Dan wasn't in any position to worry about what happened to his truck.

As it was, Seeley could have been just another motel guest departing a room. He walked athletically to his pickup, not too fast, but at just the right speed. He'd parked it down the street, away from the motel. Unlocking the driver's door, he tossed the bundled hazmat suit into the passenger's seat and climbed behind the wheel. Starting the Ford, he let it run until the idle dropped, shifted into Drive, and motored off into the silent night.

Dan Butler couldn't have chosen better. The Bit O' Rest Motel had minimal security. Only the office and parking lot had security cameras, and Seeley had been able to shift the parking lot camera's field of view before he jimmied the lock on Butler's motel room.

As he drove down the dark access road, a smile crossed his lips. Once again, things were neatly tied up. Plan B was complete and executed perfectly. Should be a slam-dunk.

At the interchange, Seeley accelerated onto I-90 westbound. If all went according to plan, tomorrow afternoon he'd make one last stop at the culvert and pick up the final package. Then, depending on the hour, he'd be back to his place in Wyoming in time to cook another mountain sheep supper. And maybe, in celebration, he'd wash it down with a couple of shots of Pendleton.

CHAPTER FORTY-SEVEN

For breakfast that morning at the hotel, Cody ordered a ham, cheese, and jalapeno omelet. He and Jillian sat in a booth in the back, away from the windows. The waiter had just set the plate on the table before him, and Cody sprinkled the folded eggs with Tabasco sauce. As he did, he studied Jillian's face. It looked puffy from lack of sleep. She kept twirling strings of hair between her fingers, grimacing.

"What?" he asked, picking up his fork.

"I feel filthy. God, my hair hasn't been this greasy since I was fifteen." A pause. "What I'd give for a shower."

"You look fine."

She raised those bloodshot brown eyes to meet his. "I look like hell. You're a lousy liar."

"A point you should keep in mind when I tell you I didn't kill Banks or Little and that my hat was stolen."

He earned a flicker of a smile for that.

"Yeah, I've kind 'a come to that conclusion." Then she yawned.

"Didn't sleep?" He took a bite of eggs.

She shook her head, stared down at her breakfast of waffles and fruit. "Chest hurt. I didn't want to take more pain killers. Figured it was time to let the drugs wash out of my system. If it gets to the point I can't stand it, I'll take a pill. But until then, I'll tough it out." She raised her eyes. "You did."

"When? I've never been shot."

"Thought you got run over by a buffalo bull."

"Yeah. That hurt. Had to blink away tears more than once in the weeks that followed."

She glanced sidelong toward the windows across the restaurant. "And after what Butler told me, I spent all night thinking about that Ford pickup he described. Every time I got up, I walked over and peeked past the curtain at the parking lot. I know that Bozeman PD had an undercover unit on stakeout, but I was still scared that pickup was out there, somewhere. That the shooter was drawing a bead on my window."

"Gets you down, doesn't it?"

She nodded, picking up her coffee and cradling it. He thought she had wonderful long fingers. Remembered holding them in the hospital. How soft and supple they'd been.

Jillian raised her eyebrows, would have taken a deep breath, but winced. "Funny, isn't it? All through college, during my course work, I never considered myself in any danger. Never crossed my mind that I would be. I was trained as an investigator. The cops who get shot? They're the ones making traffic stops or serving warrants or responding to domestic disturbances."

He gave a slight shrug. "This whole thing is insidious. Nothing makes sense. It's like everything we know is wrong. On the surface, it's meant to appear to be one thing. Like my hat at the murder scene. It's supposed to be a slam-dunk. I was at Ryman Banks' house. Set the trap and blew him away because we were enemies. And it would have worked if I hadn't been in Denver at the stock show."

"So, why kill Banks? Or Little? Why kill me? On the surface, as you say, it's made to look one way. Again, you'd be the prime suspect, except you were at home when I was shot. What's really behind it?"

"Misdirection," Cody said thoughtfully before taking another bite. "Who is smart enough to orchestrate this?"

She studied him over her coffee. "Someone involved with bison? You said your hat was stolen at the Montana meetings a month ago?" A pause. "Tell me, was anyone there from the Plains Wilderness Project?"

"Yeah. Tormey Tanner and a couple of his cronies. But they only showed up for the banquet. Probably just for the photo shoot, you know? It's not like the PWP is on anyone's 'good guy' list among the commercial bison producers. We're all terrified by what they're doing up there. Pulling down fences, building the size of that herd. Tanner claims they want to have forty thousand animals roaming central Montana in the next ten years."

"What's so wrong with that?"

Cody sipped his coffee. "They don't have the facilities to care for them. Like I said, no fences. No corrals or handling facilities. They just want those buffalo roaming around like it was 1830 again."

Her expression pinched. "So? If the buffalo roamed in 1830, why can't they roam now? It's not like a modern buffalo can't survive out there. Unlike people, they don't have cell phones, car payments, or rent."

Cody leaned forward. "Jillian, a buffalo might still be a buffalo, but the world has changed. I told you, there are more than twenty-five hundred invasive species of non-native plants living on the northern grasslands. The soil, air, microbiota, climate, it's all different from 1830. The diseases, things brought in from Europe, Asia, and Africa like splenic fever, anaplasmosis, malignant catarrhal fever, and paratuberculosis are new. Older endemic diseases like tuberculosis have been replaced with more lethal European varieties and strains. And if something like *mycoplasma bovis* breaks out in the PWP herd, they've got no way to stop it. It will roll through those tens of thousands of bison like a Biblical plague. All they're creating up there is a disease reservoir."

"They can vaccinate, can't they?"

"How?" Cody asked. "Drive around in pickups and dart thousands of animals? The buffalo up there don't have tags. No way to tell them apart. How do they know which animal they've vaccinated or missed?"

Cody sighed. "And worse, what happens when someone leaves a gate open, or a fence gets knocked down? Imagine barreling down Highway 19 north of Grass Range in the middle of the night. You come up over a rise doing seventy, and there's a herd of bison standing in the road. All you see is their eyes, their hides blending in the darkness. And, wham! It's bad enough when you hit a hundred-and-fifty-pound deer. But what about a ton of bison bull?"

"Can't they just go drive them in?"

"If they know the fence is down. And if they have enough people. But Jillian, we're talking about hundreds of miles of perimeter fence. Hell, Danny and I have trouble enough keeping our five thousand acres contained. And you don't drive bison the way you do cattle. Cats are easier to herd. Even at places like Custer

State Park over in South Dakota, they use hundreds of riders in their annual roundup."

He watched her dark eyes grow thoughtful. "What does the PWP gain from framing you for the crime?"

"If I'm locked away, I can't be around to show up at their next fund-raising event and throw cold water on their warm-and-fuzzy-happy-buffalo-please-write-us-a-check-now presentation."

Jillian considered that. Shook her head. "Doesn't work. If they've been willing to kill Banks and Little, they'd have just orchestrated your murder. Made it look like an accident and been rid of you."

"Then you think Banks and Little were the targets all along? Tanner and the PWP don't have anything to gain."

"Jen Banks does. She got the house with all the furnishings. That's at least three million. Maybe more."

Cody used his fork to toy with the last of the omelet. "She doesn't gain a thing from killing Little. I'm already set up as the fall guy. He's meaningless."

"Unless the bullet that killed Little was meant for me." Her expression tightened, gaze going unfocused.

He stewed on that for a moment, then said, "Why would Jenn want you taken out? What would she care? And what makes you think that fashion-plate Fifth-Avenue Jenn is the type to skulk around in the night with a high-powered rifle playing sniper? She might break a nail, muss her hairdo, or God-forbid get grass stains on her Donatella Versace slacks."

"Okay, granted. But Tormey Tanner had reason to hate Ryman Banks, the soon-to-be ex-husband. So, there's motive there. But not for Tim Little or me, no matter who that bullet was meant for."

"In fact," Cody told her, "Tim Little was a PWP ally. He tested all of their original bison for purity. Told

Tanner to cull out close to two thousand head. Sent them off to the packers for slaughter." He sighed. "So, now we know it was a flawed test. Those animals died for nothing. And who knows what part of the gene pool died with them?"

"Is that a reason to kill Little?" Jillian asked. "For being wrong?"

Cody considered, then slowly shook his head. "I don't think Tormey Tanner gives a rat's ass. For one thing, he made money off of those animals. Sent them to the kill floor at a time when carcass prices were knocking on five dollars a pound on the rail. For another, he doesn't care about the bison. They're just marketing props to him. Part of the grand design of his North American wilderness park with it's sprawling vistas hearkening back to a virgin purity that existed before the white man. He just needs tens of thousands of bison to make the picture look authentic."

"So, where does that leave us?"

He shifted on the chair, chewing the last bite of omelet. "Right back where we started. Who took my hat and left it at the murder scene? And what does the Butler ranch sale have to do with anything?"

"Dan Butler told me the place is being overrun by noxious weeds. Does that make sense?"

Cody leaned back, asked, "Did he say what kind?"

"Yeah, but it was like Greek to me."

"Leafy spurge? Knapweed? Palmer amaranth? Russian—"

"Yes! And I remember cheatgrass and something Japanese."

"Brome?" Cody asked.

"That was it. He said that the weeds were taking over the ranch because he didn't have the money to fight it and the US Fish and Wildlife Service wouldn't let him use poisons."

In his mind, Cody could imagine the meadows. Once they would have been lush with native grasses and alfalfa, irrigated, and productive. But as soon as the water was cut off? And without animals to make income? How many other things had Butler let slide before his tax situation forced him to sell? And more to the point, what kind of fool would buy the place knowing it had a toxic weed problem? Cody knew of agricultural properties that had been stricken from the tax rolls because knapweed or spurge had turned them into wasteland.

"Doesn't make sense," he agreed.

"I want to see Butler Ranch," she told him. "Do you know where it is?"

Cody cocked an eyebrow. "Yep. But you're just out of the hospital. It's an hour and a half each way. You sure you ought to spend that many hours bouncing around in a vehicle all the way to Gardiner and back."

"I want to go, John. I'm on administrative leave. All I'm doing here is killing time." She reached out, laid a hand on his. "You were the one who said buffalo people had to be a little more than a half a bubble off plumb. I want to see the place."

Time with Jillian? All to myself?
Damn straight!

CHAPTER FORTY-EIGHT

From inside, Jillian watched Cody pull the big Ram diesel up to the hotel entrance. Then he stepped out and rounded the truck to open the passenger door. She started to take a step. Hesitated as the automatic doors opened. It sent a shiver down her back. Sure, Bozeman PD knew that she was going out. But venturing past the safety of the lobby? Knowing that a shot could come from any direction?

Her skin was crawling as she tucked her coat tight around her; not that woolen fabric offered any more protection than that long-ago blanket had.

Come on!

She forced herself forward. Eyes scanning the mostly empty parking lot.

"You all right?" Cody asked where he held her door, curious tan eyes reading her disquiet.

"It's just weird knowing your truck is sitting where I was shot."

She winced. Pain lanced her chest as she climbed old-woman-like into the seat. Caught her breath and made a face. It eased as she settled into the leather and leaned back.

"Sorry," Cody told her.

"Yeah, it only hurts for a little while," she answered through a grin. Then found the seatbelt, considered how it was going to rest against her broken and bruised ribs, and discarded it as he closed the door.

Looking around, she'd never been in a big four-wheel-drive truck. The cab was roomy, surprisingly plush. She'd figured a ranch truck would be all about dust, worn seats, scattered tools on the dash, and a half-inch of dirt built up on the floor.

Cody crawled into the driver's seat, slipped the big one-ton dually into gear, and she heard the muffled sound of the diesel as the truck accelerated. To her surprise, it rode well. She figured it would be bouncy as all hell and painful.

"Nice truck," she told him.

Cody shot her a sidelong grin, giving her a slight bob of the hat. "Couple of years back, I had a good run at the shows. Prices were up for bison. Had to do something with the income or the taxes would have been terrible. I figured I needed a new truck more than the government needed the money." His gaze narrowed. "Funny thing, the government. Got to have a really good tax accountant, or they'll take everything you've got. Rigged game, you know?"

She adjusted the seat seeking the most comfortable position for her wounded chest.

"You okay?" Cody shot her a worried look as they headed north on 19th.

"Wow. Didn't know the ribs would be so uncomfortable."

"You sure you want to put yourself through this?"

She jerked a hard nod. "I have to see that ranch. Maybe something will pop. Like, of course! That's why people are trying to murder me. Why Banks and Tim Little were killed."

"Glad to be of service." A wry smile. "Especially since you can't drive."

She studied him. "Can I ask a point-blank question?"

"Sure."

"What do you hope to get out of this? Out of me?"

He flicked on the turn signals, timing the green light to accelerate onto the I-90 access ramp. "Honestly, I never felt so comfortable with a woman as I did with you that day at the ranch. Sounds crazy. Even to me. Nothing's happened to change that. I'm not daffy enough to believe in love at first sight, but I'm damned sure smitten. Sort of like you're a puzzle piece that just fits right. Haven't felt that with a woman before."

"Got a lot of experience with women, do you?"

"Not so much. Especially once I took over the ranch. Let's just say I don't get out much."

She stared down at her hands. "John, I'm not who you think I am. I have...well, let's call it..."

"Issues?" he asked softly. "Whatever that soul-wound is that triggers and sends you away?"

"That doesn't bother you?"

He twitched his moustache. "Sure. Makes me mad that someone hurt you bad enough to leave a scar like that. But as long as you're not America's most prolific female serial killer who specializes in men, I'll take my chances." A pause. "Besides, I've got my own demons. We've been over that. I haven't been able to walk away from my parents' murder."

"Unlike me, you're not..." She couldn't finish.

"What?"

"Damaged goods, John. I come with a lot of baggage. The kind that would wreck any kind of relationship with a man. I know men find me attractive, but that's just the wrapping. What's inside is scary as hell."

As they started the climb up through the canyon, Cody cocked his head, one hand on the wheel. "I'm not asking you to make any commitments. I just like spending time with you. Talking. Like we're doing now. Been a long time since I could just enjoy a woman's company. Hell, you might come to the conclusion that I'm just downright rude and intolerable, and you'd be better off spending your time collecting bottle caps or cheese graters. Danny doesn't hesitate to tell me every time she thinks I'm dumber than a fencepost. And, um, she tells me that a lot."

"I don't think you're dumber than a fencepost."

He shot her an almost mischievous grin. "Really? See, my good points are already shining through."

"But, seriously, John, if I have to judge you against a box of rocks, it's going to be a pretty tough choice."

Her repartee drove the grin into a wide smile. "Why, Agent Masterson, I think I have at least a fifty-fifty chance when it comes to outwitting just about any box of rocks you put me up against."

"Guess you think pretty highly of your intellect, don't you?"

"Well, I was smart enough to get you into my truck for the day. Bet there aren't many murder suspects you'll let drive you around southern Montana."

She smiled at that. "No. I guess there aren't. I'm not sure that you're still a suspect. Well, except in Barb Sampson's book. She thinks you're a bit shady and hiding something. Even then, I get the impression she's trending toward dismissing you as the bad guy."

"Good old Sheriff Wain sure has taken a dislike to me. Told me right out that if I wasn't a good and angelic boy, he'd toss my ass in jail for obstruction." A sidelong glance. "Like he had a most definite interest in you."

She nodded. "I'm not sure if it's paternal or something else."

"It's the something else," Cody told her. "When I got my lecture, it was a 'get off my turf' display rather than a 'if you hurt my little girl' warning."

She shook her head. "It never stops. God, I hate men."

"Yeah, as a whole, they're pretty shitty."

At the mock disgust in his voice, she couldn't help smiling.

CHAPTER FORTY-NINE

At the ranch turn off, Cody slowed. To his surprise, the road had been recently plowed. Taking a right off US 89, Cody drove down into the Yellowstone floodplain, winding between stands of narrowleaf cottonwoods, willows, and small groves of spruce to emerge at the old Butler Ranch headquarters.

He glanced at Jillian, seeing that she was looking wan despite having dozed most of the way up from Livingston. Now she peered around, a slightly puzzled look on her face.

The main house came off as dilapidated and worn. In places, the ancient green shingles were aged down to the asphalt to the point they were almost black above the porch and at the ends of the peaked roof. Years of sun and storms had weathered the south-and-west-facing log walls to a light gray and looked to be in need of staining and resealing. Snow had drifted under the windows and onto the porch. So had a collection of tumbleweeds. A couple of the stones in the top of the river-rock chimney needed re-pointing. The windows, however, looked modern, probably having been installed prior to the lawsuit. Behind them, the interior was dark, somehow foreboding. The place reeked of sadness.

"Look." Cody pointed at the sprawling house. "See how the additions have been built on over the years? I'll bet the wiring is old and way out of code. And you can see the logs dipping along the back wall? Means either the foundation's cracked and sinking, or there's rot in the logs."

He turned his attention to the outbuildings. A line of five ten-by-twelve log guest cabins had been built to the west on the terrace just up from the Yellowstone River and protected from the wind by a row of mature spruce trees, their tops bent by the incessant gusts blowing down the canyon. Their tarpaper roofs were all cracked and showing black patches.

On the south, the loafing sheds were blown full of snow and tumbling mustard, but occasional old pieces of rusty machinery could be seen. Some, Cody identified as parts from balers, a derelict irrigation pump, and a stack of old aluminum handline from a sprinkler system. He grimaced at the large rolls of old rusty barbed wire. Lots of them, all coiled up from when the fences had been taken down. Leaned against the wall in the back of the sheds, they reminded him of abandoned wagon wheels without their spokes.

The Cleary metal shop building with its oversized garage door looked to be in good shape and stood on a concrete pad. A couple of cords of cut-and-split firewood were stacked along the north wall and a stovepipe could be seen sticking up through the roof.

The barn, a large two-story structure, maybe forty-by-sixty, showed its age. Set on a stone foundation, rough-cut planks that had once been red were warping and in need of paint. Not only was it faded and peeling, but atop the sliding barn doors, the loft hatch was weathered down to gray wood and seemed to be sagging on its hinges. The metal roof, once galvanized, showed rust and loose panels.

Behind the barn, drifted up, the corrals consisted of splintered gray wood, alleys and pens looking pathetic, and last summer's weeds appeared knee-deep in snow. At one end, the load out was missing boards and a rusted manual squeeze chute and sorting tub looked in need of TLC.

"This would have been worth as much as twenty million?" Jillian mused to herself as she took it all in.

Cody rested a hand on the wheel and gestured toward the surrounding mountains and nearby river with the other. "Maybe more. It's not the buildings, Jill. Look around. The mountains, the Yellowstone River, and there, just north of the barn. See those snow-filled flats? That's some of the best irrigated bottom in Paradise Valley. Check out the stand of willows just below the slope. See the elk? Looks like about twenty head. And down there, maybe a half-mile down the valley, next to the cottonwoods on the riverbank. Those dark dots you see. Those are bison."

"That makes this worth that much money?"

"Uh-huh. The people from back East and out in California who have that kind of wealth wouldn't think twice about it. Location, location, location. Look at the view! The snow-covered peaks. The forested slopes. Yellowstone River fly fishing not a hundred yards from your front door. Sure, they'd bulldoze these old historic buildings. Spend another two or three million constructing a ten-thousand-square-foot mansion, add a fancy equestrian center and arena, maybe a heliport to shorten the transit time from where they've parked the Gulfstream IV. And," he added, "this is as far up the canyon as you can get. Just south of us is the National Park Boundary."

"So?"

"So, when it comes to bragging rights for the super-rich, the farther up the canyon you go, the more rugged it gets, the more valuable the land. Don't believe me? Check the property values on the Snake River in Jackson Hole. The Pitchfork in Greybull Valley, or the Antler Ranch up Wood River. The South Fork of the Shoshone above Cody. Boulder Canyon south of Big Timber. Or think no further than Big Sky south of Bozeman."

She pinched her lip. Considered. "And your Pilot Creek Ranch?"

"Yeah. Same thing." He waved a hand at the dilapidated ranch. "But with this all declared critical habitat? Sure, you could tear the old buildings down and rebuild, but you can't run cattle. Can't fence off those meadows and hay fields for fancy highbred horses. All the grass that grows in these fields? You can't cut and bale it. If you do, you're depriving those elk and bison you see down there of winter graze."

"Then, who'd buy it? Supposedly it sold for a million six."

"Someone who doesn't mind the restrictions. Doesn't want to develop it for commercial property. Doesn't want to subdivide it into a bunch of four or five-acre lots that he could sell for a couple of million each. Someone who isn't worried what the tax burden is, or what the Fish and Wildlife is going to require him to do."

"What about the invasive weeds? How do you tell?"

Cody frowned, lifted his hat to rub where the hard sweatband was biting his forehead. "Well, you can see the kochia, that's the stuff that's all brown and dead next to the barn. As to the fields, you see that slight brown fuzz sticking up through the snow? That might be knapweed or maybe spurge or star thistle. And you can see where the tumbling mustard is piled up against the back of the barn. Not to mention the tumbleweeds on the porch. So, yeah, I think Dan told you the truth."

She pointed. "But there's still elk and bison wintering here. So, it's not all a wasteland."

Cody studied the distant animals. "Nope. Not yet. But weeds 've got a foothold. That hayfield out there should be a pristine white landscape unmarred by weed stems. And if there's cheatgrass started? With just a little bit of drought, it will keep pushing the native grasses out."

He heard the engine getting louder from somewhere behind.

"Truck coming."

Turning, Cody watched as a big metallic red Chevy 3500HD Silverado appeared out of the trees and drove into the yard. The thing looked brand new, shiny, waxed, with lots of chrome gleaming in the winter sunlight. It rode high, oversized custom wheels with aggressive tires under a four-inch lift.

"Guess we'll go say hello," Cody told Jill as he reached for the door handle. "Um, just for shits and grins, let me do the talking."

"Why would I do that?" Jill asked, popping her door. Closed it as the wind tried to rip it away.

"You start off by flashing your credentials..." He shrugged. "If it were me, I'd clam up and be thinking long and hard on that 'whatever you say can and will be used against you' thing."

"Okay, Cody," she told him as she climbed down

gingerly and stepped out into the wind. "Let's see what you've got."

Cody waited until she'd closed her door. Clamped his hat down tight against the wind, shrugged into his coat, got out and walked over to the big shiny Chevy. "Hi there," he called as a man climbed down from the driver's side.

The newcomer looked to be in his late fifties, healthy, tall, clean-shaven, with silver hair slipping out from under a new-looking Scotch cap. He wore an Overland High Country sheepskin coat that looked brand new. Dark brown slacks with a knife-sharp crease were tucked into spotless Corker boots.

The woman climbing down from the passenger side was pulling on a beaver-fur hip-length coat with bone buttons, her head covered with a stylish mink beanie while her long Irish-red hair blew in the wind. Tall, with a model's face and build, Cody almost did a double take.

Something about the two of them... And then it hit him.

Tormey Tanner and Jenn Banks!

"Can I help you?" Tanner asked, stopping a couple of feet away. He was looking Cody up and down, something distasteful in the set of his mouth as he took in the worn and stained Carhartt coat, wash-pale jeans, and scuffed Lucchese boots.

"Just came by to have a word with Dan Butler," Cody told him. "Seen him around? Place looks deserted."

"He doesn't own it anymore," Tanner said shortly. "Sold it last week. Sorry. Is there something I can help you with?"

Cody offered his hand. "Well, then I guess I should say welcome to the neighborhood. I'm Bernard. Got a place just one property removed from yours."

Tanner, to Cody's immense surprise, reached out, shook.

How the hell is it that Tanner doesn't recognize me?

But the billionaire had turned his attention to Jillian, who still stood partially blocked by the Ram's hood, her rich black hair blowing around with each cold gust.

Cody stuck a thumb out. "And that's—"

"Agent Masterson," Jenn Banks called sharply. "Don't say another word, Tanner. They're the police."

Jenn stepped around the Chevy, gaze pinned on Jillian. "Is there a reason you're here, Agent Masterson?"

Jill, hands stuffed in her pockets, tilted her head so the wind flipped her hair out of the way. "We're looking for Dan Butler, Ms. Banks. After closing on the ranch, you wouldn't know where to reach him, would you?"

"No." Jenn took another step. "And this isn't a crime scene. It's private property. Unless you have a warrant, we're asking you to leave. Insisting, actually. Oh, and when it comes to warrants, I don't ever want to see you set foot on private property again unless you have one in your hot little hands."

"And you," Tanner said, a wary narrowing of his eyes as he studied Cody. "I know you. Couldn't place you 'til now. You're that damned buffalo rancher. If you're not off this property in as long as it takes to get your chapped ass in that pickup of yours and drive away, I'm calling the sheriff's and charging you with trespass."

"Yep. Whatever." Cody shrugged, touched the brim of his too-stiff new hat. "If that's how you treat new neighbors, I'm glad we've got most of the Park between your place and mine."

Retreating to the Ram, Jillian was already climbing carefully into the passenger seat. Taking care not to strain her chest. Cody waited until she'd closed her door before climbing into the driver's seat. He pushed the start button, the big Ram rumbling to life.

Then, with a farewell wave to the still-smoldering Jenn and the hard-faced Tanner, Cody shifted into Drive and wheeled wide around the gleaming red Silverado with its fancy wheels and fat tires.

Jillian, clawing at her hair in an attempt to control the wind-tangled black locks, asked, "Tormey Tanner and Jenn Banks? *They* bought Butler ranch?"

"It sure appears that way, doesn't it?"

But when he looked in the mirror, he caught one last glance: Tanner and Jenn Banks were standing there by the Chevy while the wind batted at their clothing. And nothing about the way they watched him leave was friendly.

CHAPTER FIFTY

"It's a whole new layer," Jillian told him. She'd been thoughtful for most to the trip down the valley toward Livingston. "Dan Butler insisted that figuring out who was behind the Butler ranch sale was the key to solving the killings. Ryman's death most certainly benefited Jenn, and by default, as soon as they're married, Tormey Tanner gets half of the Banks house and land."

She tilted her head. "Payback for being screwed out of the house by Ryman's handling of the divorce? Sure, that's motive. Jenn doesn't come across as the forgiving kind."

"But why kill Tim Little, or you for that matter? What does she get out of that?"

"Nothing that I can figure." She frowned at the passing ranches on the broad Yellowstone floodplain, some with millionaire-style homes, others immaculately landscaped billionaire properties with giant custom-built mega homes, designer barns, haystacks, ponds, and miles of brilliant-white picture-perfect country fences.

Cody shifted his grip on the wheel. "Tormey Tanner was at the banquet the night my hat got stolen. He and his pack of PWP cronies left before I did. One of them could have grabbed my hat. Maybe when I went up to the cash bar? Or when I got up to get seconds from the buffet line? People were getting up and down that whole evening."

"Was Jenn there?"

"Nope. And she's the kind who would be noticed. Like today in her beaver coat and chic hat. Never seen her when she didn't look like a cover model on a *Cowboys & Indians* magazine fashion extravaganza. She'd a stood out. Especially among a bunch of working buffaleros in their Levis, Carhartts, Muck Boots and leather vests. Among those guys? High fashion is a new Cinch shirt that's only been through the washing machine six or seven times."

"Were the PWP people sitting close to your table?"

Cody considered. "As I recall, they were clear across the room at a table in back. Like for a fast exit if the conversation turned ugly. It's an uneasy alliance between the PWP and the commercial producers. Granted, we're all into bison. That gives us a shared interest. Not that we all wouldn't like to see ten thousand bison roaming around northern Montana, but the producers want it done responsibly. The way the PWP is trying to do it, they're gonna have a hell of a wreck. It's not if, but when some disease breaks out up there. When that finally happens, there's not a thing they can do to contain it."

"But what would Tanner want with the Butler Ranch?"

"Now there you've got me. He can't run his bison down here. Not with Yellowstone animals already scrambling all over the place. And there's the disease aspect.

Dan Butler used to have game fences around his place to protect his beef. Both the bison and elk here carry bangs, or brucellosis. As high as sixty percent of the bison cows test positive. Not even a manager as clueless at Tanner would expose his animals to brucellosis. The state vet gets involved, the place is immediately quarantined, there's required testing, mandatory culling, it's a real mess."

"Not to mention that US Fish and Wildlife would never give approval, right?"

"Never. They wouldn't want his bison mixing with theirs. Hell, I don't want *my* bison mixing with the park herds, let alone exposed to bangs. That's why my fences are so high at Pilot Creek. It's bad enough in breeding season when one of my bulls spits out a *phisst!* at a Park bull through the fence. Things get a little Western really fast."

"What's *phisst*?"

"Buffalo bulls talk trash to each other. I think the closest translation is 'Your mother has carnal knowledge of sheep.'"

"You're kidding." She was looking at him as if he'd just told her the moon was green.

"Would I lie about a thing like that?" Cody shot her a sidelong glance. "Well, maybe that's not a word-for-word translation, but you get the idea. It's a challenge to combat. And you've never seen rage and power until you watch two of the big boys go at each other. Maybe African elephants in must tear up more scenery, but it's close."

She was silent for a while, watching the road. Finally said, "What about the noxious weeds on the place?"

Cody shrugged, one hand on the wheel. "My bet? Tanner and Banks don't know they've got a problem.

Tanner likes to call himself a rancher, likes to wear the hat and boots, talk about how many head of bison he owns...but that don't make him one."

"And, unfortunately, from the standpoint of the law, just because he bought the Butler Ranch doesn't make him the killer." A beat. "But he sure has the financial wherewithal and resources. I mean, he'd be an idiot if he was the one setting the traps and pulling the triggers."

"You think he's hiring like...a hit man?"

She glanced off at the distant snow-covered fields by the river. "I don't know what I think. Neither Tanner nor Jenn have any motive when it comes to killing Tim Little or me."

"Unless it's to ensure that I take the blame for it." Cody thumped the steering wheel. "And, remember, but for a chance phone call to you, I'd be arrested, charged, and awaiting arraignment. They came that close to making this work."

Jillian nodded absently. "Yeah. Scary as hell to think of, isn't it?"

"So?" Cody shifted in the seat. "the ball is in the bad guy's court. What do you think happens next?"

"Haven't a clue, but whatever it is, assuming I'm still supposed to be the next victim, it will probably be something different than it appears on the surface."

Which was when her phone rang.

"Agent Masterson," she said, placing it to her ear.

Cody could only hear enough of the faint voice over the rumble of the truck to know it was Sheriff Wain.

Jillian's brow lined, and she nodded slightly as she listened. "Bert, we're just north of Livingston." She glanced at Cody. "John, how soon can we be back in Bozeman?"

"Forty minutes?" he guessed.

"'Bout forty minutes." A pause. "Right. I know where it is." Another pause. "See you there, Sheriff," Jillian said, killing the call and placing the phone in her jacket pocket.

"What's up?"

She gave him a worried glance. "They found Dan Butler. He's dead in the Bit 'O Rest Motel. Said it looks like suicide."

CHAPTER FIFTY-ONE

Jillian lowered the Ram's passenger window to flash her credentials to the Bozeman police officer who stood by a city cruiser in the Bit 'O Rest's drive to divert traffic. He waved them on through, and Cody immediately parked in the first open spot, leaving most of the lot for the myriad of police vehicles, vans, and ambulance.

As he shut the Cummins down, she placed a hand on his arm. "You know you'll have to stay in the truck."

He gave her that enigmatic smile that always seemed to light his eyes. "You bet. Go work. I'll be here when you're done."

She popped the door open, eased her way down from the high cab, and felt the little spears of pain her ribs. Breathing shallowly, she wondered if there was any way to put on a coat without extending arms or twisting one's chest, then she gritted her teeth and just did it.

As she walked toward the knot of vehicles clustered outside Room 14, the irony that the numbers skipped from 12 to 14 wasn't lost on her. Whatever. It seemed that calling 13 a 14 hadn't worked out all that well for Dan Butler.

She flipped her credentials at the Bozeman officers who stood in a loose circle behind the vehicles. They nodded, whispers passing between them. While she didn't know most of them, word of her shooting had apparently made her some sort of star as they backed reverently away, some nodding, others touching the brims of their hats. One of the female officers gave her a crooked grin and hearty thumbs up of approval.

Bert Wain, his coat zipped against the cold, stood just outside the door talking to the evidence tech she'd met in Ryman Banks' foyer that day. The tech held a long gun in a plastic evidence bag, the chain of evidence tags clearly marked. The guy looked up, nodded, and Bert turned, a hint of relief in his not-so-florid face. She attributed the pallor to the cold.

"Glad you're here." Bert pointed at the bagged rifle. "We're betting dollars to doughnuts that's the beast that took out Tim Little and blasted your Glock. 6.5 millimeter Creedmoor. It's a Ruger American. Common enough around here. Nothing special about it. Just the sort of rifle a rancher would buy. Affordable, accurate and reliable."

"Where was it?" she asked.

The tech glanced meaningfully at Wain, who nodded dismissal. The tech left, bearing his prize toward the van. Wain, fingers stuck in his duty belt, screwed his face up, and said, "Laying sort of crossways on Butler's belly. Thing is, Butler's thumb was trapped in the trigger guard. Good thing he was tall man, had reach. Somehow he managed to shove the muzzle under his chin. Got that thumb on the trigger, and bam!"

Jillian felt that old flutter of unease tickle her stomach. "Suicide? You're sure?"

"'Bout as sure as we can be at this point. The guy was lying on his back on the floor beside the bed. Just had his pants on. Like he wanted it over with." Bert took a deep breath. "Doc A.C. figures time of death around midnight last night. Said the nature of the contact wound would have muffled the sound of the shot."

"I'd like to see."

Wain's expression worked. "Jill, it's not pretty. That's a high velocity contact wound that—"

"I'm familiar with the forensics of terminal ballistics, Bert. I want to see."

He took a deep breath. "It's not the sort of thing a young woman—"

"Fuck it!" She stepped close. "I'm not your daughter. Stop trying to pull that macho protect-the-innocent-maiden shit, Bert. It's humiliating and insulting. Now, let me pass."

She saw the sudden flash of anger. It ebbed just as fast to embarrassment as he stepped aside, tilting his Stetson to indicate the open door. Adding only, "Don't touch anything."

"Yeah, right," she shot back. "Like I've never worked a crime scene before."

Once inside the room, it was about what she'd expected for a fifty-year-old row motel. Worn recliner beside the window heater, cheap drapes, a queen bed with a cheesy Dacron spread. A battered-looking desk under the wall-mount flatscreen. Freestanding lamp with a tan shade on the bedside table.

A.C. France was reviewing the photos on the back of his Nikon, scrolling from one to the next as he compared them with the body on the floor.

Jillian stepped around the bed, stopped, and swallowed hard. Past A.C. she could see Dan Butler's body. Or she assumed it was him. The top of the head was missing, blown into a chunky spray that stained the carpet and walls beneath the bedside table. The eyes had been popped out of the shattered skull to leave clotted empty orbits. Blood and tissue had shot from the man's nose and the remains of the tongue hung down the cheeks. Even the teeth had been blown out.

She clamped her jaws tight, willing the tunnel vision to expand back to normal. Made herself breathe.

A.C. stood. Gave her a nod. "Agent Masterson, isn't it?"

"Yes."

A.C. indicated the corpse with a tilt of his head. "I'll say this for him, he got it right. Tough to do with rifle. Awkward, you know? Keeping things aligned, that is. Had a case once where a fella took three shots to get it done. Put the muzzle in his mouth and used his big toe. Awkward, like I said. Blew out his left cheek. Somehow he tried again. Took out his right cheek. Then, third time? He got it right and took off the top of his head."

A.C. squinted as he shook his head. "Never could figure out how he could endure the muzzle blast and shock to manage three attempts. Evidence was solid, though. His prints were all over the shotgun just like he would have had to hold it. Lifted a match for the middle of his big toe off the trigger."

She let him pass, staring down at the human wreckage on the floor. Alone in the room now, she told the corpse, "Sorry, Dan. Went to the ranch today. Met Tormey Tanner and Jenn Banks there. You said that figuring out who bought the ranch would break the case. Well, we know. And things are just as muddled as before."

She remembered that man who'd sat next to her. How he'd said he was off to live somewhere warm. How he had enough.

She took in his bare feet and torso. His left arm flopped wide, the right bent, fingers clenched, the thumb stuck out curiously in rigor.

"So, did you do it? Set that trap for Ryman? Put a bullet in Tim Little that night in the booth while he sat across from me? Was it you who came within an inch of shooting me dead?"

Why?

To frame John Cody for the crime.

That implied he had a reason to take Cody down. But to date, both men were on the same side. Besides, the man she'd sat next to hadn't come across as the kind who'd plot and hatch such elaborate schemes. He'd been an old-time hard-boiled crusty Montana rancher. The same guy who'd started into ICoHR's offices with a shotgun to settle the score.

"But I'm supposed to believe you killed yourself," she whispered to the body. "Just couldn't live with the loss of your ranch. Drowning in guilt over the crimes you'd committed."

That man who'd looked at her with steely gray eyes? Who'd dared to walk right past the Bozeman Police he knew were waiting outside the hotel?

She felt more than heard Bert Wain enter. Heard him say, "Looks like it's over, Jill. Maybe it wasn't fair, him losing that ranch. But sometimes, you take away all a man has, he snaps. Turns into someone you never thought he could be."

"And sometimes, hard knocks or not, Sheriff, people are exactly who they have to be." She thought of the expression on her father's face. Heard Uncle's head smashing through the glass and the plates and cups raining down. The terror in Uncle's eyes...

CHAPTER FIFTY-TWO

I n the quiet of her Billings apartment, Jillian sipped at her cup of tea and sat back in her dining room chair. Didn't matter what posture she adopted, after a couple of seconds, her chest started hurting. On her laptop screen, Governor Brewster and Supervisor Gaylen Meyer split the monitor. Placing the tea back on her small table, she heard the familiar hum of her refrigerator as it kicked on. Outside, the sound of traffic was a low murmur on 32nd Street West.

"It's cut and dried, sir," she said. "The Ruger rifle found on Dan Butler's chest, the cartridges in the magazine, and the bullet fragments recovered from my wounds and the slug that killed Tim Little are a match."

Governor Brewster had a contented curl to his lips, his eyes narrowing and glinting. Something about it irritated Jillian. Like the man was fighting to suppress a look of total satisfaction. That it would be over the tragic end of a rancher's life and the murder of so many people indicated something really creepy about Brewster.

"*Good job, Jillian,*" Supervisor Meyer told her. "*Your*

contributions to this case are noted. Um, has Sheriff Wain been in touch?"

"He has." Jillian stiffened, fought the urge to gasp. Shifted to favor her left side. Hurt as it might, it beat being dead.

"I think he wants to offer you a job. You going to take it?"

"No, sir. I like my position with the DOJ." She'd treated the good sheriff most professionally. Yes, it had been a good offer, but she suspected that it came with strings, the kind she didn't care to embrace. God, what was it about men?

Brewster, almost chortling, said, *"I can't tell you how delighted I am, Agent Masterson. You've done the state a wonderful service, and at great risk to yourself."* To Meyers, he said, *"I'd like to see Agent Masterson bumped up a pay grade. What do you say, Gaylen?"*

Jillian saw the sudden flash of reserve behind her boss's eyes. *"It's your call, sir."*

What was that all about?

"Then a pay raise it is! And, Supervisor, please credit this entire investigation to the agent. She did a superior bit of work breaking this case."

"But, sir," Jillian started to protest.

Brewster raised a stalling hand. *"Now, now, Agent Masterson. Humility is always an asset in one of my people, but never contradict the boss!"* The governor flicked his fingers in a sort of salute, finishing with, *"Good day to you both."*

The governor's image went dark, Supervisor Meyer's curiously pinched expression remaining.

"I didn't break this case, Supervisor. If anyone deserves the credit, it's the Gallatin Country SO, Bert Wain, and his techs. I can't take credit for this." She squinted an eye, struggling for words. "Not to mention..."

"Yes?" Meyer seemed to be waiting in anticipation.

"It doesn't feel right, sir."

"How so?"

"It's like a jigsaw puzzle where the pieces all fit together, but the picture is wrong." She tilted her head back, staring around her neat and almost-never-used apartment kitchen. "Sure, we've got the evidence. Dan Butler's prints were found all over the rifle and ammunition. Granted. But..."

She shook her head. "I don't believe the man I talked to at the hotel that night killed himself. That Dan Butler was..." She gestured her frustration.

"Go ahead." Meyer's gaze had sharpened.

"I guess I'd say beaten but not broken." She fished for words. "Does that make sense?"

He gave a slow nod. *"It does. But there's a lot about this case that doesn't."*

"Agreed. What about the ranch sale? Who bought the place, and what were Tormey Tanner and Jen Banks doing out there?"

"At your suggestion, we looked into that. It's an investment company with environmental roots. Apparently they're in the process of filing a series of applications with the county for something called a conservation development. No clue what that means. If what the governor tells me is correct, Tanner was out there to offer his input to the permitting and development plan. Oh, and Butler's suicide saved you one hell of a butt chewing from the governor for setting foot out there in the first place."

"It's a loose end, sir."

"Sheriff Wain's closing the books on it. The governor considers it closed as well."

"Is it closed, sir?"

Meyer lowered his gaze, seemed to be studying his hands where they were clasped before him. *"Jillian, don't go chasing your tail around in circles. Daniel Butler certainly had all the motive in the world. That court ruling destroyed his life, and it was Ryman Banks' case with Tim Little's expert testimony to back it up. Maybe Butler really was thinking of running when he met with you that night. Maybe he looked you in the eyes. Realized that, but for chance, he'd have killed you, too. That it was all getting out of hand. Once he got back to that motel, it all caught up with him, came crashing down, and he took that rifle and killed himself before he could be caught with it? The human mind works in odd ways sometimes."*

"Then, what reason would he have to meet me face-to-face? I didn't see my killer reflected in that man's eyes. Didn't see guilt. Didn't see curiosity. And try and figure it as I might, I still can't find motive for taking me out."

"He was setting John Cody up for the fall, remember? Butler had a lot of time to think about how he was going to get even with ICoRH."

"Maybe. Someone had to steal Cody's hat and place it at the scene. But why would Butler choose Cody?"

"He knew that Cody was perfect for the fall guy?" Meyer shrugged. *"Jill, don't torture yourself over this. If people acted logically, let alone altruistically and rationally, we'd be out of a job. Trust me, not all cases are tied up with a nice neat big red bow. There are always inconsistencies, things that, unless you're the killer, don't make sense."* A pause. *"There's no telling what was going on in Butler's head. You hear me?"*

"Yes, sir." She took a breath to composer herself and nodded. "Am I still on administrative leave?"

"You are."

"Now that John Cody's cleared, can you get a release for his personal items?"

"Sure. I'll see to it." Meyer smiled at her. *"Now, get some well-deserved rest, Jillian. Oh, and this time I mean it, stay out of trouble."*

Right. There were always inconsistencies.

She'd just have to live with that.

CHAPTER FIFTY-THREE

Cody glanced up at the gray and low-scudding clouds. All morning the wind had been gusting down the canyon from the northwest. Big fluffy flakes of snow were drifting down as he leaned on the catch-pen panels. He'd managed to capture a couple cows and a few heifers and calves in the catch pen contiguous to the corrals. A place where there was plenty of room and no one could get trapped. That morning he'd turned Rumbler and the two yearling heifers in with them. There had been the usual sniffing, dodging and getting acquainted. Bison, unlike cattle, had to be eased into a new herd. Introduced to a few head at a time to avoid fights and dominance displays that often times could become deadly.

He'd tried with 208, the two-year-old bred heifer, but she'd gone bat-shit crazy when he placed her in a holding pen with Honeysuckle, one of his older cows. Honeysuckle, outweighing 208 by close to five hundred pounds—not to mention being a dominant female—had easily put 208 in her place. It should have ended there.

Order established. But 208, instead of settling down, had started racing from one side of the pen to the other, bashing into the panels.

Cody had turned her back into the alley, let her retreat to the pen she'd first occupied.

Didn't make sense. Just wasn't buffalo behavior.

He shot a look back over his shoulder at 208 where she stood with her butt wedged in the back of her pen. The heifer kept licking her nose, huffing condensed breath, her hard hot gaze fixed on him as if he were the devil incarnate and source of all evil in the universe.

Cody opened the gate to the holding pen and let Honeysuckle trot past on her way to the herd. Then he walked down and closed the gate behind her.

What to do about 208? He was considering that, keeping track of where Rumbler, the heifers and calves, and the other cow were all grazing peacefully in the catch pen. Buffalo being buffalo. 208 could see them. That alone should have calmed her down.

The big flakes were falling faster now, swirling down to whiten his shoulders and hat. The weather guessers had said this would be a major storm. Issued travel advisories and winter storm warnings. As for the Upper Clarks Fork? Who knew? This was high country. It worked on laws all its own.

Cody stopped at 208's pen, started through the falling snow to meet the heifer's gleaming black eyes. "What the hell did that bunch do to you, girl? You're home now. No one is going to hurt you, and you can't fight for the rest of your life."

In answer, 208 made a false leap, tail up, head down, landing with a threat-grunt, her front feet together, as if to stomp him into the ground.

"Okay," he told her, backing away from the gate. "Have it your way."

Puzzled, he made his way out of the corrals, closing the gate behind him. He was halfway across the yard. Stopped. Staring up at the thickly falling snow, he listened to the silence. Magic happened when it snowed like this. Like a million feathers cascading down. The stillness so intense he could hear the soft rustling patter of the giant flakes hitting the ground, landing on his hat.

And then the sound of a motor.

Not a truck, but a car. And it was getting louder until he could hear the snow crunching as it turned down his road. Sure enough, he caught glimpses of headlights through the trees.

A snowy light-green Subaru Outback emerged from the drive, wipers on fast, and rolled its way through the snow to where he stood. He craned his head, peering through the windshield as the car stopped. Heard it shift into park, and the driver killed the ignition.

"Jill?" he asked as she popped the door, swung her feet out, and slowly stood.

"Hey, John." She was smiling, the first flakes of snow landing on her raven hair. "Got something for you. Open the passenger door."

He walked over, opened the door, and found his old black hat on the seat. "I'll be damned. How'd you get it?"

"Case is closed. I had Sheriff Wain clear it from evidence. As to how it got to be in Ryman Banks' foyer? Guess we'll never know."

He walked over to where she was standing, reached out and placed the old hat on her head against the falling flakes. "There. Looks good. But, glad as I am to see you, what are you doing here?"

She was studying him through shy and almost reserved eyes. "I'm on leave. All it took was a couple of days at home, and I'm climbing the walls." A slight shrug, accompanied by a pinch of the lips. "Barb Sampson dropped the hat off last night while she was in Billings for a medical appointment. I thought, what the hell, I'd just drive it down."

"You know it's supposed to snow like a bloody bastard, right?"

She glanced up at the falling flakes, the brim of the hat already sheathed in white. "Yeah, well, I didn't think it would be this bad. Couple of times in the last half hour, I was thinking maybe I'd made a mistake."

He glanced at her tires. "Um, you came up here on bald tires?"

She followed his gaze. "I've been meaning to get those changed. Then there was this case that cropped up. Sort of distracted me."

Cody gave her a lopsided smile. "Got time for a cup of coffee? My kitchen's always got a place for you."

"Thought you'd never ask." She started for the house, matching step. "Where's Danny?"

"Off to the Rez. Some kind of trouble with her niece. Shoshoni side of the family. Said it might be a couple of days. Maybe more." He inclined his head. "How's your wound?"

"Hurts." A flicker of smile crossed her lips. "Periodically, I move just wrong. Stitches come out next week." A pause. "But, John, it sure beats the alternatives."

He kicked the snow from the step as he helped her up to the porch. Stomped the white stuff from his packs and beat the inch-and-half of snow from his hat before he opened the door. Then he slipped out of his buffalo coat and slapped the snow off it. She'd stopped to stare at the fire, burned down now. He hung his hat and coat, then helped her out of hers before hanging everything under the old Marlin lever action to drip.

He studied the old hat thoughtfully. "Yep. See the place where old Night Rain blew bloody snot all over? What the hat didn't catch ended up in my face. Still, she won her class, helped win the ranch the Classic Producer trophy in Rapid City that year."

Her eyes had taken on a dark reserve. "Bloody snot. Of course. You'd be surprised what other horrible things are on that hat." An eyebrow lifted. "And I let you put it on my head?"

He led her into the kitchen, pulled out a chair, and stepped to the coffee machine. Loved the fact that he could glance sideways and see her reflected in the mirror. Wondered what a gift it would be to see her there for the rest of his life.

"Guess you got your wish," she told him as she eased into the chair. "Everything points to Dan Butler as the perp. Hard to think he sat there, right next to me just days after he tried to kill me. What kind of brain works like that?"

"You sure he did it?" Cody asked softly, placing a cup under the dispenser as the Capresso heated.

He felt her eyes burning into the back of his head as he pushed the brew button and the machine whirred.

At her deep sigh, he turned. Her gaze had gone distant, a slight shake of her head shifting the raven locks spilling over her shoulders. "Everything's cut and dried. That Ruger rifle killed Tim Little, and but for a bit of luck...?" She shivered, winced, and barely stopped from touching her side. "John, his prints were all over it. Same with the ammunition. 6.5 Creedmoor like they dug out of my side."

He placed her coffee on the table before her. "Funny,

isn't it? I heard there wasn't a single print on the shotgun that took out Ryman. Not a single clue anywhere. No fibers. No hairs. It's all meticulous until poor old Dan decides to kill himself. Then, all of a sudden, he doesn't care?"

He made his own coffee and seated himself across from her. Her eyes were on the mirror, its reflection filled with the curtains of falling snow obscuring the mountains outside.

"My boss told me not to chase my tail in circles over the little bits that didn't make sense." She sipped the coffee. "I liked to think of the case like an onion, but when I got to the middle and found Dan Butler, it was somehow brown and rotten."

Cody sipped his own brew. "Saw on the news that you're the hero of the day up there."

Her lips pursed, again the distant gaze, "Had a long talk with Barb Sampson about that when she dropped your hat off. It's like I'm the opposite of a scapegoat, but instead of taking the blame, they're pushing the credit into my lap. Making me into someone I'm not. Governor's behind it, I think."

"Politics?"

"Or misdirection." She said it absently, then cued. "Where did that come from? Just popped out of my head. Why?"

"What would Brewster care about misdirection? He's got a year before he's running for re-election."

The dark reserve was back. "Hell, I don't know. Not sure what to think anymore. Maybe that's why I'm down here. I needed to be with someone who wasn't fawning, sulking, or preening. Everyone's acting differently around me these days. I just need honesty."

"And I thought you only came down for the coffee."

He gave her a wink. "It's all right, Jill. Take a load off. There's no judgment here. You can just be yourself."

A flicker of smile died on her lips. "Oh, sure, John. Which part of myself should I be? The insecure out-of-her-league newbie with no self-confidence, or the one with nightmares and flashbacks who wakes up shivering on the floor under the bed the next morning?"

A gust of wind roared through the trees, pattered snow against the kitchen window. Cody turned in his seat, watching the wall of white blow down around the eaves. "Jill? That's whiteout. You ask me, the last thing you should be considering is trying to drive out of here on four bald tires."

She arched a slim eyebrow. "And what are you suggesting?"

He gave her grin, and said, "How about hot chocolate and peppermint schnapps in front of the fire? I'll have to change the sheets first, but you can have the folks' bedroom."

"And where will you sleep?"

"My room. Just like always." He paused. "Funny. Never could talk myself into moving into that big room."

Another gust rasped and whistled around the logs, a curl of snow dancing past the window.

"Hot chocolate and schnapps in front of the fire, huh?" She took a deep breath, winced as if it caught her healing ribs just wrong. "Guess that wouldn't be so bad."

CHAPTER FIFTY-FOUR

"**S**hhh! Don't make a sound."

Uncle's voice sent a tremor through her. Painful.

"Now, be my precious little girl," Uncle cooed.

Jillian gasped, the pain stabbing her chest, but not so bad as the fear of what was coming.

"Let's play our special little game." The words were so soothing...so frightening.

Jillian huddled against herself, whimpering, "No. No. No. Please!"

"There's my good girl. And when Uncle's done, he'll give you a treat."

She felt the blanket being pulled back, the cold air on her body.

"Please! Please!" She jammed knuckles into her mouth to stifle the scream that...

"Jillian? Jillian! It's okay."

"No. Please. Don't!"

"Jillian? You're safe. Safe. You hear?"

"I'm a good girl. Please. I'll be a good girl."

"Jill! Damn it! Wake up!"

The dream flickered, faded as Jillian blinked her eyes open. She was panting, the cold sweat chill on her body. When did she get so cold?

She didn't recognize the hard floor she lay on. Wood plank. Her body was curled on an old Navajo blanket, her knees tight against her throbbing chest. A strange chest of drawers stood against a log wall not three feet in front of her.

"Jill? You okay?"

She jerked, Uncle's voice mixing with the man's.

"Please?" she implored. "Don't..."

Feet shuffled to one side.

She glanced up, froze. John Cody, wearing only blue jeans, leaned over her. A bed was behind her, sheets trailing to the floor. Bright light blazed down from a fixture in the wooden ceiling above Cody's looming head. Images of Uncle flashed in her mind. Reaching out, like Cody now reached out.

"Here," Cody's soft voice said. "Let me help you up."

Uncle's hand on her arm, rough, callused.

She trembled at Cody's touch. "No!"

Then Cody was crouched down, eyes concerned. "It's a dream, Jill. A flashback. You're at Pilot Creek Ranch. You're safe."

She sucked a half-panicked breath, shook her head. "God, it's always so real."

Cody nodded, his light brown hair and dark beard haloed by the overhead light. "Yeah. I can tell." Again he reached out. "Here. Take my hand. Let me help you up."

She gasped at the pain as she unfolded herself and sat up. "Damn! My ribs..."

"Yeah. Easy now."

That's when it hit her. The old, oversized T-shirt he'd given her to sleep in was wadded up around her midriff.

Everything below was bare. "Oh, God. I don't believe this is happening."

But she let him help her to feet. Pulled the T-shirt down to cover herself. The shivers really set in as the chill took over. Played hell with her throbbing ribs.

"Why don't you climb under the covers?" he told her. "I'll be back with a cup of something warm."

"I'm so sorry." The horror of it, the humiliation and embarrassment... "I need to find my things. I have to go home."

Cody, eyes kind and knowing, shook his head. "It's still blowing a gale out there. On those tires, I doubt you'd make it out of the yard. Come on. Let's get you warmed up."

"God, John. I... I'm so...I just need to get out of here."

"What happened to Uncle?" he asked gently.

She hesitated, finally exhaled the words. "Dad...beat him to death. And I... I..."

She pushed past him, found her clothes at the foot of the bed. Still shivering, she grabbed up her panties, started to pull the on, and glared at him. "Do you want to get out of here so I can get dressed?"

Instead, he seated himself on the edge of the rumpled bed, arms crossed. "So, what do you do at home when you have a night like this?"

"I sit up for the rest of the night cradling my gun to my chest, okay?" she snapped as she pulled on her panties. "There, now you know just how fucked-up I really am."

He nodded, reaching up to pull sagaciously at his beard. "It's said that God created man, but it was Smith & Wesson who finally made women equal. Sounds good to me."

Seeing that he wasn't leaving, she tugged on her pants. Reached for where she'd left her bra and shirt. Figured to hell with the bra and pulled her shirt on over Cody's baggy T-shirt. Slipping her boots on, she grabbed up her purse and headed for the door.

He followed her down the hall, flicking on the lights, and then finally to the front door where her coat hung on the rack amidst hats and coats beneath the old Marlin lever-action rifle.

He said, "I wish you wouldn't do this," as she tugged her coat on and opened the door. The cold hit her like a right hook, snow pattering wetly on her face. Despite the yard light, she could barely see her Subaru through the blizzard—a mere mound in a world of swirling white.

"Oh, hell," she whispered in defeat.

Cody gently closed the door, a wry glint to his eyes. "Come on. Let's put you back to bed. And how about this? I'll loan you a pistol to tuck close, and for added protection, I'll stay with you. Stand guard. Just like I did at the hospital. Deal?"

Jillian closed her eyes, a feeling of absolute defeat and humiliation sucking at her guts. She felt the tears break past her lids to trace down her cheeks. "Why are you doing this?'

"I guess because I really like you. Tonight? Sitting by the fire, sipping cocoa? That was the best night I've ever had. I could do that. Every night. Just sit and watch the light in your hair. See the sparkle in your eyes."

"Then pick me up naked and screaming from the floor?"

She opened her eyes to see his questioning tilt of the head as he said, "Maybe, if you knew you were safe and loved, those dreams could be replaced by something better."

"You're a lunatic, John Cody."

But she let him lead her back to the bedroom. And, yes, he did just as he said. Gave her a big Smith & Wesson .44 and sat there propped up against the headboard as she slept.

Which she did.

The rest of the night through.

CHAPTER FIFTY-FIVE

That morning over breakfast, while snow continued to fall, Cody had mentioned going out to "cake" the buffalo. So, Jillian now found herself wrapped in a real honest-to-God buffalo coat, riding around in a ratty old wreck of a 1995 Dodge 2500 flatbed with a large white metal hopper on the back. By pushing a button, an auger shot out pellets: half-inch-by-three-inch cylinders of compressed double-molasses-injected twelve-percent-protein plant matter. With all four tires chained up, they idled their way across the winter pasture, the bison swarming around, bounding and snuffling in apparent joy. To Jillian it was sheer magic.

Bison were nothing like beef cattle. They charged each other, leaped, danced, and milled in an athletic way cattle couldn't have dreamed of. She'd never have believed the big animals could have been so fast, so nimble on their feet. And there was a definite pecking order.

"The cake has molasses, and buffalo have a major sweet tooth," Cody told her as she snuggled in the buffalo coat. She had to. The passenger-side window was stuck at halfway, so the six-below air was nipping at her nose.

"Seriously?"

"Like kids at a candy store." He pointed at a large cow that dashed at two others who were snuffling in the snow for cake. "See her? That's Saky, short for Sacajawea. She's the lead cow, just turned twenty. Three of her daughters have won grand champion female at the national Gold Trophy Show and Sale. She runs the ranch. And that cow there, the one with the blue ear tag? That's Pepper. She's number two and Saky's best friend. One of her bull calves was grand champion at Dakota Territory and helped win us the producer of the year award."

"What about the bulls?"

"The big old guys, like Smoke and Red Stone, are out in the river pasture. After about age eight, they become what we call bachelors and value their own company. But come breeding season, they'll be back. Knock these younger guys, including Rumbler, here, out of the way. It's the old dominant cows who are the heart of the herd. Lot of these new producers, the ones just getting into the business? They'll sell off their older cows like they do in the cattle industry. It's a mistake. These are bison; they live to be twenty-five and these old cows set the standard for behavior for the rest of the herd. If the old cows are mellow, don't get excited, the younger animals won't either."

She hugged the coat tighter, wondering at how warm she felt. That morning Cody had emerged from a back room, handing it to her and saying, "Here, you'll need this. It was mom's. Looks to be around your size."

She'd tried it on, feeling oddly humbled and honored, and, sure enough she was warm and toasty even though the truck's heater didn't work and the snowflakes that blew in from the open window coated the sleeves in white.

She asked, "What about this purity thing? Carly Joyner kept harping on that."

Cody pointed to a stunning-looking cow, dark with a forward hump and long shaggy hair on her shoulders and front legs. "That's Brionna. She won grand champion female as a bred two at Agribition in Canada a couple of years back."

"She's beautiful."

"She's what they call a woods-cross. Turns out she had two of Tim Little's "cattle" genes when Danny and I tested her. About half of the animals you see would qualify for killing based on Little's TGS test. The other half passed Little's genetics test. Now, looking at them, can you tell the difference?"

"No."

"Neither can anyone else. Including the other TGS companies."

Cody hit the button to dispense more cake, before adding, "You know, when you think about it, it's sort of like the Nazis. How much Jewish blood could a person have before they were sent to the gas chambers? Was one distant great-great-great-great grandmother enough? In the case of bison? Just one beef gene condemned thousands of buffalo to death."

She was considering that when Cody called, "Hey! Look! It's Buttercup!"

"Buttercup?"

"Yeah! She's a bottle baby. Want to pet a buffalo?"

Jillian fixed on the rambunctious bison knocking each other out of the way for cake. A human would be flattened like a pancake. "Are you out of your mind?"

Cody flipped the steering wheel, heading back to the

corrals as he leaned his head out the driver's side window calling, "Come on, Buttercup. Come get your cake."

Jillian craned her neck, watching the cow bounding along beside the truck. The other bison were still milling around where Cody had left a line of cake.

At the gate to the corrals, Cody stopped the truck, saying, "It's all right. We can get out now. Buttercup won't hurt you. At least, not on purpose. Sometimes she doesn't know her own strength, and if other bison are around, sometimes she has to get away from a dominant animal. Fast. So don't be in her way."

"Right." Jillian reached for the door handle, brought a stitch to her damaged ribs as she wrenched on the mechanism, but the door sprang free. She walked tenuously around the front of the dented old truck to where Cody was standing by the hopper, feeding cake pellets to the bison cow who was almost as tall as he was. She'd never been this close. Never realized just how big a buffalo was. And Buttercup was eyeing Jillian as she crunched the last pellet Cody had given her. A silver line of drool leaked from Buttercup's lips.

"Here," Cody told Jill, handing a couple of pellets. Jillian felt her heart thump as she tentatively extended a hand, was surprised by Buttercup's gooey tongue as it curled around the cake and snaked it into her mouth to crunch.

For Jillian, the moment was amazing. She fed another cake, awed to look into Buttercup's gleaming eyes, seeing flecks of blue amidst the brown irises. Then she extended her hand, touching the wiry black hair, feeling how firm and thick it was. For his part, Cody was smiling, one hand on Buttercup's muscular shoulder. As if the man was absorbing Jillian's wonder.

"Buttercup," he told the buffalo as he fed another pellet, "this is Jillian. She's a special friend of mine."

"It's not a dream. I'm really here," Jillian said softly. "My God, I'm petting a buffalo." She ran her fingers through the thick fur, awed at how the snow mounded on Buttercup's back, totally insulated.

Cody glanced back. "The herd's coming. Better get back in the truck before they get here."

Jillian forced herself to move, feeling almost trance-like as she walked to her door, clamped a jaw against her tender ribs, and climbed in. Once seated, she pulled the door closed as the first of the cows arrived. And, true to Cody's prediction, Saky made a leap at Buttercup, who, quick as a flash, skipped sideways and away through the space where Jillian would have been standing.

"What do you think?" Cody asked, an arm resting on the steering wheel.

"I think I'm in heaven. What comes next?"

"Want to help me check the perimeter fence? Means a little ride on a snowmobile."

"Can I wear this buffalo coat?"

His smile was the only answer as he pushed in the clutch and shifted the old Dodge into first gear.

CHAPTER FIFTY-SIX

I t took two days before the highway department opened the road to the Upper Clark's Fork past the town of Crandall. Seeley had postponed his trip to keep an eye on the news. As usual, stories about Dan Butler, the sensational murders, and what it all meant faded away to new and more salacious news. Seeley, having had no more notices from the client, figured it was time. He packed his truck. Left his house at three that cold and clear morning, tires crunching in the virgin snow covering his drive.

His destination was the parking area the plows kept open for the snowmobilers and cross-country skiers to access trails over The Plug from the Wyoming state line to the Montana town of Cooke City.

The ferocious storm that had blanketed the mountains for two days had left White Mountain and the Cathedral Cliffs looking like a magical wonderland in the moonlight. Below Beartooth Butte, snow-rimed trees and splendid crags were gilded in blazing white. Soft meadows of unbroken and drifted snow shone in the predawn. All in all, well over a foot had fallen in the valley bottom, more on the towering heights to either side.

Just to be safe, Seeley timed his arrival at The Plug to just before sunrise. In the dawn sky—glowing a mystical purple, orange, and indigo—the last stars struggled against the growing radiance. He wheeled the F 150 into the plowed lot, parking beside the high snow berm. Closer to the trailheads, other vehicles, snow-covered, along with empty snow-machine trailers waited for their owners to return.

Seeley stepped out in the predawn, watched his breath condense and slowly rise in the still air. Then he reached in the back seat for his insulated white snowsuit. Slipping it on, he pulled the hood up, snapping it tight around his face. The white balaclava he used to cover his nose and mouth. Finally, he reached his cross-country skis out of the F 150's pickup bed and snapped the bindings closed on his boots. Tugging his thick gloves on, he slung his pack onto his back. Took one last look around to ensure no one was watching and withdrew his Gunwerks Nexis rifle chambered in 6.5 PRC. This he slung over his shoulder. Side-stepping, he climbed awkwardly over the piled snow berm and down the other side to the new-fallen powder. Minutes later, he was hidden by the trees.

Damn! He loved hunting in the depths of winter. And this would be so much more satisfying than poaching. Dumb animals never had a chance. But humans? Oh, yes, the most dangerous game. Not that Seeley Atherton would ever give John Cody so much as a hint before the bullet blew him away.

The client hadn't made his wishes known one way or the other, but this thing with John Cody? It was personal.

The guy had thrown sand in the works too many times. Not just with the hearings, the fund raising, and legal testimonies, but he'd kept Seeley from finishing what he'd started with Agent Masterson. Slipped out from under the legal wrap Seeley had so cunning laid to trap him. And, on top of it all, the son of a bitch and his polluted half-breed bison sat blocking access that would allow true bison to expand their range down the Clarks Fork Valley.

"Sorry, you piece of shit," Seeley muttered, breath frosting the outside of the balaclava. "Bet you're gonna wish you'd spent the rest of your life in jail. Would'a beat ending up dead."

CHAPTER FIFTY-SEVEN

Jillian blinked awake and stared up at the now-familiar ceiling, aware that the first light was graying the ranch yard beyond the bedroom window. She eased herself around to find the bed empty. Cody was already up. Probably had breakfast started.

"So, Jillian," she asked herself. "What the hell are you doing?"

Some sort of a decision was coming due. What had originally been planned to be a down-and-back trip to deliver Cody's hat had turned into three days and nights. Somehow, from Cody sleeping atop the covers, keeping guard, he'd ended up under them. And last night, she'd awakened to find herself sleeping with him spooned around her. Warm. Safe.

I slept the whole night through.

That realization shook her.

As did both the trepidation and fear that if she didn't stop this, he would want to cross that final boundary. And then what? On the few occasions she'd tried to have sex with a man, to prove that she was normal, all had ended in disaster. The first time, she'd frozen, every muscle knotted and tense. Like she was a paralyzed. The other times, she'd ended in tears, just lying there as she chewed on her knuckles and endured.

Maybe her brain might be terrified, but the cravings in her traitorous body sure weren't.

She eased out of bed, slipped off the big T shirt and dressed carefully. In the bedroom mirror she could see that the bruise was fading. Not that she was any judge, but the sutures where they'd removed bullet fragments looked like they could come out.

"I could do that for you," Cody had told her. What set her back was that he wasn't kidding. That he'd taken them out of bison, out of Danny, and even himself more than once.

Backcountry ranchers, she was discovering, were a breed unto themselves.

She wandered into the kitchen, smelling bison sausage and cooking pinto beans simmering in a red chili sauce. "Smells heavenly."

"How'd you sleep?" Cody asked from where he stood over the stove, a spatula in hand. After stirring the beans, he cracked a couple of eggs and dropped them into the mess.

"Straight through." She stopped, quizzical. "Did you give me the gun last night?"

He shot her a measuring look. "You didn't ask for it."

"Son of a bitch," she whispered, stepping over to the coffee machine to place a cup, and push the button. After filling the cup, she seated herself at the table to stare at the mirror. Beyond the yard, the trees where heavy with snow, the forest and slope beyond looking like montane wonder.

With the spatula, Cody removed the sausages then spooned the beans and eggs to cover them. With a flourish, he placed the plates on the table. Toeing the chair out, he seated himself and handed her a fork.

"You and I have to talk," she told him, then took the first bite. "God, that's good!"

"Growing up in Texas, you learn to cook." He arched an eyebrow. "What are we talking about?"

"Danny's coming back today. The road's open. I should be going home."

His tan eyes had taken on that evaluative gaze. "Sore after yesterday? I was afraid checking fence on the snow machine might have pushed your ribs too hard."

She smiled. "No. That was a blast. That's the problem. Every day has been great. Driving the cake truck through the bison? Seeing them frolic and chase each other? That was magic. Never been that close to buffalo! Watching you work with 208. I mean, wow. Even if she's still trying to kill you. It's... It's..."

"What?"

"Is trying to fix broken females a hobby of yours?"

He chuckled, took another bite of beans. "Maybe. She's a lot like you. Did you watch her yesterday? It's me that she's got it out for. Surprised me. She seemed to know that you weren't a threat." He gestured with his fork. "That tells me that it was a man who made her hate people."

"Bison know the difference?"

"You bet. Sometimes it can come down to the color of a hat, the way someone walks, and there's a host of other signals, smells, sounds. They know and they remember."

She frowned, stirred her egg, seeing that he'd left the

yoke half runny. "John, if I don't leave now... I mean, you and I..."

"Then don't go."

She stared him hard in the eyes. "We're sleeping in the same bed. One of these nights..."

He shrugged. "Whatever. I'm happy to just hold you. Nothing else implied or expected."

"No urges?"

"That's what rolling over on my other side is for."

She closed her eyes, leaned her head back. "There you go again! Making it so hard."

"That's why I roll over."

"I *meant* that you make leaving hard. Why can't you be an asshole like every other man? Then it would be easy."

He placed a hand on hers, that smile bending his beard around. "These are some of the happiest days of my life. But—pay attention here—whatever you need to do for yourself, to find yourself, come to grips, or whatever, do it. Go back to Billings if you think you need to. Stay here and help me with the bison. Whatever you need. I'm for it."

She shook her head. "What is it with you?"

"You just seem to fit, is all. Like you're a part of me I didn't know was missing."

"Yeah." She took another bite of sausage then pushed the plate back. "That seems to sum it up, doesn't it? Listen. I'm going for a walk. I need to get my head straight before I do something dumb."

He nodded, lips pursed. "See you when you get back. Oh, and don't take any chances with the bison. Remember what we talked about?"

"Yes, John. They're still wild animals." She stood.

"Sometimes I wish I was, too. Maybe then I'd know what I wanted out of life."

CHAPTER FIFTY-EIGHT

The fence had a been a pain in the ass until Seeley figured out how to use the long rifle barrel short the hot wires against the ground wire. Wiggled his way through the high-tensile wires, and then carefully snaked the Nexus between the wires without shocking himself.

Someone had passed recently on a snowmobile. He stepped onto his skis and refastened the bindings before setting off through the trees.

That had been just after sunrise.

Now he lay just where he wanted to be, beneath the low-spreading branches of a spruce tree. His white insulated suit blended with the snow; the branches broke up his silhouette. From his vantage, he could see the ranch house below not one hundred yards across the snowy flat. His pack braced his rifle, the position giving him a perfect cheek weld. Through the scope, he watched John Cody through the kitchen window. The guy was cooking breakfast.

Perfect.

It never paid to rush a shot. Not on a hunt like this. Not when he had all the time in the world and could savor the knowledge that his victim was clueless. Had no hint that his life was but mere minutes from its end.

Taking a breath, Seeley charged his lungs, then let it out. The crosshairs bumped with each heartbeat as they settled on Cody's broad back. Bang. That would be it. This was a straight shot through the window. No deflection. Unlike what he'd figured for the Tim Little shot. And this was domestic glass, thin. Not the thick commercial stuff. The bullet would strike within millimeters of the aim point.

Cody turned. In the scope's field of view, Seeley watched another person enter the kitchen. A woman. Long black hair. He could just see a sliver of her back as she did something out of sight and reappeared a minute later with a cup of coffee. Seating herself at the kitchen table, she was facing him. In the scope's magnification, he could make out her...

"Son of a bitch," he whispered into the balaclava. "Agent Masterson. Right here. You and Cody, together. This just gets better and better."

Cody seated himself, the broad back blocking Seeley's view of Masterson.

Lined up as they were, the most likely scenario was that the 147 grain bullet, given its sectional density, would blast right through Cody and then take out Masterson. And he'd had a good look. She wasn't wearing any shoulder holster. Just a button-down blouse. Loose, but close-fitting enough that Seeley knew she wasn't wearing body armor underneath. Two with one shot.

He sucked his lips, thinking as they ate breakfast. The bullet would lose a mere fraction of its energy before blasting through Cody's back. In addition, Seeley would have time. He could ski down to the house, make sure that everything was tidy at the scene. Maybe even doctor it a little, make it look like some sort of argument between them that got out of hand?

Who knew until he could study the scene. Muddle the evidence.

"Two for one," he muttered, taking another breath. Settling the crosshairs, he began computing where to place the bullet so as to maximize damage to Cody and still hit center of mass on Masterson. Seeley was about to massage the trigger when Masterson stood, shoved her chair back, and soured the shot.

Seeley waited, breathing easily.

Then, to his disgust, Masterson walked out of the kitchen.

"Well, shit. Guess we'll have to do this a different way."

Which was okay. Seeley Atherton had all day.

Moments later, he heard the front door slam. Glanced around to see Jillian Masterson walking across the ranch yard. She headed right for the corrals, passed through a gate, and disappeared down the central alley.

Seeley returned his attention to Cody. The guy was up, carried plates to the sink—which was out of Seeley's line-of-sight—and did the dishes.

"Come on." Seeley waited. With the suppressor can on the Nexus, the only sound would be the hypersonic crack and the impact of the bullet on glass and flesh. Out in the corrals, Masterson might not even realize what had happened.

So, then what?

"Maybe I'll just go down and look her in the eyes," Seeley said with a grin.

No sooner did he make the decision than Cody

turned, walked over to the table, his full torso visible through the window. The man seemed to pause, as if staring straight across the field and right into Seeley's scope.

"Adios, asshole."

Seeley put gentle pressure on the trigger, heard the crack as the Nexus recoiled. For a second, Seeley lost the sight picture in the scope. When he found it, he could see the bullet hole in the glass right where Cody's heart would have been. Must have flattened John Cody on the spot.

CHAPTER FIFTY-NINE

The snow crunched under Jillian's boots as she crossed the ranch yard. Her Subaru still huddled under that thick blanket of snow. Might have been a symbol of her indecision.

Puffing out a breath, she watched the condensation rise in the still air. Heard the distant cawing of a raven. Behind it all came the soft grunting of bison out in the winter pasture. A pleasing sound, and so different from the lowing of cattle.

Do you want to leave this behind?

She hadn't expected to cleave to the bison so. Maybe it was in the blood? All those thousands of years of her Shoshoni ancestors? And, getting right down to it, the hundreds of thousands of years of her European ancestors, too. They had lived with and hunted bison through most of humanity's evolution.

At the corrals, she unlocked the clip on the gate chain, opened it, and stepped into the main alley that ran between the pens. As the cold nipped her nose and cheeks, she walked down to 208's pen. Stopped, and gazed into the two-year-old's dark eyes.

"So, what do I do?" Jillian asked. "Forgive and forget?" She knotted her fists. "What if there're some things in life that you can't get over?"

208 shifted, flipped her tail, and to Jillian's surprise, yawned, the breath rising from her mouth.

"Sorry if this conversation is boring you."

She heard the sound, like someone cracked a whip in the cold air. It barely echoed. Perhaps a tree had broken under the weight of the snow somewhere? As if in answer, the distant ravens cut loose with a series of clicks and squawks.

Jillian sighed, finding no answers with 208 and strode down to where she could see the rest of the bison out in the winter pasture. Most were bedded down in the snow, looking like dark wedges. A sort of cuneiform against the deep white. The sight calmed her.

"I could be happy here, I think."

As if three days was enough to really know who this Cody really was. Besides, there was her job. She'd be receiving a raise, a promotion, and was at the start of a promising career. What was she supposed to do about that? Leave it all behind? Run off to become a buffalo rancher's wife?

Wife?

It was just three days. When had the idea of marriage ever entered into it?

"God, Jillian. You're out of your head."

She let her gaze drift across the bison-filled pasture to the snow-filled spruce and fir trees, then up to the white-gleaming heights where the peaks and ridges of stone rose to the winter-pale sky. Stunning country. Pure. Actual wilderness. The haunting heights called to her.

Peace was here. But she needed to go home. Get some space between her and Cody and his magical healing buffalo ranch.

She turned, started back. Was halfway up the alley when the man in the white snowsuit stepped through the gate and left the chain hanging to clang against the metal. As he turned, he slipped a long-barreled rifle from his shoulder. Unhooking a white balaclava, he had a wide face with a week-old beard. Dark eyes fixed on her. Sprits of hair poked out around the tightly fitting hood. The man's wide lips broke into a smile as he started toward her.

"Hello, Agent Masterson! Me? I'm the Buffalo Warrior. You know, the guy who shot you. Sorry about hitting your pistol. If the light had been better, I wouldn't have had to bother you with this follow up visit. Couldn't get to you in the hospital. That Cody was a real pain in the ass, wasn't he? Glad that I finally got to even the score with that son of a bitch. Got him through his kitchen window."

"Excuse me? Killed Cody? Who the hell are you?"

"I told you. Call me the buffalo warrior. I do the dirty work. Wire up shotguns, shoot people through windows. Steal cowboy hats. Free bison. Should have killed you that night outside your hotel."

"You shot me?"

The man glanced around. "Right nice place ol' Cody had here. Would have worked better if we could have pinned your murder on him. Guess I'll just have to make do. Won't even need his hat this time."

Jillian instinctively reached for her missing shoulder holster, stopped short, and swallowed hard. "For God's sake, why?"

"Do you know the greatest power of all?" His smile widened as he strode down the alley toward her. "It's the power to take life, and nobody knows you did it. John Cody? Dan Butler? Leaving a fall guy is like an art, don't you know?"

She laid her hand on the gate to 208's pen, lifted out the chain and pulled the gate open across the alley between him and her. Anything to block his relentless advance. As if the metal tubing would stop a bullet. She backed away, shaking her head.

"You bought the Butler ranch?"

"Me, oh hell no." He kept talking through his smile as he walked up to the gate. "Not that I don't get paid well, but not that kind of money."

Keep him talking, Jillian.

"Was it you who took the box out of the safe?"

That seemed to catch him by surprise. "You know about that?" A chuckle. "Yeah. Insurance, you know? The client doesn't know I've got it. Something to bargain with in case everything goes sideways. Old Ryman, who'd a thought he was such a sneaky grifter? Glad I took him out."

She kept backing away, her eyes locked with his. "What do you want?"

"I want all these filthy private ranches and their stinking cattle out of the last great wilderness in America. Make this country free again for the bison and bears and deer and mountain sheep. This was a paradise once. Before the white men came and trashed it all."

"My people weren't white. They're Shoshoni!" she cried.

The gunman hesitated, a slight pinch behind his eyes. Then he feigned a shrug as he stopped at the gate. "Sorry.

Guess you're just collateral damage. But then, Indians been taking it in the ass since the beginning."

She thought he might follow her down the alley as she backed away. Instead he braced his elbow on the open gate and lowered his cheek to the stock, finding her in the scope.

"Gotta finish what I was hired to do back in Bozeman."

"For God's sake, why? The case is closed!" Jillian froze. A crawly tingling sensation spread through her guts. She was staring into the little round hole in the suppressor can.

Movement at the edge of her vision. A blur of brown.

The heifer seemed to appear out of thin air. The gunman screamed as 208 hit him low in the hips. His rifle flew from his hands. Head down, back arched, tail standing straight up like a flag, 208 drove the "Buffalo Warrior" into the steel panels lining the alley. Shouts and shrieks mixed with the metallic clangs of bone and cartilage cracking against metal. 208 threw all of her might and rage behind the charge, crushing and distorting the gunman's body as she pounded it against the alleyway.

Jillian gasped at the fury of the attack. The man was on the ground in a heap, but 208 didn't stop. As she unleashed her pent up rage and terror, the air seemed to vibrate. Raw power radiated from the animal's straining muscles. 208 was clearly crushing evil and blackness from the very earth.

Then the heifer backed up with the impaled body still on her horns. The man's legs and arms flopped. Dropping her head, 208 tossed the body high; it turned a limp somersault and smacked headfirst onto the frozen ground. Leaping, 208 slammed both front hooves down on the man's chest. Again and again. The crackling ribs and bones could have been muffled firecrackers. The body kept jerking, the head lolling as the man's dark eyes blinked, his mouth a soundless O. With each impact, the victorious bison grunted, huffed, and blew hot breath over his bloody face..

Jillian fought to slow her hammering heart.

When the man was clearly dead, 208 uttered what sounded like a disgusted huff and stopped. She fixed her dark and depthless stare on Jillian, licked her nostrils. Then, gave a faint shake of her head, as if to say, "Well, I feel better."

Jillian softly said, "Thank you."

The heifer turned and walked calmly back into her pen. The only sign that she'd been involved was her deep panting.

"Jill!"

She turned.

Cody, the old Marlin lever gun gripped in his hands, came down the alley at a dead run. To her surprise, he was barefoot in the snow, missing a coat, his hair flying.

"He said he'd killed you!" she cried. She had to step wide to avoid the mangled remains in the dirty snow as she closed 208's gate.

Then she was in his arms, hugging him close, heedless of the hurt in her ribs.

Cody ran fingers through her hair, "That big mirror in the kitchen blew up. Like, crack, shatter, and there's glass all over. And there's this bullet hole in the window."

He pushed her back, face paling as he took in the trampled body that leaked blood and fluids to stain the trampled snow. "When I got my wits together enough, I ran for the rifle, jacked a cartridge into the chamber. Then I came at a run."

Jillian studied 208. The big heifer stood relaxed in her

corner of the pen. For once, she wasn't stressed, wasn't fixed on Cody with that deadly gaze. She ground her teeth, just loud enough to be heard, and yawned.

CHAPTER SIXTY

Seated behind the wheel, Jillian turned the Ram dually off the pavement west of the little settlement of Clark, Wyoming, and took the dirt road. Cody rode in the passenger seat, arm propped on the windowsill, his old O'Farrell hat pulled low. The destination was easily discerned; a host of Park County Sheriff's vehicles crowded the yard before the small house and its out buildings. Behind it, rising like a mighty wall, the Beartooth front shot up from the flats to rake the sky.

Jillian pulled off the road just far enough to be out of the way and glanced at Cody. "You ready?"

"Guess so." He gave her a short nod. "Let's go see who Seeley Atherton really was."

She waited for Cody to get out and close the door before popping hers. A woman learned that in the Wyoming wind.

Closing the pickup's door, Jillian pulled her coat tightly about her and led the way past the line of parked vehicles. One of the deputies approached, his collar up, wind tugging at his hair. "Can I help you?"

"Agent Jillian Masterson, and this is John Cody. Madison Wade sent for us."

"Got it." The deputy pointed. "Go on in. I think they're mostly finished with the evidence recording. Stuff's bagged. You know the drill."

Leaning close, she told Cody, "The drill means, don't touch nothing."

They passed a Wyoming Game and Fish truck, the warden labeling cuts of meat, a hide, and some bones on the tailgate.

"Whatcha got?" Cody asked as they passed.

"On top of everything, the guy was a major poacher. Shoulda seen what we recovered out of his freezer." He pointed. "And that shed back there? Found a couple of ram's heads we've been missing from the mountain sheep herds. And then there's the mule deer, elk, and a couple of moose racks. This closes a major case for us."

At the door to the old frame house, Jillian stepped inside. The place wasn't much. Kitchen and living room all in one. Off to the back she could see what looked like an addition with a cheap dining room table and a big picture window that looked up at the Beartooths. Three deputies nodded at her before stepping out with bagged evidence.

Deputy Wade, talking to a medium-sized man wearing jeans and a leather vest, emerged from the door that led into a small bedroom. She said, "Thanks, again, Byron. Send the bill to the department."

The man, balding, and in his fifties, nodded to Jillian as he passed, a tool kit in one hand.

"See you made it," Wade called.

Jillian followed the deputy into a cramped bedroom filled with a reloading bench along one wall, twin bed, and gun safe. The latter was open, displaying a variety of rifles and handguns.

"Needed Byron to crack this thing," Wade said, her gray eyes looking satisfied. "Got dies, bullets, powder, and all the makings for the handloads we recovered from Atherton's rifle up at your place. Not only that," she pointed at the long cardboard box on the bed. "That was out in the trash. It's the shipping box for a Ruger American 6.5 mm hunting rifle. Funny thing. It's the same gun your Dan Butler is supposed to have committed suicide with."

"Atherton said he'd set Butler up." Jillian fixed on the guns in the safe.

Wade scratched at the back of her neck. "Yeah, well, Mr. Butler's family will probably appreciate that he didn't kill himself. Course, it comes at the knowledge that Atherton murdered him. We've got the remains of a couple of hazmat suits out in the burn barrel. No telling what the state lab can get off them."

"What else do you have?" Jillian asked. Cody was bent, hands dutifully in his pocket, staring thoughtfully at the guns in the safe.

"You remember the cell phone we took from his body up at your ranch?" Wade asked as she wrote a number a scrap of paper she tore from her notebook and handed it to Jillian. It was a 406 area code. "That number mean anything to you? We called it, got no answer. Tried to run it down but it's a burner phone. Atherton had some pretty suspicious texts in his messaging service. Found it again in the contacts on his laptop. It's listed only as 'client.'"

Jillian studied the number, shook her head, and stuffed the piece of paper in her back pocket. "What else did you get from his computer?"

"Wow," Wade told her. "Talk about a social media presence, this guy, the Buffalo Warrior, was something. Some of the stuff he posted about ranchers, about the livestock industry, and especially about developers? Sick shit. He thought of saving wilderness as a sort of war. Considered humans to be a sort of infestation, like rats introduced to a pristine island. That we had to be eliminated from the environment to reestablish the purity of nature."

"And at the same time," Cody noted, "he's poaching wildlife? How did he justify that?"

"Got me," Wade told him. "Like I said. Sick son of a bitch."

Jillian pointed to a strong box sitting on the edge of the reloading bench. "What's that?"

"Don't know. Found it in the safe. Byron said it wasn't his kind of lock. We'll break it open when we get it back to the barn."

Jillian said, "Try 111222 for the combination."

Wade gave her a sidelong glance. "Think so?" She input the numbers on the rolling lock plate, the latch springing open. "Son of a bitch. How'd you know that?"

"Looks about right for the one missing from Ryman Banks' safe. Atherton said he'd taken it for insurance. Leverage, he called it. What's inside?"

Wade, her hands cased in Nitrile gloves, carefully lifted out what looked like a leather-bound ledger book. Touching the covers with the tips of her fingers, she opened it. "Looks like accounts." She fingered to the last page with numbers in columns. "Hmm. Damn. Two million, seven hundred and sixty-six thousand fifty-eight dollars and forty-four cents?"

"But whose bank account?" Cody wondered. "Atherton's? Or Ryman Banks'?"

CHAPTER SIXTY-ONE

Cody was driving them south from Chico Hot Springs on US 89 toward Gardiner. Jillian had been surprised when her phone buzzed. Listening, she stared sightlessly at the snow-capped mountains ahead.

The day was sunny, warm for this late in March. The high country gleamed a remarkable white against the almost Navy-blue sky. Jillian glanced out at the passing ranches, cattle grazing in the pastures, center-pivot lines waiting for the coming of spring. The two of them were headed back through the park to Pilot Creek Ranch where Jillian would pick up her car prior to driving back to Billings, and her latest investigation.

It had been Cody's idea. The Plug had been plowed to open the road to Cooke City. He'd offered to take Jillian for a getaway weekend at the Chico Hot Springs. They'd rented the Caboose—a charming railroad car outfitted with a bed and bath that overlooked the resort. Another of her growing liaisons with Cody. Intimacy, with some

fits and starts, had come easier than she had ever anticipated. Maybe it just took the right man.

Jillian lowered her cell phone and pressed the red
"end" icon as she killed the call. Frowning, she stared at
the highway. After what Supervisor Meyer had just told
her, her relationship with Cody wasn't front and center in
her thoughts.

"What's the word?" Cody asked. "You spent a lot of
time listening. Kept saying, 'sir' so I guess that was your
supervisor?"

"Yeah. Gaylen had an update." She shifted in the seat.
"Remember that ledger we found at Atherton's? They've
been working to decipher that back account. Trying to
crack the code. Okay, they know it was Ryman Banks'
ledger, taken from his safe. So they finally figured out his
cypher to identify the bank and account number. Turns
out the account was closed the Friday before Banks was
murdered."

"By whom?" Cody asked, shifting his grip on the
wheel.

"No clue. That's where it dead ends. Two point seven
million. Transferred to a numbered account in the
Caymans. And then, poof."

"So, someone got away with Ryman's loot? Are we
back to his grieving wife?"

Jillian considered, remembering the expression on
Jenn's face that day in Ryman's office. "I don't think so.
We know that Atherton took the box with the ledger. If
Jenn was involved, she wouldn't have mentioned it that
day in Ryman's office. Wouldn't have wanted to be tied to
the missing money."

Cody flipped on the signal, punched the accelerator,
and blew past a slow-moving Sysco semi before pulling
back into the right lane. "Granted, he was a slimy lawyer,

but where'd Ryman get the money? Who'd fork over that kind of dough, and for what kind of favor? Was someone buying him off?"

"Who?" She shifted, thankful her ribs had healed to the point they rarely caused her pain.

Cody squinted an eye. "Here's two-and-a-half million. Don't sue me? Too many holes in that."

Jillian leaned back, stared out at the broad Yellowstone Valley as the road skirted the eastern uplands with their partially forested and grassy slopes. "Wonder what Dan Butler would have said to that?"

"Here's his old place," Cody told her. "Coming up on the right. Looks like someone's been doing a lot of the work on the ranch road. It's paved."

"Turn in!" Jillian cried, grabbing the Oh Shit handle on the dash as Cody hit the brakes. He barely made the turn.

"You know, the last time, they threw us out." He was giving her his warning glance from under his old hat brim. The once-stolen one with the bloody buffalo snot on the crown.

She shot him a look back. "Yeah. I know. Call it a hunch."

Cody wound his way down through the trees, the new asphalt dark against the fading patches of snow under the trees. Breaking out into the bottom lands, it was to an entirely different vista. Heavy machinery stood weekend-idle, including a track hoe, backhoes, a loader, and small caterpillar. Piles of dirt lay next to recent excavations. Forms for a new basement filled an extensive hole where the old ranch house had stood. The barn, guest cabins, sheds, and pole barn were gone, as were the loafing sheds and corrals. The entire area had been bladed flat. Surveyor's stakes with fluttering flagging tape could be seen extending down into the hay fields, and the center post irrigation system was missing.

"Holy shit," Cody whispered as they slowed.

A late-model green Subaru stood by a twenty-eight-foot fifth wheel RV off to one side. As Cody slowed to a stop, the door opened and a woman stepped out.

"I'll be damned," Jillian muttered under her breath. "Of all the people."

"Jenn Banks?" Cody asked, his eyes still on the heavy equipment. "Coming to tell us to scat?"

"Nope." Jillian popped her door, not needing a coat in the warm spring air. She flipped her hair back, walking across the freshly bladed ground to where Carly Joyner stood, arms crossed, her blonde hair shining in the sunlight.

"Agent Masterson," Carly greeted. "What a surprise."

Jillian stopped a pace short of the woman, met that pale green stare. She gestured to the construction. "Thought this was all critical habitat? That it couldn't be developed."

"It is, and it won't be," Joyner told her, those cold green eyes unwavering. "It's an entirely new concept we're introducing. No-impact ecological cohabitation. That survey line in the meadow? That's for the tram towers. Those plots down the valley? They sit on either bedrock or on nonproductive soils. Each luxury habitation will be elevated on a column. Like a water tower with a limited footprint to minimize disturbances."

"Houses on pillars? Seriously?" The disgust built.

"You get the idea," Joyner continued, voice like syrup. "Imagine, Agent Masterson, a community that seems to hang in the sky with wildlife grazing undisturbed below. The land open and free. You can have your morning coffee while looking down on bison, elk, and deer. Not to mention the occasional grizzly passing through. All in their perfect state of nature. This will be a landmark community." She pointed toward the cottonwoods masking the river. "And, of course, private access to some of the finest fly fishing in the world. All accessible by the elevated tram. We expect that US Fish and Wildlife, the county and state, even the environmental community will sign off on this by the end of the year. The governor assures me that state of Montana's fully behind it."

Jillian's disquiet built. "So, why do I suspect that Tanner and the Plains Wilderness Project are invested in this, too?"

"Money, of course. This will be worth millions. Too bad we lost the last round to list Yellowstone bison. But we'll find a new angle. Try again. Eventually, we'll get that listing. And by then, we'll have this project as a successful blueprint and can expand, buying up bankrupt ranches for a song."

Jillian's fists knotted as she fought the urge to reach out and strangle the woman. "You know that you've got a problem with noxious weeds? That US Fish and Wildlife won't let you spray?"

Joyner broke out in laughter. "What? No, I wasn't aware. Not that it matters. You see, dear, it's the government. They have regulations and responsibilities for the management of critical habitat, and we're a high-visibility project. We know the law, and if Fish and Wildlife doesn't manage the noxious weeds according to their legislative mandate? We'll sue. But trust me, they won't let it get that far."

"How much is this going to cost to get off the ground? I mean to build this...?" It hit her like a thrown rock. *Like, the amount missing from Ryman's secret account?*

"So, it all starts to make sense."

"What does?" Joyner's expression remained cool.

Jillian nodded to herself. "You knew that Ryman was skimming funds. Falsifying records. The accountant had found discrepancies in the company books. How long had that been going on?" A cold chill ran down her back. "Are you the person who ordered me to be shot?"

Joyner's lips twitched, a gleam in her eyes, but she said nothing.

Jillian swallowed hard, reached up to place fingers on the still-tender spot where the bullet had struck. *I'm face-to-face with the monster that almost killed me.*

The cold chill corkscrewed down her spine.

She was back, in the darkness of the hotel parking lot. The lights in the lobby bright. Walking toward the door.

The bullet hits.

Drives into her side like a fist. The smack as copper and lead explodes on her pistol mixes with the whip-like crack in the air.

And she is down. Like the shit kicked out of her. She can't breathe...

Jillian shook her head, the image shredding. She sucked a deep breath, fixed herself: Butler Ranch. Mid morning. Yellowstone valley. The trees down by the river thick with buds.

Joyner was staring at her through suspicious eyes as she asked, "Are you all right?"

Jillian made herself think. "And then...and then Tim Little's murder. It didn't make sense until now. Sure, his test was debunked. The myth of bison purity was on its last legs. But he was sharp enough after all those years with ICoHR to figure out that you were the only person to really gain from Ryman's death."

No waver could be seen in Joyner's cold green gaze. "I don't know what you're talking about, Agent Masterson. You, yourself, broke the case. Exposed that lunatic,

Atherton, for the sick murdering crusader he was." A pause, Joyner's gaze sharpening. "Thank you for getting him before he could kill me, too."

Jillian shook her head in amazement, her heart continuing to pound. "Oh, you were never in danger. You used him, just like you exploited Ryman's and Tim Little's deaths to create sympathy. To rake in a couple of million more in donations. And, Little's death, it was reported, almost swayed the appeals court. Would have if the new genetics tests hadn't been so rock solid."

Joyner said, "You're insane. I'd place my money on Jenn."

"Uh-huh. She was here that day after the ranch sold. She and Tanner. So, whatever's afoot, she's still in the game."

The temperature in the cold green gaze dropped another ten degrees. "I have no idea what you're talking about, Agent Masterson. And, I'd beware if I were you. You're a smart young lady. You solved the case. You're the charmed darling of the hour at the DOJ. Rest on your laurels, my dear."

Cody had walked over and now took a position behind Jill's shoulder.

Through gritted teeth, Jillian said, "My God, you're a cold and calculating bitch. Atherton's 'client.' I remember that hesitation in your office when I said Cody had an alibi. You'd forgotten that Stock Show was the same weekend, or you'd have had his ranch, too. Decided to have me killed when I didn't jump on the Cody bandwagon, because, hey, who'd look closely when a Montana agent had been killed?"

"These are wild accusations, Agent Masterson." A slight tension lay behind Joyner's lips as she added, "Probably brought on by post traumatic stress. Poor woman, but coming so close to losing your life? It's no wonder. If I could offer a word of advice, I wouldn't rave in public like this, my dear."

Jillian lost it. Started forward, reaching out. Saw the sudden fear in Joyner's eyes. Only to have Cody clamp a restraining hand on Jill's shoulder and pull her back. "It's not worth it. Ease down."

Cody jerked a thumb over his shoulder. "So what's the giant building for?"

"A community lodge," Joyner told him, recovering her poise. "Like the one we'll build where your ranch house now sits. One of these days. When we finally drive you and your polluted half-breed abominations off the land."

It was Cody's turn to take a half step toward the woman, his eyes narrowing. "Yeah, well, better pack a lunch, wear your working clothes, and tug your hat down tight, Carly. 'Cause it'll be a fight."

"Maybe," the woman rejoined.

"I'll bring you down, you know," Jillian told her.

"No, you won't, Agent Masterson," Joyner responded. "All you have are wild accusations. Where would you find probable cause?"

Cody's hand on Jillian's shoulder pulled her back. "Come on, Jillian. She's won this round."

"No. I'm going to—"

"Look at me." Cody spun her around to stare into his tan gaze. "Do you trust me?"

That she did came as a revelation.

"You've got to know when there are battles you can win, and those you're doomed to lose. Don't play in a rigged game you can't beat. Not today. She'll destroy you."

Jillian jerked a quick nod as her heart continued to pound. Let him lead her toward the pickup.

Then she stopped. "Just a minute." She slipped her phone from her back pocket, turning to where Carly Joyner was grinning, arms crossed and one leg forward.

From memory, Jillian typed in the number and pressed Send.

"Calling someone?" Joyner asked. "I wouldn't get my hopes up that..."

The ring could just be heard—an insistent buzzing from the open fifth-wheel trailer's door.

The startled look on Joyner's face was followed by confusion and then panic. The woman turned, made a dash for the RV.

Jillian, screamed, "Stop her!" and ran for all she was worth.

Made the flying leap. Got a hand on Joyner's shoulder and pulled. Jillian's feet tangled with Joyner's and they hit the ground hard. The impact, coupled with Jillian's weight, drove the air from Joyner's lungs.

Before the woman could squirm away, Jillian slipped her arm across Joyner's throat, choking her down. Joyner squirmed, her struggles weakening. Feeling her ribs aching, Jillian said, "Carly Joyner, you're under arrest for the murders of Ryman Banks and Tim Little." And then she proceeded with her Miranda.

In the trailer, the phone had ceased to ring.

"Jill? What the hell?" Cody asked as he caught up.

"You got something in your ranch truck we can use to tie her up with? Just long enough for the Sheriff's Office to send somebody from Gardiner or Livingston?"

"How about some Gallagher high-tensile buffalo fence wire? If it's good enough for bison, it ought to hold a skinny pissed-off woman." He started back for the truck, then stopped. "What makes you so sure she did it?"

Jillian tightened her forearm on Joyner's neck when the woman tried to buck her off. Didn't take but seconds for Joyner to gasp and submit.

"John, when the SO gets here, they're going to find that burner phone. The one belonging to Seeley Atherton's so-called client. That's what rang in the trailer. Remember? The slip of paper Deputy Wade showed me? That's the number I just called."

To Joyner, Jillian added, "Looks like probable cause after all, doesn't it?"

CHAPTER SIXTY-TWO

Watching the little orange calf as it struggled to its feet filled Jillian with a sense of hope and relief. The birth had looked difficult. 208 had alternately stood, stretched out on her side, strained, and stood again. Sometimes she'd whirl, as if to sling the stubborn calf like mud from a spinning tire, and then she'd stop, hunch, and strain until the front feet protruded. Finally, she'd laid down and squeezed that little wet bundle of buffalo calf out onto the grass.

The day was chilly, though sunny, with patches of puffy clouds that shredded on the surrounding high peaks as they blew past. Under the trees, and on the timbered north slopes, old snow banks were rotten with the melt, and Jillian could hear the Clarks Fork's muted roar from beyond the perimeter fence.

Jillian quietly cheered as the calf struggled up, stumbled between 208's back legs, and found the nipple. It was critical for the calf to suck down that first feeding of colostrum. Cody said the little bison wouldn't survive without it.

"Quite the sight, huh?" Danny asked as she came to lean crossed arms on the corral panel. The elbows on the old woman's jacket were worn through and frayed. Fits and starts of the western breeze teased Danny's long ponytail. The lines in her weathered brown face hinted of a wisdom and serenity that was confirmed by the knowing brown gaze that warmed as she watched the cow and calf.

Jillian indicated 208 where the newly official "cow bison" stood with Buttercup. "Turns out that she fit her way right into the herd."

"Having a calf does that," Danny agreed. "Hey, I had my doubts. Thought Cody was crazy for buying her. Funny thing, huh? She just had to kill a guy, and just like that she's all settled down. Felt that way myself a time or two."

Jillian grinned in reply. "Guess we all have our demons. Good for 208. Me, I'm still working on killing mine."

"Naw," came the call from behind as Cody came striding down the central alleyway. "It's been weeks since you needed to sleep with the pistol."

He was wearing his old black felt O'Farrell, a silk kerchief around his neck. The Levi's fleece-lined coat hung open to expose a buffalo-hide vest and Pendleton wool shirt. A beaded Shoshoni belt buckle with a red rose against a white background gleamed in the light. Jillian thought he looked really good in a pair of jeans given the way they fit his muscular legs.

"How would you know?" she asked. "Most of that time I've been up working with the Gallatin County DA. Lot of testimony and preparation in being a key witness. Even in an open-and-shut case like this."

Cody settled on the corral panel, pressing snugly

against her and taking her hand as he studied 208's calf. "Look at the hip and shoulders on that little guy. I just knew she'd drop a hell of a calf."

"You know it's a bull?" Jillian asked skeptically. "How?"

"By the horn buttons that you can see on his head. Heifers are usually slick-headed when they're born." He fixed his tan eyes on hers, a question behind his gaze. "And how's the case lining out?"

Jillian took a deep breath. "Speculation in the DA's office is that Joyner's going to strike a plea bargain. Billy Blood is no fool. He's putting out feelers. Says Joyner is willing to testify that she wasn't alone in the deal. That there are connections to someone big in Helena. And, wow, suddenly the pressure coming from Brewster's office is intense."

She paused, a piece of the puzzle falling into place. "Of course."

"Of course, what?" Cody asked.

"No wonder the governor was so desperate for an arrest back in the beginning. He and Banks were good friends, after all. Partied together. And, who knows what else they did?"

"Think they'll get him?" Danny asked.

"Never can tell," Jillian admitted. "It's politics. They always cover their asses."

"How long can you stay this time?" Cody asked.

"Three days. Then I have to be back in Bozeman." She glanced at him. "Got any ideas about what we could do to pass the time?"

"Haven't a clue," Cody told her mildly. "I'm open to suggestions."

"Woah!" Danny cried, slapping her callused hands to the metal panel. "What's happened to young people these days? If you can't figure that out on your own, I'm outta here." She turned, started up the alley toward the barn. Stopped, and called back, "You be good to her, *Taipo*. Woman like Jillian, she could get any guy, so don't screw it up!"

Then the old woman headed up the alley in a bow-legged stride.

"That true?" Cody asked. "You could get any guy?"

Jillian pulled him close, wrapping her arms around him. "It is. Now, if you'll recall, the first time I came here, it was in hopes I'd take you back to Montana in custody. It just took me a little while longer than I initially planned. But I've got you right where I want you."

And she tightened her hug just to make the point.

A LOOK AT: PEOPLE OF THE OWL

The Earliest Americans Book One

New York Times bestselling authors W. Michael Gear and Kathleen O'Neal Gear masterfully bring to life an ancient America, long forgotten in the mists of time, yet strikingly relevant in today's world.

Four Thousand years ago, in the lower Mississippi Valley, a civilization thrived that would lay the foundations of the great Indian Nations. In a long-lost land of forests, swamps, and hidden waterways, A boy is thrust into leadership of America's first city, forced to become a man before his time.

Salamander, only fifteen winters old, would rather chase crickets and marvel at blue herons than navigate the treacherous politics of his clan. But when his revered brother is slain, Salamander is thrust into the role of leader in what will one day be known as the American South's first city.

Burdened with the legacy of his brother's two wives—who despise him—and a marriage to the daughter of his mortal enemy, Salamander must forge alliances to secure the trade goods his people need to survive. Yet, in a world where enemies lurk in every shadow, and assassins strike without warning, Salamander must grow from boy to man, and from a reluctant leader to a formidable one.

Can Salamander navigate the brutal landscape of ancient politics and emerge as the leader his people need? Or will the passions of the human heart devour him before he can claim his destiny?

AVAILABLE NOW

ABOUT W. MICHAEL GEAR

W. Michael Gear is a *New York Times, USA Today,* and international bestselling author of sixty novels. With close to eighteen million copies of his books in print worldwide, his work has been translated into twenty-nine languages.

Gear has been inducted into the Western Writers Hall of Fame and the Colorado Authors' Hall of Fame—as well as won the Owen Wister Award, the Golden Spur Award, and the International Book Award for both Science Fiction and Action Suspense Fiction. He is also the recipient of the Frank Waters Award for lifetime contributions to Western writing.

Gear's work, inspired by anthropology and archaeology, is multilayered and has been called compelling, insidiously realistic, and masterful. Currently, he lives in northwestern Wyoming with his award-winning wife and co-author, Kathleen O'Neal Gear, and a charming sheltie named Jake.

ABOUT KATHLEEN O'NEAL GEAR

Kathleen O'Neal Gear is a *New York Times* bestselling author of fifty-seven books and a national award-winning archaeologist. The U.S. Department of the Interior has awarded her two Special Achievement awards for outstanding management of America's cultural resources.

In 2015 the United States Congress honored her with a Certificate of Special Congressional Recognition, and the California State Legislature passed Joint Member Resolution #117 saying, "The contributions of Kathleen O'Neal Gear to the fields of history, archaeology, and writing have been invaluable..."

In 2021 she received the Owen Wister Award for life-time contributions to western literature, and in 2023 received the Frank Waters Award for "a body of work representing excellence in writing and storytelling that embodies the spirit of the American West."

www.ingramcontent.com/pod-product-compliance
Lightning Source LLC
Chambersburg PA
CBHW012239260626
47157CB00025B/3287